I0599779

TO HAUNT
and TO HOLD

True Sloan

Copyright © 2025 by True Sloan

All rights reserved.

No part of this book may be reproduced in any form or by any electronic or mechanical means, including information storage and retrieval systems, without written permission from the author or publisher, except for the use of brief quotations in a book review.

This is a work of fiction. Any resemblance to actual persons, living or dead or actual events is purely coincidental. Although real-life locations or public figures may appear throughout the story, these situations, incidents, and dialogue concerning them are fictional and are not intended to depict actual events nor change the fictional nature of the work.

First published in the United States of America by Lake Country Press & Reviews.

Cataloging-in-Publication Data is on file with the Library of Congress.

ISBN: 979-8-9931082-2-3 (Paperback edition)

ISBN: 979-8-9931082-3-0 (Ebook edition)

Author Website: https://truesloan.com/

Editor: Tara Sexton

Cover Artist: Talita Asami

Cover Design: Rae Valtera

Interior Art: www.instagram.com/lulybot

Formatting: Juliet Bridges

Author Photo: JrayMay Photography

Lake Country Press
Publishing & Reviews

To anyone searching the skies:
I hope you find your cotton candy ones.

Trigger Warning

The material of TO HAUNT AND TO HOLD mentions sensitive topics relating to:

blood, body-horror, death, depression, grief, mental health, murder, self-harm, substance abuse, and suicide.

Four White Walls, Porcelain Tile, A Pool of Blood, and A Dead Body

May 30

I think sanity looks good on a lot of people, but as the single light bulb illuminating my kitchen highlights my reflection against the darkened windowpanes, I realize I am not one of them.

How can I be? In one minute, I'll fix my gaze on the sun until all I can see is him.

My father loved sunrises so much that on the day he died, he became one, and as the orange beams of the sun crawl along the earth and burn through my reflection, I search for him again. All I can do is stare, until the light scorches my retinas and black spots invade my vision, so overwhelming I have to jerk my head to the side as tears gather in the corners of my eyes.

"Is this it?"

I blink a few times, the tears blurring my vision as I meet

the heavy stare of my cousin. The pain contorting his face is a mirror of my own. "Is what it?"

"Where he died." Caleb walks through blood he can't see, not noticing the scarlet footprints he tracks across the kitchen floor.

My father always talked about how the pink and yellow hues made cotton candy skies, but as sunlight streams through the window, the only thing I see is how the sun bleeds into the clouds and saturates the sky, the same shade of red my father bleeds onto the kitchen floor.

I don't know which is bloodier, my father or the sunrise.

I nod and swallow the sudden urge to throw up, forcing myself not to locate my dad's Trace. Hard to do when it's only a couple feet over, just beside the leg of the dining room table. I can still see it from the corner of my eye. The Trace begins with my father standing, his face quivering in pain before he claws at his chest as the heart attack begins. He falls, his head catching on the edge of the table with a sickening thud. Blood pools, passing the third cracked tile from the table before filling its crevices. Then it stops, the whole scene reversing only to play again and again until it's more than a crack in my sanity—it's a crack in my soul.

But like the blood, Caleb can't see this either. No one can see the Trace but me and if I can still see the remaining essence of my father, then the last drink I had wasn't strong enough. While alcohol won't drown out the ghosts that haven't moved on, it will temporarily drown out the remaining Traces of the dead that have.

Caleb approaches me, the slippery slide of his shoes raking chills up my spine. I flinch away from him, fighting back a scream as he walks through the Trace—*through* Dad.

Dad's body flickers like a hologram before becoming whole again like it's taunting me, appearing as if he's rooted to this earth when I know damn well he isn't.

Caleb holds up his hands in surrender as my best friend Hadley enters the kitchen behind him. "Whoa. Still just me." He casts a glance over his shoulder. "And Hadley. Hey, Sunshine."

"Caleb," Hadley greets with a slight blush before giving me a sad smile. "I'm going to miss you."

"Me too." I lay my head against her shoulder, not for my own comfort, but because I know it'll mean something to her if I do. I'm already leaving her, so the least I can do is leave the sunshine girl with a smile.

She wraps me into a hug. "Are you sure you can't stay? You're nineteen. You could rent an apartment."

I shake my head at the hope strengthening her voice, my chin brushing the cotton of her shirt. "You know I can't afford it."

She squeezes me tighter. "Don't forget to call. Love you, Audrey."

"I won't," I promise.

She wipes at her cheeks as I pull away.

I bite my lip, guilt eating at me when I have no tears of my own to offer, but my ability to cry was lost with my father. "Love you, too," I add hastily.

A monotone drone masks my sincerity, but Hadley doesn't falter in rewarding me with a smile, knowing the slightest bit of disappointment will make my pain worse. Caleb is right: she's straight sunshine, and everyone is drawn to the light she produces when she smiles. Even I can be beckoned out of the shadows just for a glimpse of it.

There's something about her that ensnares Caleb too, because his attention doesn't stray from Hadley until she leaves. Then, he's grabbing my suitcase and hauling it to the door. "Come on, let's go." He throws an arm around my neck and pulls me to his side, but I duck out from under him. If he's looking for affection, he should've gone to Hadley. I've had enough hugging for a lifetime.

"Go," I encourage. "I'm right behind you."

My cousin blows out a breath. Neither him nor my uncle wanted me to stay here the past week, but I had to burn Dad's Trace into my brain before I left. I hadn't even bothered to glance up in the last moments I saw him alive to absorb the details of him. I never imagined I would need to, so I do it now—after today there will be nothing left of him to hold on to.

"Don't . . ." Caleb trails off, searching for the words. "Think too much." He winces at his own choice of words. "*God.* I suck at this."

I glimpse back at him and shoot him a reassuring smile. "I don't think it's something anyone is meant to be good at."

He presses his lips into a firm line and nods, knocking his fist lightly against the door on his way out. When I hear it shut, I pull the small gray flask out of my pocket, watching through the window as Caleb loads my luggage into the car. His girlfriend, Quinn, lounges in the front seat with her bare toes pressed against the dashboard. I snort and unscrew the cap.

"I bet her feet stink," I find myself saying to the Trace, like it's him I'm speaking to and not a poor imitation of my father.

I inhale a pained breath when I'm greeted with nothing

but silence. I step away, turning back to the manifestation of the death scene. Watch Traces long enough and you'll more or less feel yourself go mad. Can't say where I fall on that scale, when for the past week, every spare moment I've had has been spent here, in this kitchen that reeks of bleach and failure to suppress the stench of blood.

I throw my head back and chug it until the vile liquor is gone. Wiping the back of my hand across my mouth, I focus on the Trace, tilting my head slightly. I thought it might help me picture Dad's face clearer when I thought about him, but now I'm not sure what watching his Trace has done to me. For days I've thought about reaching out to touch it, some sickening hope festering in my chest that it may hold the last bit of his warmth. I never fully convince myself to do it, because if I were to reach through him and feel nothing but cold empty air, I'm not sure my heart could take it. Inebriated, I may avoid it yet.

Four white walls, porcelain tile, a pool of blood, and a dead body. Nothing out of the ordinary, except for the fact the body belonged to my father. His body begins to fade out of view as my chest starts to burn. The Trace replays one last time, the edges blurring more with each second. Then it's gone. And with every agonizing sip of liquor, I become normal again—as normal as a nineteen-year-old girl who sees ghosts can be.

If I didn't know what waited for me on the other side, I would've killed myself by now. I'm still kind of contemplating it, to be honest, and if morbid humor doesn't convey how tired I am of Caleb and Quinn fighting, I don't know what will. I've already dealt with their bickering for the past couple of days, all because Quinn hates that Caleb calls Hadley 'Sunshine.' While I can't exactly blame her, they're at each other's throats and we've still got a whole summer to go before they head back to Texas for their freshman year of college while I remain here for my own.

They've been dating since sophomore year of high school, and it shows. They're both obviously tired of each other and stay together out of comfort and fear of never finding anyone better, but neither of them has the courage to admit it. And the second I mention something about it, I'm the one who's crazy. Considering what I see on the daily, I do what I can to steer as far from the word as possible.

We still have another thirty minutes—that's right—thirty minutes of absolute hell to go until we're at Windhaven. And if hell is their grating voices and earsplitting whines, the smell of her feet is a purgatory of its own.

I prop my elbows on the console between them and smile. "Y'all fight like a married couple," I say, chewing on a stick of gum to mask the alcohol on my breath.

Who are on the brink of divorce, I don't add. Instead, I place a hand over my mouth just in case the comment tries to sneak out. Because I do that—say words I think are fine to speak until I look up and find everyone wide-eyed. Then I know I'm terribly wrong.

Quinn twists in her seat and shakes her head. "He drives me insane." She forces herself to laugh at an unnaturally high pitch. I cover my ears and lean back into my seat to create some distance. "Tell him to shape up, Audrey. He'll listen to you."

"What the hell do you mean I need to shape up? I'm not doing anything."

"Stop cussing at me. That's so dead."

I fight the urge to laugh, because dead is the perfect word I'd use to describe this relationship. All they need to do is dig a six-foot hole and bury it. I might throw myself in it while they're at it.

"I'm not cussing at *you*; I'm cussing in general."

Quinn folds her arms across her chest and shifts her whole body away from him.

Caleb's knuckles tighten around the steering wheel. I don't know why he tolerates her, but the only reason *I* do is because she makes me look like the sane one.

Quinn drags in a long breath before she speaks. "Audrey, are you excited to move to Windhaven? It's cool you get to live at a hotel."

My grip on the seat belt tightens. Windhaven Hotel sits on the edge of Raven's Nest Cliff, overlooking the Gulf of Maine. The terrain is rocky, the elevation fluctuates, and the pine trees scale high and low as they overlook a cerulean blue, crystal sea. The pine scent is strong, the air there so crisp it almost hurts. Caleb loves it, but I associate the smell with near-death and gag on it every time.

"Not that excited."

I never wanted to live at Windhaven. If it were up to me, I'd live with Caleb and start college back home in Texas, but Uncle Hank and Granna thought staying in the town where I did everything with my dad would be too 'traumatic.' Considering the constant torment this curse puts me through each day and the fact I've already seen his Trace, I don't think it can get much worse.

"I'm a little excited. I won't have to worry about you and your little friend tagging along on our dates anymore." When I don't reply, she follows with, "You've been there before?"

I peer at Caleb through the rearview mirror, raising an eyebrow to silently ask what else he told her.

He meets my gaze, apologetic.

Traitor.

I make sure he catches sight of my middle finger before dropping it back into my lap.

"I went to Windhaven to visit Granna once when I was five."

"And never again?"

"No," I answer, acting oblivious to what she's fishing for. "Granna usually came to visit us."

"Did you like it?"

"Nope."

"Why?"

"Oh, look," I cheer as we pull up to a dirt road. "We're here."

The three of us stay silent as we drive up the winding road. It's a sunny day, but the woods surrounding the property are so thick they cast a veil of darkness over the land, leaving only the thinnest streaks of sunlight passing through the leaves. Through the window, it's a blur of evergreen.

My whole body trembles, every hair standing as chills race down my body. I feel the restless spirits that reside on this property, their shifting crawling across my skin like an itch I can't reach.

"Whoa, is that a graveyard?" Quinn exclaims, pressing her face into the glass.

The bodies buried in the ground are different, like

weights attached to my ankles that drag as I walk. The lighter the weight, the deeper they're buried. Every sensation is distinct, but the ice coating them is all the same. A hollow coldness, a chill that'll never escape my bones no matter how warm my skin might be.

Caleb nods. "It's been there since before Granna and Grandpa bought the property. Our aunt and grandpa are buried there."

And soon, Dad will be, too, his headstone engraved with something that won't matter as it'll end up neglected, infested with moss and eroded away until it's not even legible. I'll never know what words the headstone will read because I won't be visiting his grave. Graveyards make me uneasy. The knowledge that I'm stepping over skeletal remains doesn't sit right with me.

Quinn asks me something, but I'm too distracted to catch it. While the strong presence of the buried bodies is only a few feet from me, I don't feel any active spirits attached to them. Everyone in the graveyard has moved on.

That's not all, though.

A strange flutter spreads through my chest, overpowering the sips of alcohol I've snuck at the past few rest stops. They're muted in comparison to my distance from the grave-yard, but I can sense them, all four of them.

Ghosts reside here.

"You good?" Caleb asks as air struggles to enter my lungs.

A break in the wind causes the trees to stop moving.

"I'm good. Thinking about Dad, you know?" He doesn't, not how I do. Blood and sunrises.

"Do you want to get out and stretch for a moment?"

"Get out to *stretch*," I snort, giving him a knowing smile.

9

He shushes me and gestures for me to keep it down with his hands before making sure Quinn's oblivious to what we're really talking about.

I turn over my shoulder to find the graveyard is still within walking distance. My smile fades. We should get out just to relieve ourselves of Quinn's feet fumes. God knows I could use the fresh air.

"No," I say instead. "We're pretty close to the hotel. Let's go."

The tires crunch over gravel, the wind growing stronger as we near the clearing. The sun shines through the windshield as we exit the woods into a large, open space vacant of trees and covered in a mass of wildflowers, the hotel smack in the middle. At the edge of the road stands a blue wooden sign that reads 'Windhaven Hotel' in cursive letters. The white paint of the letters is chipped, the sign more weathered than the last time I saw it. Through the window, I can hear it creaking as it moves back and forth in the wind. Cicadas chime faintly in the distance.

"Not bad," Quinn says to Caleb. "That's a hotel? It looks like a castle." She glances over the intricately carved stone, the off-white color standing out amongst the trees and the sky behind it.

"It was a lighthouse at one point, but Granna wanted it to appear like the castles in those old Disney movies, so they added onto it every chance they got."

I follow his finger to the highest point—the top of the lighthouse. The stone around it is eroded and stained in comparison to the added on three stories, the blocks so bright, they reflect the gleam of the sun.

But even the deception of the sun can't mask the shadows

clinging to the fissures or the fractured walls the hotel hides behind its sturdy doors, broken and splintered from the paranormal activity within them. Appearances are cheap. If you want the truth, see where the light stops shining.

Climbing out of the car, I pop the trunk and unload my suitcase, eyeing the hotel as dread washes over me. Every step is like wading further into the depths of dark water. I never know which step will submerge me or how many breaths it'll take me to asphyxiate.

Swallowing, I shift my gaze to the edge of the peninsula where a man sits, his legs crossed as he rests on the edge and stares out at the vastness of the ocean. I step forward and prepare to call out that he's too close to the edge when he turns around, watching me through the wet strands of hair plastered to his face. I hesitate and take in his appearance. He's fully clothed and completely drenched, droplets running down his cheeks. He meets my eyes, slamming his fist into his chest so hard it caves in before he retches up gallons of water. An impossible amount for any human.

And that's how I know he's a ghost.

One.

Death by drowning, huh? Worst way to go, I've heard.

He continues watching me as the last remains of water dribble down his chin. Then he places his hands behind his back and presses forward, his sternum popping back into place where it belongs.

The other three are close. While I feel them all, I can never tell whether someone is dead or alive until I find the cause of death. When ghosts die, they still operate like the living. Aside from a few obvious things—like flying and going through walls—they appear like living people, just like the man on the edge of the cliff. If not for the water and his concave chest, I would've mistaken him for being alive. But the young girl sprawled out on the bottom of the stairs leading up to the entrance? I know she's a ghost. People don't lounge in front of hotels with two-inch gashes in their heads, blood staining their lilac tank top.

Two.

She can't be more than fifteen, with pale skin and dirty blonde hair parted to the left. Too *young*.

"Oh, he's cute," she says to herself as Caleb and Quinn approach her. Not aware of the ghost ogling at him on the step, Caleb walks through her form with his and Quinn's bags.

She clenches her teeth at the uncomfortable sensation, her apparition buffering. "Asshole," Little Miss Ghoul spits out, knowing he can't hear or see her.

Caleb shivers, his shoulders involuntarily moving. "I just got the fucking chills."

Quinn rolls her eyes.

This is why I have to think before I speak. Calling out to a ghost that no one else can see but me? Not a good look when you're faking normal. After all this time you'd think I'd be better at it. I'm not.

Slamming the trunk closed, I drag my own luggage forward, taking in the building when I spot her on the roof. She's older than the previous two ghosts, and unlike the others, she's smiling straight at me, like she's happy I'm here. I spy at her, feigning interest in the scenery beyond her to divert any suspicion she might have. Her smile gradually fades until her lips are tilted downward and she mumbles words to herself that I'm too far away to hear. A gust of wind rushes by, blowing the hair off her shoulders to reveal her swollen, purple neck. Death by strangulation. I can pick out the individual finger markings.

Three.

Does she know I can see her?

Shaking her head, she narrows her eyes at me quizzically. I still, not allowing a single breath to pass my lips as if that will be enough to stop her from putting two and two together and doing what she wills with it.

Finally, she sinks through the roof, fleeing somewhere inside the hotel. I follow her movement down to the window below to find a boy sitting on the edge of the windowsill, one leg dangling off the side. I take in his appearance. Brown curls on his forehead, plump lips pulled into a frown, and tired hazel eyes scanning the property with precision before landing right on me.

I search for signs of injury but find nothing except a thin white scar circling his neck. It's healed. The fatal injuries of ghosts don't heal—they remain as fresh as the day they happened.

Not a ghost, then.

Maybe he's a Trace? I silently count and wait for something to happen, but by the time five seconds pass, he's still sitting there. No death. No replay. Just a living, breathing person.

Then he does the strangest thing of them all: he falls from the window.

A scream rips through my throat as he falls five stories, his body landing with a sickening thud. I've seen plenty of dead bodies and Traces over the years, but I've never seen someone die right in front of me in real time. Nausea tunnels through my stomach. The fear of witnessing his soul leaving his body levels me to my knees.

"Audrey!" Caleb and Quinn drop their bags and rush over. "What's the matter? Are you hurt?"

I grab onto Caleb's arms, glancing up at his worried face. "That boy. He fell out the window!"

"Where?"

I point a trembling finger to the boy's broken body, shoving my face into Caleb's chest to avoid the scene. "There! Under that open window!"

Caleb speaks each word softly. "Audrey, there's no one there."

"What?" I pull out of his grasp to see for myself, sprinting over to where I saw him fall.

He's right. The boy is gone.

If not for the blood painting the grass, I would've questioned if what I saw was even real. Maybe it's not. Maybe the alcohol combined with the stress of my dad's death, and my abilities, are altering my reality. Creating hallucinations. Maybe I am going crazy.

Or maybe . . .

Four.

Do Turtles Have Souls?

June 1

The composure Caleb demonstrates should ease the rod of tension in my body and allow me some solace that he's not horrified by my outburst. Instead, it does the opposite. His nonchalance digs deep into my nerves, grating against them because it's as if he *expected* this.

My state of mind is a subject that comes up a lot in the family and since most of my family is now dead, all of it is exclusively from Caleb's dad. It's an endless loop of: is she okay? Do we really think she's sound enough to be making her own decisions?

So, I can't say I blame him for the calm he's exhibiting. It's hereditary at this point. Not everyone has a cousin who was sent to an asylum when she was six for claiming to see the paranormal. And this incident occurring just after the untimely death of my dad? The cherry on top. In his head, I'm sure the mental breakdown makes perfect sense. He probably thinks I'm stressed. Depressed. Crazy. And while I'm all of that and more, I'm not the actual product of a mental illness like everyone believes I am.

No, I'm perfectly stable.

I just see ghosts.

And if they saw half of what I've made myself immune to over the years, they'd be losing their shit ten times over.

Quinn side-steps five feet to the left of me with a newfound wariness. I bite back a wide grin and lean toward her before I cry out.

She jumps. "What the hell, Audrey?" Clicking her tongue, she stops in her tracks and folds her arms across her chest.

At least everyone believing I lack my sanity is good for something. I even catch Caleb smacking his knee from my peripherals in laughter before forcing himself to straighten up and be a dutiful boyfriend to Quinn by pretending her freak out didn't just make him lose his shit.

I giggle, even when Caleb grips both of my shoulders and guides me up the rickety blue stairs to the double paneled doors.

He feigns aggravation. "Not funny."

"You laughed harder than I did."

He bites down on the inside of his cheek to smother his smile and shushes me before opening the door and allowing me entrance. "After you."

I quietly release a sigh of relief. Little Miss Ghoul is no longer occupying the step below the top one. A good thing, too. I don't know how she would've reacted when she realized I wouldn't be able to walk through her. No, when my foot hit her, unlike Caleb's and Quinn's, it would've been solid. Then one more ghost would have the knowledge that they can touch me. And what they do with that knowledge when they find out? Well, let's just say there's a reason ghosts are viewed in such a negative light. Sadistic motherfuckers.

I enter the foyer, noting the interior hasn't changed at all. The walls on the first floor are still built with the same stained, dark brown wood and decorated with blue accents. Two staircases wind up to the second floor, the whole room completed by the crystal chandler Grandpa imported from Italy decades ago. It's Granna's favorite piece, her prized possession.

One memory from this place I hold onto is lying on the floor side by side with her, staring up at the ceiling as she admired the way the light shining through the glass panels reflected off the crystals, creating a kaleidoscope of colors bouncing against the off-white walls on the second floor.

"Wow," Quinn says in awe, totally disregarding my previous behavior and turning to me instead of Caleb since they're still not talking to each other. I must be the lesser evil. "I can't get over how peaceful this place seems. I feel like nothing bad could happen to you here."

If nothing bad could happen to you here, there wouldn't be a graveyard.

I brush my fingers over the cold metal of the flask in my pocket, fighting the urge to whip it out for a drink.

Caleb stares at the empty front desk. "Where's Granna?"

I point at the heavy oak door to the left. "Check the library."

He nods, grabbing the brass handle and twisting it, Quinn and I hovering behind him.

As soon as the door opens, small sniffles fill the room.

Inside, Granna sits beside an older woman on the orange loveseat who dabs her eyes with a tissue. She pats her shoulder and whispers soft words of comfort.

"Whoops." Caleb steps back. "My bad, we'll come back—"

"Nonsense." The crying woman stands and faces us, her nose red. "Come see your grandmother. She's been anxious for you to arrive for days." She sits back down and proceeds to blow her nose. "She won't stop showing me pictures and talking about the two of you."

"Uh, okay," Caleb says, leaving the luggage by the door before strolling over. He takes a seat in a lone chair and leans back, throwing his arm over the back of it. Quinn rolls her eyes, having no choice but to sit on the opposite side of the room by herself as I sit next to Granna.

"My sweet girl." She gathers me in for a hug.

I hug her delicate frame, patting her twice on the back before extending my hand to her friend. "I'm Audrey. Nice to meet you."

"Audrey, this is Linda Harper. She's been a close friend for years. Her family owns an estate a few miles down the road."

She firmly grasps my hand. "You're even more beautiful than the pictures your Granna has shown me. You're quite the looker too, young man. Just like my grandson."

"Appreciate it," Caleb says with a charming smile.

"Thank you," I chime in.

"Caleb," Granna chides. "Aren't you going to introduce us?" She gestures to Quinn, who looks up from her phone.

"Yes, Granna. This is Quinn—my girlfriend."

"Hi." She waves.

The two older women nod at her in acknowledgment before shifting their attention back to us. Linda tosses her tissue into the woven waste basket. "I'm sorry you kids had to witness such a scene. My grandson is in the hospital right now. He hasn't been doing well for a while."

Granna shifts beside me, bowing her head slightly.

"I'm sorry to hear that."

"Thank you. We've all been sending prayers his way. I believe in miracles."

I don't.

"You're more than welcome to visit him with me if you'd like. I could use some company. Everyone else seems to have given up on him. He's running out of visitors." She directly addresses me. "I'm sure he'd love to hear a pretty girl's voice."

The boy in the window crosses my mind. I look down at my folded hands braced on my lap. They're still shaking. I could barely handle seeing that ghost. The toll of the hospital would be far greater. It would be crawling with ghosts, Traces, Shut-Eyes, maybe even Bygones. At least here I know what to expect, so for the most part, I'm safe.

Well, as safe as anyone who sees ghosts can be. So really, not at all.

"Oh, um, thank you for the invite. I'm not sure if I should—"

"Now don't be selfish," Granna scolds softly. "Of course, you'll go." The words die on my tongue as she stands abruptly. "I'm going to walk Linda out. I'll show you to your rooms afterwards."

Linda rises and wraps her thin shawl around her shoulders, bidding us goodbye before heading into the foyer with Granna.

I sink back into the couch, knowing there's no way I'm going to the hospital with her. If the death of my own father couldn't get me to step foot inside one, what makes Granna think a living boy I don't know would be any different?

I peer through the glass of the window in the lobby as Linda drives away. The two ghosts in view pay no attention to her and go about their business, Vomit Boy lying on his back in the grass near the patio as Little Miss Ghoul sits on her knees beside him, something cradled in her hands. The other ghosts are nowhere in sight, but their presences are not far off, and the thrumming beneath my skin informs me that one of them is on their way to the others this very moment.

I unlatch the window and lift it a few inches to catch what they're saying.

"Look, I found a baby turtle."

"Let me see," says another boy, one whose voice I haven't heard before, but whose presence I know too well. The one who—for some odd reason—threw himself out of the window. Ghost Number Four flies into view, landing beside Little Miss Ghoul. His body isn't broken and twisted at unnatural angles like the last time I saw him. He's in perfect shape, muscles flexing beneath his tan skin and not a droplet of blood on him. I frown at his lean body, the cut of his jaw.

I suspect if he wasn't dead, I would think he was hot.

Little Miss Ghoul holds out her hands, opening her palms to him. He leans forward, the waistband of his

Calvin Klein underwear visible from beneath his jeans. I blink and lean closer. A ghost in designer briefs? He wears Calvin Kleins and jumps from windows, go figure. I've got to say, not exactly what I pictured to be haunting this place.

"You see this?" he asks the drowned spirit. "Think that's the offspring of the turtles we saw picking at your bones?"

Vomit Boy covers his face with both arms. "Ugh, don't remind me." He rolls onto his side to heave more water, groaning as he drops his head into the grass. "I tried to shoo them away too, but they kept swimming back. One of them ate my fucking pinky toe."

Ghost Number Four smirks down at the turtle. "I bet you just wanna grab a piece of plastic and ram that thing straight through the nostril." He mimics the motion with an imaginary piece of plastic, biting his bottom lip.

Little Miss Ghoul clutches the turtle to her chest. "Why would you want to do that?" she yells.

"Just kill it. Who knows, maybe it's got some pent-up turtle rage that'll keep it from moving on. Then"—he bares his teeth in a sadistic smile and croons—"you can keep it forever."

"Do turtles have souls?" Little Miss Ghoul taps her chin in thought as if she's actually contemplating it.

"Man, why would you tell her that? No, we're not killing the turtle and I don't want to ram it in the—"

I shut the window.

When Granna comes back inside, her face is tense, lips drawn into a thin line as she closes the door. I step closer, Caleb and Quinn's arguing a faint ring from the library. "Granna?"

Her eyes shoot open, her pupils shrinking in the light. "Audrey," she says. "You frightened me."

Naturally. I've spent so much time watching ghosts I've learned to move like one. Fast. Silent. Just until I've found the right time to make myself known.

"Are you okay?"

Her forehead has a sheen of sweat on it and she's lost in thought. Haunted. I know the expression well.

"Let's discuss it later, Sweet One. For now, let me get the three of you settled in your rooms."

I nod, following her. Caleb and Quinn are quick to hush and back away from each other as soon as Granna enters the premises, clapping her hands in excitement. "Come on, kids, time to take you to your rooms."

We exit the library, our steps echoing throughout the foyer as we walk up the stairs. The steps gradually wind as we ascend into the northern wing of the inn, Granna's private residence reserved for family who live there or visit. The guests have access to anywhere before this point. My Aunt Rachel lived here with Granna for a while, but she didn't think she had enough privacy and stayed in the guest wing instead. The one time I visited, I slept in her room and every night I'd fall asleep to movies she'd project onto the clear space of the wall above the top of her bed. We'd lay on the opposite side of the bed, our toes pressed against the headboard.

She died by suicide nearly ten years ago, a couple years after my visit. Granna couldn't step foot in Windhaven for a while after that, but eventually, she healed. Windhaven became a place of light instead of darkness once again.

But me? My visions are slick with shadows, and the sun is

nothing but a white orb whose warmth can't penetrate my skin. All I know are shivers, my skin prickling anytime a ghost is near me, and the cold touch of the undead that follows.

"Quinn, this will be your room," Granna opens a door with a golden twelve plated onto the blue door before giving Caleb and Quinn a pointed look. "I expect you two to know better than to ever enter each other's rooms?"

"No," Caleb responds automatically, smirking when Quinn stifles a laugh.

"Of course." She shakes her head. "You're kin to your grandpa. He never listened when a pretty lady was involved either."

Caleb covers the side of his mouth with a hand as he leans in and whispers, "I think she just called our dead grandpa a slut."

I force my lips up to give off the impression of amusement. I'm just about to make a comment of my own when my body fills with ice. It's freezing, yet there's a trace of warmth, almost like walking through the cold while holding someone's hand. My whole body is numb, but that little bit of warmth stands out from everything and becomes the temporary epicenter of my being. The spot of heat comes and goes, in and out like it has its own heartbeat. Yet despite that small speck of comfort, I can't help but shake from the sensation, whipping around in the direction it comes from only to find nothing except a small gust of air brushing against my skin.

Something else disturbing about ghosts? They move fast. What was once standing behind me could've disappeared through the floor and vacated another room. The creaking of the floor and walls have an alert of their own and always

23

groan in protest when a ghost goes through and disrupts the atoms within the structure.

I close my eyes, trying to focus on the sound of my own breathing instead of the creaking but it's no use. The eyes burning a hole into my head are maddening and the only image I can conjure behind my eyelids is of my father on the floor, a canvas of white tile painted with his blood. I expect a wave of nausea to hit me at the cruel picture, or some innate reaction that indicates my body knows it's a brutal image of my father, but my stomach doesn't churn in the slightest. I've become completely desensitized.

The realization weighs heavy on me as Granna continues to show us to our rooms, Caleb being the next to turn in for the night. As we approach the end of the corridor, we come face-to-face to a door plated with the number thirteen. Caleb stares ahead with unease. "Granna, you're trying to curse me!" He walks backward.

Granna slams a hand to her chest and gasps. "Good heavens! Why would you think that?"

He points ahead as if that's enough explanation and looks at her sideways. "That door's got a number thirteen on it!"

"So?" I ask, with a shrug.

"Don't you know thirteen is an unlucky number?"

My lips quirk up. "I didn't realize you were superstitious. What do you think is going to happen if you go in there?"

"I don't know. A lot of things could happen. I could fall. Break my neck."

"I'd plan your funeral," I offer, as if I could even step foot in a graveyard.

He narrows his eyes at me. "You would."

"Quinn can give a dramatic speech about what she loved most about you."

He lets out a dry laugh. "That would be inappropriate, considering it's my dick."

As Granna scolds him for his language, I grab my luggage pushed off to the side and drag it into the room. "Don't worry, Caleb. I'll take the room."

He frowns. "Are you sure?"

I hum in response. *How juvenile.*

"You're not superstitious, Audrey? Not worried about bad luck or anything?"

A sardonic smile pulls at my lips. "Nope. Bad luck is the *last* thing I'm worried about."

He accepts my statement with a nod. Granna sighs and uses the master key to unlock the room after mine, warning Caleb of another talk he must endure in the morning about using profanity. He agrees before pulling me aside specifically to inform me he's here if I need him, that he's just a text away if I find myself battling with my inner demons. It's a nice gesture, but I stopped battling my demons a long time ago. They reside in my head, and I can't tell the difference between them and the real ones anymore.

Once Caleb has shut the door, Granna follows me in the room. As I take in the baby blue speckled wallpaper, she smooths her dress before taking a seat and gesturing for me to join her. "I'm so glad you and Caleb remained close throughout the years. Since neither of you have siblings, you're the closest thing each other has."

"I'm lucky to have him," I admit, taking a seat on the bed beside her.

"And him, you."

Granna folds her hands as we lapse into silence and works them back and forth. I recognize the mannerism instantly. Dad would do the same when he didn't know how to approach a topic. Ghosts he could talk about with no problem, but as soon as sex and periods were involved the man would wring his hands senseless until the words came to him. A part of me is relieved even something as small as this is living on in someone else.

"I was a little distressed earlier."

"I could tell." I run a finger along the carved wood of the bed frame, remembering the expression of pain that settled on her face before vanishing like the ghost in the hallway. Not a trace left behind.

Granna lived with Dad and I for a few years after Aunt Rachel's death. She would confide in me, telling me of her happiest memories with Aunt Rachel to cope with the grief and give me some memories of my own, since all I have of Aunt Rachel is a summer's worth. A summer's worth is hard to stretch into a lifetime, so I was grateful for the stories and know them so well, I can't tell which were hers and which were my own.

"It's just—" She takes a shaky breath. "There's been so much death here."

What gave it away? The fatalities? The fact that locals have cultivated legends around this place? Can't say I didn't notice. The four ghosts move around, their presence emitting from deep within my bones as we speak.

"Granna, do you believe in ghosts?"

She blinks a couple times as if she's trying to decipher my question. I keep my gaze trained on her, willing her to respond. Finally, she says, "I do not. Your father always did. Why? Do you?"

A swell of emotion builds in my chest. He only believed in them because of me. I shrug, turning away to examine the trinkets displayed on the dresser in order to hide my smile. "Just curious. I hear locals say this place is haunted."

"No, not haunted, just full of misfortune. First your grandfather. Then we lost your Aunt Rachel to"—she lets out a strangled sound—"Suicide."

I place my hand over hers, keeping quiet as she continues.

"It's not even just them. Over the years, there's been so many accidents. A couple tourists here and there. Linda's grandson. Your own little accident from so long ago." She squeezes my fingers, her expression burdened by guilt.

I cringe, remembering what it felt like to have water fill my lungs, to claw at the surface only to find myself still trapped in that watery hell.

Her gaze travels around the room. "It's this place, Audrey. I should've known there was something so incredibly wrong with it when your grandfather and I found out the property came with its own graveyard. I should sell it after how it affected this family, but I can't bring myself to do it. Windhaven is still my home. It's where I built my life. Oh dear, do you think that's selfish?"

I shake my head, nearly too riled up from the flashback to find the words to console her, so close to choking on imaginary water that I can't find any comfort.

"Peter didn't think it was either. Your father . . . he was the one I didn't expect to go soon. As ridiculous as it sounds, he was nowhere near here, so I always envisioned him and you living forever. I miss him."

Was it delusional of me, the girl who sees ghosts, to think he'd live forever too?

I take another moment before trying my voice. "I'm okay though, aren't I?"

It's meant to be a nice sentiment, something relieving, but as my tongue grows heavy with lies, I'm forced to face the truth I deny.

I'm more dead than alive, and it fucking scares me.

I've always felt like I was in-between the dead and the living. But after Dad died the scale tipped. And coming back here has tipped it even further. I fear what's going to happen when I'm weighed all the way down.

"I'm okay," I find myself repeating. "Linda's grandson is too. He's alive and breathing. And Aunt Rachel? She had a mental illness. It killed her."

There's a bitter note in my tone and I consider the possibility that I'm angry. Angry that she had a choice. Angry there was something eating at her mind so bad she felt like there wasn't one. I lose people so easily. Teeter a little too close to the edge and they're gone.

Granna stares forward, eyes glazed over with unshed tears. "It may have killed her, but I saw the erratic behavior. I heard her talking to herself. I saw her tear her room apart, yet I didn't connect the dots. I did nothing. I failed as her mother when it really mattered. In Rachel's case, it wasn't the land. It was me."

I've never thought much about my relatives and the circumstances surrounding their deaths. They died from natural causes—natural meaning not murdered if that counts

—and in this case it does. The property had nothing to do with that, not like Granna thinks it did. There's nothing more to it, and maybe it's time both Granna and I realize that. Maybe it's time we move on.

But the shift in the air, the temperature dropping, and the icy wind grazing lightly against my skin has a language of its own, one that tells me moving on isn't possible here.

Ghosts swarm these halls. The walls beg for release as they bend and break to the weight of their beings—because Windhaven is a land scarred by death and these cotton candy skies are tainted.

Is He Trying To...Haunt Me?

June 2

A knife of anxiety wedges in my chest so deep, any attempt to pull it out would be suicide.

I can't explain what triggered this feeling, but the sinking sensation in my stomach worsens. Hand on my stomach, I pause, recognizing the swell of irritation in my body is no longer my own. Whatever I was feeling has been stomped out to make room for the presence of ghosts. There isn't room within me for both.

There's no staggering between the apparitions. The four of them are huddled balls of energy and while I can't pinpoint their exact location, I can tell they're to the east of me, conversing somewhere in this hotel. I wonder what they're talking about, if it's about me.

My heart sinks, the knife of anxiety sliding even further into my body until the hilt is pressed against my chest and the tip sparks enough fear for my body to once again be my own.

It's an irrational fear; the ghosts can't possibly know I can see them. I'm too careful about noticing presences.

I try to breathe, but the musty air does nothing but remind me of how alone I am. How vacant this room was before I was the one occupying it and that the person who had it before me could be *dead*.

I grab the bottle from beneath my bed and chug a couple gulps of the liquor, screwing the cap back on as creaking floorboards intrude my thoughts. I glance up to find Ghost Number Four standing in front of me as I sit on the end of my bed.

Examining the label on the bottle, I read the print before taking in his form and sighing wistfully. Too bad alcohol can't drown him out like it does the Traces.

Hands shoved into his pockets, he paces around my room, taking in the clutter of my unpacked luggage and the pictures of Dad I've pinned onto the wall. In one of the pictures, we're in front of the White House fence, me on top of his shoulders as he holds my hands. I was too young to remember that day, but the sheer happiness and sun shining on us sends a warm flutter through me every time I see it. He stops at the dresser, pulling a hand from his pocket to mess with a perfume bottle. He glances into the mirror at me for a second, then in a swift motion, hurls the perfume bottle across the room.

I watch as the bottle hits the floor. His eyes harden in laser sharp focus as he awaits my reaction. Is he trying to . . . *haunt* me? I direct my attention to the bedspread to avoid the intensity of his gaze. How would a normal girl react to paranormal activity?

Letting out a deep sigh, I throw my head back and let out a dramatic scream.

He clutches his stomach and laughs, slapping his knee when he doubles over.

I roll my eyes. Idiot.

I stop mocking him in my head when a knock sounds on my door. Face flushed, I grip the sheets. My nails dig into my palms as a prickle of sweat forms on my forehead. For a moment I think it's the rest of them. They're all coming for me and they're going to haunt me until I lose what's left of my mind, but ghosts don't knock. They fly through walls, which is considerably worse, but it means it's not them.

For now.

A muffled voice speaks from the other side of the door. "What's up, cuz?"

The apparition is gone.

I let out a shaky breath and haphazardly stash the bottle back in its hiding place. "Damnit, Caleb!" I scream as he lets himself into my room followed by Quinn, who casually glances around the room before plopping onto my bed.

I still as the bottle rolls beneath my bed, the liquid sloshing against the glass.

Caleb takes in the balled-up sheets in my fists along with the baby blue knit blanket that covers me. He pinches the corner between his fingers and grunts. "Someone needs to tell Granna these old blankets ain't it. They all smell like someone died under them. Quinn's got the same one in yellow. I got pink."

And Aunt Rachel had purple.

"Newsflash Boogey-man," I say, relief unraveling in my chest when neither of them discovers the bottle. "Someone probably did die in them."

Caleb shivers at the thought while Quinn rubs at the

goosebumps forming on her arms. I smirk, then snort as I drop my head down onto the pillow. If a sentence is all it takes to freak them out, how would they get through the day in my shoes? Their minds would be in pieces. I saw a ghost claw their own face off last week and all I did was put my AirPods in so I wouldn't have to listen to that God awful screaming.

"So." I break the silence as the two recover. "What're you doing here? It's nearly one a.m."

A mischievous smile forms on Quinn's face. "Tell her."

I focus my vision on him and raise an eyebrow.

Caleb's smile mirrors Quinn's. "We got alcohol."

"No way," I chime in sarcastically.

Meanwhile, I have a whole bottle of Disaronno and a half-empty bottle of Malibu that I've been using to refill my flask under the bed. With Dad dead and gone there's no one to miss the contents of his liquor cabinet but me.

They share another smile. "Yes, way."

My sarcasm couldn't be more lost on them. "What's the plan then?"

"Well, since Granna stays in this wing too, we thought it would be a bad idea to drink in any of our rooms."

Granna's old fashioned that way. If she had a say, we wouldn't have a drop of liquor until we're twenty-one, but I had my first drink a few days shy of nineteen and Caleb's been drinking at parties even longer.

"Yeah," Quinn agrees. "I'm crazy when I'm drunk. Loud too."

I nod a reply, unable to trust my voice in fear of my words slurring.

"It's worse when she's on drugs."

33

"And I do a ton of those."

"Just socially though," Caleb adds like it matters. It doesn't, not when my already bad impression of his girlfriend has shifted more towards crackhead than the lunatic I'd initially pinned her as.

Quinn sighs in annoyance. "He doesn't like it. Won't go near them either and if I do them, he'll completely ignore me for days. And I'm always like what is wrong with you, dude? I'm your girlfriend."

Sounds pretty toxic on both ends, but I'm not one to get involved in something that has nothing to do with me. Besides, I'm more interested in the fact that she does drugs. I've never tried them. I always figured it would make what I already see ten times worse, but I can't deny my curiosity, considering what alcohol does to my abilities.

"Anyway." Quinn shakes her head. "We're getting off topic. The plan is to go in an empty room at the end of the east wing so there's no chance of her finding out. Caleb swiped the master key earlier—"

He grins, holding up the key and giving the keyring a jingle.

"—so, are you down or what?"

I'm slow to process her words, tugging my sock further up my ankle when the four ghosts disperse. As they disband, one passes so dangerously close to us that ice crawls up my spine, frost spreading slowly over each vertebra.

"Yeah," I finally say, rubbing the back of my neck to ease the tingling. "I'm down."

Sliding out of the sheets, I place my feet onto the hardwood floor. A creaking sound puts me on high alert, my eyes flitting back and forth until I can determine the floor really is just protesting from old age and not the occupancy of a ghost. Quinn looks down at my feet, examining the thick white socks that bunch around my ankles.

"Thick socks in the middle of summer? Are you not hot?"

They both stand with bare feet, Quinn fanning herself with her hand.

I shrug. "My feet get cold. Bad circulation." Which is true, but it's more about hiding what's beneath the socks than keeping my toes warm. As if on cue, my right ankle starts itching. I shift to fight off my discomfort, wanting nothing more than to rake my fingernails down my skin until it bleeds.

She gives me a look as if she knows better, eyes flitting from my wrists to my ankles. "Yeah, okay. Sure."

It's like an open-handed palm to the face when I conclude why. Huffing out a breath, I flip my palms up and hold my wrists out to her. "Looking for something?" I challenge.

She gives me a smile with a mocking edge. "Just making sure you're okay."

Caleb eyes her warily. "Enough with the attitude, Quinn."

"I don't have one."

"You do," Caleb tells her. "You can never just be nice."

"I'm blunt," she defends.

"No, you just care about what you think more than other people's feelings."

Quinn marches up to Caleb and gets right in his face. "Well, I'm not your little Sunshine, Hadley," she seethes. "I'll say what I think. I'm not going to smile and keep my mouth shut like she does just to make people like her more."

Caleb steps back. "What does this have to do with Hadley? She's Audrey's friend."

"You call her Sunshine," she spits, crossing her arms and walking in front of us. "If you like her so much, go be with the bitch."

"Don't call her that," I interrupt. "If Caleb wanted to be with her, he would. He's with you, Quinn. Does anyone understand why? Nope, but you're who he chooses to be with."

"I'm with you," he assures her.

She glances between us in disgust. "Like you're doing me a favor. No, *I'm* with you. I've always got options."

Even I can't conceal my surprise. I've never heard her be so mean to him.

Caleb's expression cracks, fault lines of sadness running through his face. He turns to walk away, but Quinn reaches out and grabs his hand. He stops but faces the other direction. After a second of hesitation, he finally rips his arm out of her grasp and slams the door behind him.

"Caleb," Quinn cries running after him. "I didn't mean it."

I follow her down the dark hallway, my feet thudding against the orange and brown patterned carpet as I stagger, having drank twice from the Malibu bottle in the last hour. I watch as she grabs onto Caleb only for him to tug away.

"I'm sorry," she says through snot and tears.

"You're always sorry."

"I love you."

I peer towards Granna's door. Her coming out here suddenly doesn't seem like such a bad thing anymore. These two need a mediator—or maybe a psychiatrist. I don't know.

I'm not knowledgeable enough about relationships to be stepping between them.

Caleb stops pushing her away and throws his head back, staring at the ceiling as she latches onto him. "I love you too."

"Come on," I interrupt. "Y'all are going to wake her."

I walk past them, my unease uncoiling with each step the further away I get. I was the reason Dad's relationship went to shambles. If I hadn't been burdened with these abilities, Mom would've stayed. They would still be together, and he wouldn't have been alone when he died. She would've been the one to properly grieve him instead of me, his sorry excuse of a daughter who looked at him bloody on the floor and felt nothing, thought of nothing except how the blood pooled around his head reminded her of the sunrise.

I shudder at the thought of someone other than me being the one to find him, the scream that would've ripped through their throat. Would it have left their vocal cords in pieces? I never screamed, so mine are whole. If I had sustained physical damage in that moment, would it have alleviated the mental one I'm burdened with now?

With a tear-stained face, Quinn nods and sniffles. Caleb lets out an exhausted sigh and follows me the rest of the way as we head downstairs to the first floor. We open the door leading to the stairwell at the end of the hall. This one is caged within walls, the window ledges so high I can barely see out of them. The moon casts an eerie glow onto us that resembles a spotlight.

I take a step into the stairwell, the contact throwing off my balance as the energy shifts in the air, so dense it rings in my ears like static.

Something's off. My head swivels toward the inner wall, the buzzing growing louder.

With Caleb and Quinn on my heels, I trudge forward, blinking when darkness creeps into my vision. I rub at my eyes, but the shadows stay.

It's the alcohol, I convince myself.

"Come on, you two. Hurry."

They're spooked themselves, clutching onto each other for comfort. Caleb offers me his free hand, but I brush it off. Quietly, I turn the brass doorknob, trying to prevent another ear-splitting creak from echoing down the hall. When it opens further, I quickly duck into the room, the other two right behind me.

Caleb shuts the door, leaning all his weight against the door and sliding to the ground like it was the most stressful situation of his life. Quinn places her hand on her racing heart, as much adrenaline coursing through her veins as Caleb's. I can't share in their excitement. My adrenaline is wasted on the ghosts.

I lie face down on the bed, scrunching my nose when I smell the knit blanket beneath me. "You're right, Caleb." I roll over. "They do smell like death. Quinn, check under the bed for a body."

Her lip curls up, prompting me to smile.

"Told you." He catches his breath and flicks the light switch on.

The ceiling spins as the room is washed in a soft pinkish glow. I rub the material between my fingers. The blanket I'm on top of is purple.

Aunt Rachel.

"So, what're we drinking?" If they brought Mike's Hard

Lemonade or White Claws, that's it. I'm ending it right here and now.

Caleb raises an eyebrow at my eagerness. "Uh, tequila." He shakes his head and takes off his backpack, pulling out three plastic neon shot glasses.

"I want orange." Quinn snatches it.

Caleb picks green, so I take pink. He pours liquor in each of their glasses before pouring mine. The second the alcohol is in my glass, I lick my lips and throw my head back, downing it in one go before letting out a satisfied sigh and holding my glass out for more.

There must be a million rooms in the hotel that resemble hers.

"Already?" Caleb hasn't even put down the bottle.

Quinn sniffs at her shot, lifting her gaze as he speaks.

I keep my arm held out with the glass in my grasp. "Mhmm."

He shrugs and pours me another one. I swallow that one too, the alcohol fueling the fire in my chest.

Caleb brings his own shot to his lips, slightly sipping it before pulling a face. He sets down the glass. "How come I've never noticed you've drank before?"

Probably because I've only been doing it since Dad died.

"I don't know. It's nothing I do often."

Now that I'm four shots into the hour—two back in my room and two here with these guys—I find myself flopping down again on my back, my head near the edge of the bed as the other two sit crisscrossed beside me facing each other. Quinn huddles into Caleb's side in an affectionate gesture that he's eager to return with an arm around her shoulder and a kiss on her head. I don't think he notices she's only being so loving because she said something nasty.

My eyes slide open and shut until my vision blurs. I slowly start keeping my eyes closed longer and longer. Then I can't keep them open anymore.

The first thing I notice when I wake up is that my throat is dry and scratchy, begging for a glass of water after what I just put my liver through. My eyes are so heavy I can't bring myself to open them. I groan, rubbing at my temples.

"Morning," Caleb says from somewhere beside me. "I passed out."

"Blacked out, you mean. What time is it?"

"Three a.m."

Someone shifts beside me. "Shut up," Quinn says hoarsely.

Smoothing back my hair, I finally open my eyes.

Above me hangs Aunt Rachel with a rope around her neck, her milky eyes fastened on me. A strangled scream leaves my throat. I claw at the sheets, struggling to get them untangled from my legs. I flail, falling off the bed right onto my knees, pain searing through them as the impact busts the skin wide open.

"What?" Caleb jumps to his feet, eyes rapidly scanning the bed. "What's happening?"

I choke on air as I fight to inhale it in my lungs. My chest spasms off rhythm.

"Audrey, breathe!"

Caleb holds me as I gasp and heave. Only when I force

myself to look up to where Aunt Rachel's body hangs is she gone, the thick rope wrapped around the ceiling fan gone. Now she stands on top of the bed, her heels digging into the mattress as she zigzags her hands across the wall as if she's searching for something, her hands forming a triangular pattern.

It's not Aunt Rachel's actual body or ghost. It's her Trace.

My lungs burn as if they're on fire.

In. Out. In. Out.

The order chimes through me as Caleb pulls me to my feet. Once I've gained control, I step closer to the edge of the bed, hand pressed against my heaving breastbone as I try to get a better look at the last five seconds of her replay. Quinn blocks my view, stepping in front of me with her hands on her hips.

"What the *hell* is wrong with you?"

I quickly school my face. "Nothing is wrong with me," I snap, before biting my tongue to gain composure. "It was just a nightmare."

Caleb shakes his head, holding his fingers up like he's trying to piece it together. "That makes no sense though, you were just talking to me."

"I was half asleep." I try to peer past the two of them.

They invade my space, Caleb towering over me as Quinn looks at me like I'm stupid. Stupid, because I'm definitely not crazy.

"Audrey, your eyes were wide open."

"It was a nightmare," I insist. "I saw Dad. I saw him die." My expression crumbles as I recall seeing his Trace.

A sympathetic look crosses Caleb's features. He relaxes his posture, stepping back to give me space. Despite Caleb's resolution, Quinn doesn't back down, even when he grabs her shoulder.

"Well?" she presses.

I cock my head to the side. "Well, what?"

"I asked what the hell is wrong with you."

"Me? You just admitted to me you do drugs!"

"Quinn," Caleb speaks softly, pulling her back. She yanks away from him.

"No!" She scowls. "I'm tired of catering to your schizophrenic cousin! Like, I'm sorry her dad died, but the bitch is screaming for no reason. There's obviously something wrong with her and I'm tired of you pretending like it's okay. No wonder we heard your dad considering putting her in a looney bin! If not for Granna, she'd be—"

A seal on my memories breaks open, as fresh as the day they happened. The musty smell of the air turns to the metallic scent of blood. I try to quash it down, but I can't stop it from overpowering me.

"Quinn," Caleb hisses. "That is way too far. You don't understand what she's been through."

"I don't have to! It's not hard to act normal."

"I'm done with you!" Caleb raises his voice.

Quinn protests, their arguing erupting into a full-on screaming match. I peer past them both, still unable to get a clear replay of my aunt's Trace when Quinn grabs me by the arms, her nails digging into my skin. "What the hell do you keep looking at?"

I shove her away from me. "Stop," I yell, finally at the edge.

She cowers on the bed like I just struck her.

I take a deep breath and slam my eyes shut before spinning away from them. "Caleb, get her out of here."

"Audrey—"

I point to where blood runs down my calves, small droplets staining the floor. "I don't have the patience to deal with her right now. Both of you, just leave."

Gathering her off the bed, they quickly duck past me. My harsh breathing slows down, the anger eating away at me slowly subsiding. When I calm down and the echo of their footsteps finally disappears down the hall, I concentrate ahead of me.

I catch Aunt Rachel at the beginning of her Trace again, her hands forming a triangle as she zigzags them across the empty space above the headboard. Something about the shape of her hands and the way they're moving looks familiar, but I can't place them. It dwindles on the edge of my mind.

The Trace continues, a rope catching around her neck. Aunt Rachel falls back onto the bed, kicking at the sheets as she claws at the rope around her neck, tearing her skin up in the process. Her body rises off the bed until she's hanging there, fighting to keep the life in her as the rope strangles it out.

It's horrifying to watch, but I can't stop. I watch it again and again. Watch it until I can feel the scratchy rope forming a noose around my own neck. Watch it until I find myself swallowing down the sickness that follows.

And with bloody knees and wet cheeks, I fall to the floor, the full force of her Trace slamming into my body like a pile of bricks. I slouch there, lips parted, pulse throbbing in my throat. Memories from over the years spiral through my mind chaotically. I was always told Aunt Rachel died by suicide, that she hung herself, but now that I stand here, watching her Trace over and over.

One time.

Two times.

Three times.

Four . . .

Never once does she put the noose around her own neck.

That's when something clicks, the gears in my mind coming to a halt once they're finally in place. Aunt Rachel didn't kill herself.

She was murdered.

Don't Fuck With Ghosts

June 7

*A*unt Rachel didn't kill herself.

I can't think of anything else or remember what anyone has said to me in the past week since I found her. Even my awareness of the four ghosts has faltered. Sometimes I pass by them speaking to each other, mistaking them for other guests of the hotel when glancing out of the corner of my eye, only to turn back around to find them gone, their whispers vanishing with them.

It's like my thoughts overpower their presence. I wish I could find relief in it, but like the lost souls on the property, the matter I'm made of is just as restless. All I want to do is tell someone about it, but the question of my sanity is something I'm not willing to put on the table. Two days in a psychiatric hospital was enough. I've claimed to see things that everyone else said weren't there.

But they *must* be.

I've seen too much. Know too much. *Felt* too much for them not to be real.

I can't go back. Yet despite that, I can't let go of what I just discovered. I need answers. Sure, I've come across murdered ghosts with unfinished business, but I've never felt the overwhelming need to dedicate sweat and blood into helping them. But this one hit too close to home. I need to gather evidence, so much that no one can deny the truth: Aunt Rachel *didn't* kill herself.

I'm going to find who did, then tell Granna she *wanted* to live and eliminate the unnecessary pain ravaging her from within.

Pulling on my white Nikes, I tie my laces, carefully dragging my right sock down to reveal my ankle. A blood spatter stares back at me, begging to be washed away. It's stained my body since I was six. I'm nineteen now, but that hasn't deterred me from searching for ways to rid myself of it. Nothing ever works and 'blood on your hands' doesn't ring half as true as it does now. Blood that touches you in this spiritual plane colors you forever.

It's permanently etched into my skin, a constant reminder—*don't* fuck with ghosts.

Covering the mark with my sock, I climb to my feet and march straight to the person who'll be closer to this than anyone.

"Hey, Granna." I descend the stairs with a small smile, faltering in my step when I find the four ghosts loitering in the lobby.

She glances up from the reception desk where she sits with a pen clutched between her fingers, motioning with a wave for me to join her. I continue my stride to the bottom, dropping down on the stool next to hers and leaning forward to examine the paperwork.

Ghost Number Three's—Bloody Mary as I've decided to call her—gaze is unnerving as she watches me. Her bloodshot eyes are the product of the blood vessels in her eyes exploding due to the lack of oxygen when she was strangled. Paired with her purple neck, she's what I imagine my sleep paralysis demon looks like.

I pretend she's not an incarnation of my nightmare and turn to Granna as I attempt to block them all out and act normal—and by normal, I mean not run out of the room screaming.

"New guests coming?" I pinpoint the last four digits of a credit card number on the end of the paper, indicating they paid in full for a month.

"Yes." She sighs, taking her glasses off. "Two ghost investigators. They said they wanted to interview me about all the deaths over the years on the property. I told them absolutely not, but they still insisted on coming." She sighs again. "To each their own."

"Ghost investigators?" I eye the paper warily and prop a hand under my chin. "Right. Locals tell stories about the Windhaven being haunted."

"Windhaven is not *haunted.*"

Glass beads clank together above our heads as Ghost Number Four swings on the chandelier.

I give her a pointed look before peering up toward the ceiling. "If you say so."

"Please don't tell me you believe your Aunt Rachel haunts these very halls," she remarks bitterly.

"If you're going to swing on a chandelier, you need to sing

SIA as you do it," Little Miss Ghoul calls out from her seat on one of the couches. Vomit Boy chuckles from beside her.

These halls are haunted all right, but Aunt Rachel's not the one haunting them.

"Can I ask you something?"

Granna's shoulders sag as her expression softens. "Sure, Sweetie. What is it?"

"Lately, I've been thinking of Aunt Rachel."

She pushes the paperwork to the side and folds her hands. "Of course, you have. I thought you being back here might . . . disturb some older memories."

I picture the small pond behind the hotel, my heart racing as my chest tightens. "A few of them."

She pushes a stray silver strand behind ear and takes off her glasses to clean them. "Rachel loved having you here. She adored you."

"How did she do it?" I don't need to elaborate. I see for myself she knows what I'm asking as her face slackens, her eyes glossing over as the memories sear her mind.

"Why must you know?"

I shrug as if I don't know the answer. "Closure, maybe. I feel like I've seen her ghost since being here." Trace, really— but close enough.

"Metaphorically that is," I add, my tone hardening. I don't want to give anyone else a reason to toss me back into that hell of a hospital again. "I'm not crazy." I prod at the pen she was writing with. "Not like Mom thought I was." Not like Caleb's dad still thinks I am.

Granna straightens up in her seat at the mention of my mother. "Of course not. You never have to fear anything like *that* happening again. And Rachel . . . She hung herself on the ceiling fan in her room. I found her the next morning."

"Did you keep the medical report?"

"Heavens, no. The medical examiner kept it for their records."

"That must've been terrifying."

It was merely a Trace and it gave me a breakdown. I can't imagine walking in on the actual day it happened. I doubt the sunrise bled for her like it did for me.

Her expression darkens. "It was the hardest day of my life."

And for the first time, there's someone more haunted than me, someone with more shadows clinging to them, pulling and sinking them like they bear the weight of a rock. Grief festers like an illness, until it leaves nothing but an empty, living corpse.

The roar of the engine blasts throughout the Windhaven property, attracting the attention of not only the guests who lounge on the limestone patio overlooking the sea, but the ghosts as well. Each of them follows the noise, Little Miss Ghoul and Vomit Boy being the first to appear in my rearview mirror as I slouch in the passenger seat, my knees pulled to my chest as I wait for Caleb to come back.

"I wish I had gotten my license," Little Miss Ghoul says longingly, gazing at Caleb's car in admiration.

"I wish I was alive," Vomit Boy quips, retching up ocean water as soon as he does. He continues coughing. Little Miss Ghoul rolls her eyes.

"What about you?" She questions someone beside her, the mirror angled in a way that obscures them from view.

"I wish they would run me the fuck over."

I sit up, angling the mirror towards me until he's visible. There he stands. Ghost Number Four with blood smeared on his cheek. I expected nothing less from him.

The other two notice as well.

"What happened to you?" She reaches up for his cheek only for him to frown and smack her hand away.

"Caroline, what have I told you about touching me?" he demands.

"Not to."

He nods in satisfaction. "Exactly."

"I was just trying to be nice."

"You're not nice. Don't think I didn't see your grubby little ass harassing that teenage girl the other day."

Like he can talk.

"I just wanted to try on her lip gloss, but she started screaming that it was floating. It was annoying, so I wanted to scare her." She smiles sinisterly. "Besides, you joined me, remember?"

A grin slides across his handsome face. "I only came around in case she took her clothes off." He groans. "It's been too long since I've been able to do it to a girl myself."

I continue to watch the exchange. So Little Miss Ghoul's name is Caroline. Interesting. Besides the little bit of mischief I picked up at the end of the conversation, I can't help but think of how human they seem. Ghost Number Four though? A complete psycho—a complete psycho I have yet to find a nickname for, because Fallout Boy seems way too easy when my first impression was of him falling out of a window.

"Um, what're you doing?" Caroline questions.

I snap back to reality when Ghost Number Four drops onto the hood of the car. I feign nonchalance as he peers through the windshield at me, fidgeting with my nails so I don't accidentally make eye contact with him.

Through my peripherals, I watch as his eyes run across my face. "Counting her freckles."

"What freckles? I didn't notice any."

"They're small and light, but they're on her cheeks and across her nose." He presses his palm flat against the glass level with my face.

A flush creeps up my neck as the car door opens. Ghost Number Four retreats as Caleb climbs in, buckling his seatbelt. I blow out a breath.

"She's still mad?" I ask when I see his clenched fists around the steering wheel.

"When is she not mad?" He snaps. "But yes."

"Gotcha." I rest my cheek against the hot window.

"We've been texting, but I wouldn't let her in my room the past few days. I went to hers just to let her know you and I were gonna head out for a bit and that I needed some space, but it was an argument the second I told her. I'm just tired of it."

"Did Granna notice anything?"

He shifts the gear to drive and pulls forward. "Yeah, she said she doesn't think Quinn is the one for me, that I would need to be with a sweeter girl since I'm more sensitive. One who doesn't bring out the worst in me."

He literally calls my best friend 'Sunshine.' Who he should be with has never been more obvious to me. I snort. "She's not wrong. You cried a lot when we were kids."

He laughs. "You rarely cried at all."

"It's the trauma."

The easygoing smile drops off his face as he focuses on the gravel road.

"Caleb," I draw out, half-heartedly knocking my fist into his shoulder. "I'm kidding."

His face is marred with concern. "Are you?"

Not at all. "I'm fine," I say tersely.

He lightens up a fraction. "Okay. Where to first?"

Deception is easy when he's desperate to believe it.

"Old Orchard Beach." Then to the medical examiner.

"You got it."

The drive away from Windhaven brings me the most peace I've gotten in days, including before I left Texas and the empty house I no longer call my home. It's true what they say, home is where the heart is, but I lost mine. And while I don't know when I'll get it back, I don't need to join the two broken halves to find ease in my surroundings. With each mile, awareness of the four ghosts grows weaker, until they're nothing. While there's a faint shifting of others, it's more subtle, barely noticeable.

I'm free.

Old Orchard Beach lacks the bustle of ghosts Windhaven has, but it's got its own movement through the lapping of waves against the shore and the grit of sand between my toes as my heels sink into the earth like it wants me to be a part of it. Another wave crashes over the shore, the disruption of the sand beneath the rippling water and reflection of the sun making it look like beige marble. I like the chaos of it all. Everything is pulsing and moving, reminding me of something I often forget: *I'm alive.*

"Are you sure you're going to be okay by yourself? I can go with you, then we can go get my game from GameStop," Caleb says as he laces his shoes.

I shake my head. "I can go alone. Meet back here at four?"

"Got it." He heads the other direction.

I leave the beach and make my way into town, cutting through buildings and streets as my phone lays out a virtual map for me to follow.

"Arrived," my phone says in a robotic voice.

I glance up to find a red brick building with tinted windows. Swallowing, I walk forward, the skin on my arms prickling as I sense the bodies inside, a few sleeping presences within the walls. And most significant of them all, a single ghost. I spot her immediately, clutching a teddy bear in her little arms. A ghost girl, no older than three or four. Her lips are blue. Poisoning.

While I make it a point not to interact with ghosts anymore, I can't find it in me to ignore her.

I pass through the door, raising my hand to wave at her. She smiles back, lifting her own hand to wave enthusiastically. Inside, I walk up to the lady sitting at a desk in front of the computer.

"Hi," I greet. "I'm looking for the autopsy file of a deceased family member."

She ceases typing and meets my eyes. "Name?"

"Rachel Woudstra." I flash her my driver's license. She prints some documents and gathers them into a manila folder before handing it to me.

"Thank you." As I take it from her, something catches on my finger. I pull it off to find a sticky note containing a login and password to the files. When I peer up, the receptionist is gathering her things, not realizing it got caught on my folder.

"Have a nice day." She goes through a door to another room, shutting it behind her. I watch through the window as she pulls out a lunchbox.

Outside, I take a seat on the edge of a fountain. The little ghost girl plops down beside me, kicking her legs back and forth as I scan my surroundings. "So," I say once a person walking down the sidewalk is a good distance away. "What's your name?"

"Tilly. What's yours?"

"I'm Audrey."

"Hi, Audrey."

"Hi. What're you doing here by yourself?"

"I'm waiting for my mommy."

"Where is she?"

She frowns, squeezing her teddy bear to her chest. "She was here with me. I saw her. But . . . she went to sleep and then—and then she disappeared. She was right here!" She points to the spot beside her. "She laid down right here and went to sleep."

Through the babble I understand the gist of what she's saying. Her mom became a Shut-Eye. She hasn't moved on in so long she fell asleep, trapping this poor child here alone. Once ghosts lose the motivation to keep existing, they fuse into structures, gradually sinking into them until no part of them is visible. I've woken a few on accident before, but I'm grainy on how to do it. It's not something I encounter enough to learn. It's a good thing—for me at least. The more ghosts in the wall, the better, as long as I don't think too hard about them being there.

"Do you want her back?" I'm surprised when I find myself sympathetic towards the young ghoul. Maybe because I almost became one myself.

She presses her cheek into the bear's worn fur. "Yes."

Taking a deep breath, I close my eyes, and inhale the air. It smells like a summer day, the wind tinged with the faint scent of grass and soil. The fountain behind me bears a metallic scent as well—pennies scattered along the base. The wind runs across my skin and whistles in my ears. I search for it, that dormant presence within. I sense the Shut-Eye behind me, sleeping within the fountain. Finding them is never an issue, but now that I have, it's unclear. I step forward, a loose coble stone shifting beneath me. I jump back in surprise, feeling a deeper vibration reverberate beneath me.

She slowly becomes visible, her still form in the fetal position at the bottom of the fountain in what essentially looks like a watery grave. She rises slowly from her slumber, her hair soaking wet as she begins coughing up the water in her lungs, disoriented as she searches her surroundings.

There, I did it. It probably wouldn't work if I attempted a second time, but once is all I need.

Her eyes latch onto mine. That's when I grab her. My fingers twist around her wrist until she lets out a soft cry, unable to look away from where I'm gripping her. "You can touch me."

It's not a question. Her eyes are wide with fear, wondering why the living can suddenly grab the dead, because pain is something she probably hasn't felt in a long time.

"You need to move on."

"Your eyes—"

"She's trapped here because of you. She won't move on without you." I point to her child, who stands to the side, her head tilted as she watches.

"They're glowing." Taken aback, she backpedals. "Get away from me."

"You left your daughter," I whisper harshly, the summer breeze stirring my hair as my lower lip wobbles at the admission. Suddenly I'm not talking to the ghost anymore. I'm talking to my father.

Like the wind she flies back, slamming against the stone of the fountain so hard she cracks it. *What just happened?*

Her daughter follows, floating and landing right in her arms. "Mommy!" She rests her head against her shoulder, but her mother does nothing but stare at me, clutching her child as hard as she can. One second passes by. Two. Then they're gone, fleeing somewhere far away.

Something slices my hand. I look down to realize the file is clutched between my fingers. I hold it up, flipping it over. I'm just about to slide it into my backpack before I glance around to find a woman staring at me. Her hair is wrapped in a fuchsia scarf, a billowing silk skirt flowing past her ankles. Her fingers are decorated in rings, a blue crystal pendant hanging around her neck. She drops the basket of fruit in her hands. "All-seeing eyes," she whispers, her gaze searing into me. "What *are* you?"

"What do you mean?" I step forward. "Can you see them too?"

She holds out a hand to prevent me from coming closer. "Demon," she decides. "Demon! You're a demon!" She screams in hysteria, attracting the attention of the people around her. They run over to her and suddenly the world falls silent. My ears begin to ring. I can't hear what she's saying anymore, but she's pointing to me. People look at me in accusation, some making a move to approach me. That's when I run.

I run so fast the summer wind slaps my cheeks, tears stinging in the corner of my eyes. My feet hit the ground so hard my heels ache, my shoe catching on a crack in the cobble stone. I fall, but quickly get back up. Looking behind me, I'm terrified there's someone coming after me. I'm so worried about what's behind me that I don't see what's in front of me, or that I've stumbled into a graveyard. *Oh no.*

Ghosts and Shut-Eyes rise around me, my anxiety and fear awakening them. It's the one part of my ability I haven't mastered yet. They come toward me, some of them weighing my body to the ground as they latch on, feeding off my energy and draining me.

This is why I can't step foot in a graveyard. Too many overwhelming feelings. There's a sense of fear I can't control because all I can think of is the dead bodies and how my father will soon be buried in the ground among them—how Aunt Rachel is already six feet under.

More climb onto me, but I can't control my fears enough to make them stop. They attach themselves to me, try to possess me. I'm weak right now. That's why they think they can do it, but they can't; I'm clear of mind and alcohol isn't nearly enough to cloud it. I sense the frustration in them as they grab onto me, trying to enter my body and get out of this rot. And despite so many holding me down, I still manage to climb to my feet and run.

It's like leeches are all over my body. They're cold, wet, and they hurt. I'm sweating, the sun burning into my scalp, my hair sticking to the back of my neck. My bones feel too big, like my skin is stretched over them too tight. A few more steps and my legs give out once more.

With no warning, it all stops. All at once, my body becomes light again. My energy comes back, and the wind seems to perish, nature at a standstill. When I open my eyes, there are no ghosts around me. Instantly, I peer up and know why. Stained glass shines above me, the sunlight catching the golden glass of a cross, informing me there is a greater force at work.

Maybe Dad did find a way to remain with me after all.

When Caleb sees me, he tells me I look like death. And I'm desperate—desperate to tell him what that actually looks like. That it's not always white sheet ghosts and creatures with gray dead skin and blood-red eyes. That it's a boy damning the whole world as he repeatedly slams his fist into his chest to throw up an endless supply of water. That it's a girl putting on a flower crown right before ogling scrawny, sixteen-year-old boys as they tan on the patio. That sometimes, it's an attractive maniac attempting to kill himself for the millionth time, despite the fact he's already dead.

I don't tell him though. I never do. And since *I* think the shit I'm witnessing is ridiculous, anyone else would too. At this point, I don't know whether to fear the ghouls or laugh at them anymore. Individually, that is. When the four phantoms come together, there's something unnerving about them, hence why I can never make myself known to them. Ghosts will switch up on you fast. One moment, they're offering to help you and the next, there's blood smeared down the hallways because of said help.

I can still remember what the blood tasted like: coppery poison.

Caleb parks the car, stopping just as the front bumper brushes up against the small rope fence separating the hotel grounds from the woods. Cracked wooden planks stick out from the grass, worn rope looped through the holes and hanging low. While the property is still a part of Windhaven, Granna keeps it blocked off since it's easy to get lost in the denseness of the vegetation and rocky slopes.

I can't smell the pine of the tree in the air, or feel the breeze run across my skin. Thanks to the ghosts assaulting and overwhelming each of my senses, they were kicked into overdrive, ultimately fusing out about a half hour after the haunting. Thankfully, when I lost my sight, it was in the car, and only for twenty-minutes. My ears rang for about ten, and now I'm stuck waiting for the rest of them to go back to normal.

Despite that, there is one thing I feel: the file. It sits at the bottom of my backpack. What's supposed to be a light folder of paper is like a rock sinking me into the sea, and even though what's in the file rattles me down to my bones and sparks fear in my core, it also gives me something else: purpose. If Dad's heart was so quick to give out on him, who says mine is any stronger? That it can keep carrying the pain of losing him? If I don't have this, I have nothing.

Retreating into the foyer, I bid Caleb goodbye as he heads the opposite direction to search for Quinn, who Granna says went down to the beach for a swim earlier. He groans in frustration and makes his way to the stairs carved into the side of the cliff. Alone in my room, I sit in the middle of the bed, the file spread in front of me. I slip my finger beneath the flap and hesitate. Sighing, I scoop up the file. Clutching it to my chest, I walk to the edge of my window. I push back the torn lace curtains to revel in the sunlight. I peer out to sea, glad Granna didn't give me a room with a view directly to the pond behind the hotel. It's hard enough starting each day knowing this place is the root of my abilities.

Yet I'm not a ghost. I just feel like one, having six senses instead of five. And while not all of them are intact right now, one sense never seems to fail me. My awareness of ghosts. They were all outside when Caleb and I pulled up, but they've already moved on—not to heaven or hell, if it exists— but to somewhere else on Windhaven land.

I'm just about to open the file when all my senses heighten, restored as I detect a change in the air. It becomes thinner, the matter of the room shifting. A tingle spreads over my skin as my nerves erupt in my body, begging me to run. The floorboard behind me creaks in two separate places.

Ghosts. Two of them.

Right behind me.

Water floods past my feet, soaking my socks as Vomit Boy walks up. He chokes, gurgling as he attempts to speak, only to spit it out.

"Shit!" He screams, a nasty burp erupting as he coughs up more. "That one hurt so bad."

"Suck it up, Bryce," the psycho ghost says. "I got myself off at the bottom of the ocean last week. Drowning is not as bad as you're making it out to be."

"Dude, you're demented. But anyway, look at her—" He cuts off, gurgling his words as his throat fills with water.

They're silent then, but I feel the psycho ghost's footsteps as he approaches, circling me. I freeze, my body still as a statue. I keep my gaze trained on the ocean, trying to act as nonchalant as possible and not give away the fact I can see him.

"You should've heard her scream the other night." He snickers, standing face-to-face with me as his eyes rake down my figure before lingering on my cheeks. "I can't get enough of those freckles."

Bryce walks in front of me as well, but unlike Phantom of the Assholes over here, he keeps his distance from me. The circling doesn't stop, his fingers lightly hovering an inch away from my shoulders as he moves. Goosebumps erupt along the tops of my arms as if the tip of a knife is poised above my skin.

And when a miscalculated shift of my feet sends me stumbling backwards, he catches me, his hands firm as they grip my arms. The dimensional wall between us shatters, the shards gathering around our feet.

"I can . . . feel her," he tells Bryce, voice low with awe. "She's soft. *Warm.*" His fingers lightly sink into my flesh. I school my face to conceal a reaction because if I was anyone else, his hands would've gone right through me.

"Ryne, look at her eyes."

Ryne.

He hesitates, letting go to resume his appraisal. "What about them?"

"They're glowing."

Halting in front of me, he leans forward, his hazel eyes boring into mine. I'm left with no choice but to gaze deep into his own, unable to stop myself from examining the green flecks in them. The file is still clutched between my fingers, my sweat dampening the papers.

Ryne's pupils dilate. He blinks a couple times, his eyes narrowing, but never leaving my own. Then as quick as lightning, a sharp pinch on my waist. I can't stop the squeal of pain that follows, or the glare that comes after.

"No way," Ryne breathes, a crazy smile slicing across his face. "She *can* see us."

RYNE

June 8

It's like an openhanded slap across the face when it dawns on Ryne that I've been able to see him this entire time, except instead of it causing some hostile reaction, his smile widens as if the realization is exhilarating. I expected wounded pride, anger—emotions I can deal with, not *this*.

"Stay the fuck back."

Both the ghost boys oblige, stepping back with their hands up in surrender, one narrowing his eyebrows while the other stares at me not the slightest bit bothered. I stumble backward, chest heaving and one hand in front of me to prevent them from coming closer while the other rubs the sore spot on my waist.

Bryce stares at me as though *I'm* the ghost, backing up as if he fears me as much as I do him, his soggy footsteps making a mess on the floor.

Ryne is a different story, elated as he watches me. "You

can see us," he repeats in disbelief. "You're alive and you can see us. I think—"

"Think what?" I snap, as the ache from the pinch dulls.

"I think I wanna touch you again." As if in a trance he reaches forward.

I dodge his outstretched hand. "Do it and I'll smack you."

A twisted smirk carves into his face. "Go ahead," he challenges, raising his chin. "I'll probably like it."

"You're sick."

As if coming back to his senses, Ryne straightens. "Actually, I'm dead. Crazy what death does to you, huh?" His eyes sparkle. "I'm Ryne. This is Bryce."

Bryce continues staring at me, the bead of water sliding down his temple resembling a nervous sweat. Then he's gone. Spirited away, leaving nothing behind but the echo of a faint gagging sound.

Ryne doesn't waste time glancing over to the spot where Bryce once stood and instead keeps his eyes trained on me, a predator watching his prey. I anticipate the pounce, keeping my body on high alert, every muscle tensed.

"I think he was bad with women when he was alive." He refers to Bryce, his gaze roaming. "Let me touch you again." He steps forward, his gaze hooded.

Another step back. "And you?" I ask, trying to distract him. "Are you bad with women? No living boy has ever asked to touch me right after we met." Or at all for that matter. No one's got the balls.

He laughs. "Not at all."

I stiffen, my lips parting in awe at how easy it is for him to recall the days he was alive. I've never met a ghost capable of remembering their previous life. Most can't. It's what makes them dangerous—inhumane—because they have no memories of right from wrong. The only thing they can remember is how they died and sometimes why they haven't moved on. The reasons? Never good if they felt strong enough for it to keep them there.

"Why haven't you moved on?"

A shadow crosses over Ryne's face, his carefree demeanor gone and replaced with something darker. "I don't know."

Okay, next question. "How did you die?"

"Someone slit my throat." He mimics the motion with his finger, but instead of lightly sliding his finger along his throat, he actually drags his nail across his skin, blood spilling from the thin red slash.

I stare at him unfazed, wondering if he's trying to scare me. He grins, revealing a full set of straight white teeth before muttering something under his breath that sounds a lot like, "tough crowd."

I ignore his games. "Why?"

"Again, I don't know."

"Do you know anything?" I ask in irritation.

He wipes the blood from his finger onto his jeans, leaving his throat bloody and soaking into his shirt. "I remember *mostly* everything up to my death."

Invading the ghost's space like he did to me, I maintain eye contact with him. The corner of his mouth raises even more as he tilts his chin down to get a better look at me, his cold breath fanning across my lips. I scowl at him, swiping my finger across his bloody throat before leaning forward on the tips of my toes. His mouth slackens as I draw a red heart on his cheek. He smears the blood and peers down at his stained fingers, eyelashes brushing his cheek.

"Stop with the antics," I say. "I've seen ghosts much scarier than you."

I can't tell if he's impressed or amused. Maybe a mix of both.

He bites his lip as he stares at me, the grin widening. "When I try to recall people from memories, their faces are blurred along with everything about them."

Whether he remembers his past life or not, it's safe to say this one is completely insane. I know what he's doing to himself hurts, but he's putting up with pain because he wants to make me uncomfortable. Too bad I've been in this spiritual world a lot longer than he has and it'll take more than a little blood to set me off.

He chuckles to himself and wipes off his hands. The slash on his neck oozes more blood with the movement. Why does he do it to himself? The questions pile up along with the urge to ask him everything. "Why did you throw yourself from the window—the first day I came?"

He perches on my windowsill and shrugs. "I was trying to kill myself."

I swallow. No wonder Bryce said he's demented.

"Why?"

"So many questions."

I give him my own version of a twisted smile. "Well, then it's a good thing you've got nothing but time to answer them."

His own smile widens. "And *you* don't have enough of it." He tilts his head to get a better view out the window, the curtains billowing around him as the salty ocean air mixed with pine enters the room and the sound of the waves crashing against the cliff surfaces. "I've spent the year as a ghost. It doesn't matter how many times I stab myself or how often I throw myself out the window. I'm still here."

Silence forms between us, neither of us knowing what to say next. Until he does.

He lifts his head. "How come you can see me?"

A shaky laugh leaves my lips. I clamp my mouth shut as soon as the sound cuts my own ears. Can't have him thinking I'm as crazy as he is, though. He already might.

Gaining my composure, I sit on my bed, tucking my knees to my chest as I smooth my dress down. I keep a sharp eye on Ryne, watching for the slightest movement that might suggest he's going to hurt me.

"I guess the same way you became a ghost. I died."

This piques his interest. He turns his back to the window, his full attention on me. I note how close he is to the edge. If he leans back even a bit, he'll fall out, but I guess that's the point.

"When I was five, I drowned in that pond behind the hotel. My dad said I was dead for two minutes."

Two minutes. All it took for the ability to form. It shouldn't have been that easy.

"From there," I continue, "I started seeing ghosts and Traces."

My throat burns as I recall first discovering what I could do—the things I asked ghosts to do for me without knowing the consequences.

"Traces?" Right, he wouldn't refer to them the same way I do.

"You know, the last seconds of someone's life—their remaining essence."

He nods. "Traces. I like it. You screamed the other night when you saw Rachel's."

"You know about Aunt Rachel?" I climb on my hands and knees to the edge of the bed and lean forward. "You were there when I saw her?"

Ryne takes in my current position, presumably looking down the front of my dress. "We *all* know about Rachel. Especially Judith. And yeah, I was there."

I cut off his view. "Oh, Bloody Mary? And I didn't feel you there." Which I shouldn't be so surprised about since I was terrified.

He fixes his gaze on me and lets out a low whistle. "Bloody Mary, huh? Don't let her hear you call her that." His voice softens a fraction. "You can feel me?"

"Your presence, yes. Now tell me about Bloody Mar— Judith."

"Not much to tell. She's been dead longer than all of us."

"She must know who killed Aunt Rachel," I conclude. My legs bounce. "You need to take me to her."

"Why should I?"

"Because I can help you move on."

He rolls his eyes. "Alright, Melinda Gordon. What're you gonna do? Help me kill myself? Push me out the window so I don't have to?"

I stop myself from biting back that he does that just fine on his own and focus on the important facts of the situation. "Better. I can do what you can't. I can leave the property." Unlike me, he's bound here for an eternity, or until he decides to move on. But since even he doesn't know why he hasn't, it's safe to say he never will—at least he won't without my help.

"I can research who you are. I know what you look like and that you died at the hotel. How hard can it be?" A couple hours of work in exchange for a meeting with the ghost who saw who killed Aunt Rachel seems like a fair deal. I'd say he'd be insane not to take it, but it wouldn't have any meaning since he *is*.

"You're sure?" he questions.

I nod. The surest I've been about anything since Dad died.

He peers up from beneath his lashes. "And you swear to me, no matter what, you won't give up on me?"

"Yes. I . . . I swear," I draw out cautiously, a prickle of sweat running down my back at the weight of his words. His eyes are hard, cunning as they search for the smallest trace of deception. I wonder if he's been dead for so long that the gears in his mind have grown rusty. If he can't remember what it's like to put them to use and trust someone blindly. But most of all, I'm curious if he's forgotten how to be hopeful. Maybe he won't let himself be. All I know is that if I don't put my hope into him, I've got nothing to believe in. Then there's nothing to stop me from completely unraveling.

As if sensing my fear, he strolls over with his hands in pocket, his smile deepening as if he's a shark and smells blood. All he's missing is razor sharp teeth, but even without there's something cutting about his smile. If he widens his lips a fraction more, I might just bleed.

Like a quick gust of wind, he's suddenly on top of me, one of his knees pinned between my own as he leans into the edge of the bed over me, his cold fingers wrapped around my throat.

"Good." He squeezes, not enough to hurt, but enough to

disrupt my airflow. I kind of like it, the way he softly threatens to end me. I like it, but I hate it. Hate the thought of being bound here but crave the thought of confirming I'm not insane.

Ever since Dad died, life has felt like a fever-dream. It's about time I wake up. Ryne's breath is so cold it puffs out of his mouth, the tendrils like smoke as they caress my skin.

"Because my death isn't a quick Google search like the others. Every year, there are memorials for both Bryce and Caroline. Every year, people come crying and cursing God for taking them away, wondering where the hell they'd be today if given just a little longer. I've been dead for a little over a year, yet no one has ever come to grieve me. And since I recall having a family, you know what that means, right?" He lets me go and moves away.

I sit up on my elbows. "They don't know you're dead. No one does."

"Right. I'm considered missing. So really, if it comes down to it, I'm going to need you to dig up my body. Can you handle that much, Melinda?"

"It's Audrey." I hiss at his stupid Ghost Whisper reference.

"I know. I hear *everything*."

Who needs walls to talk when you've got ghosts?

"Fine. What about you?" I demand. "Will you still help me if Judith doesn't know who killed Aunt Rachel?"

He crosses his heart. Then his gaze travels from my eyes back down to my neck. There's something detached about his eyes. They've grown dull, unfocused.

I prod at my neck. "Why did you do that?"

He looks as confused as I am, his form leaning against the

wall. Just as he opens his mouth to answer, Caleb bursts through the door, breathing heavily in excitement. "Audrey! Come downstairs! The ghost investigators are here—holy shit."

"What?" I ask, glancing into the corner of the room at Ryne who watches Caleb.

"Your neck. It's covered in bruises."

"You wanna tell me what happened?" Caleb is concerned, but overall furious. His brows are drawn together, his lips pressed so tight that they're losing color. For once, I have no explanation. Nothing that will make sense. "Who did this to you?"

There's really no one I could pin this on. I could tell him it was Quinn, but that would be a lie. Still, it doesn't stop me from considering it.

"A ghost," I say, my words dripping with sarcasm, but I'm dead serious. If he'd look hard enough, he'd see through the façade.

"That's not funny."

But he never does.

My mouth edges up. "No one's laughing."

Caleb swallows. "There are handprints around your neck, Audrey. Someone obviously tried to strangle you."

Guilt is evident in Ryne as he examines his own hands like he can't believe he was the one to do it.

"Don't know your strength?" I whisper under my breath, catching Ryne's attention. "You ghosts never do."

He swallows, his hand trembling as he runs it through his curly hair.

Ghosts have a lot of strength, but how could they possibly know when their hands go straight through any living person they try to touch? When I was younger, I didn't possess the same discretion as I do now. It made me susceptible to becoming a ghost's personal punching bag. Maybe that's why the pain doesn't bother me now. I'm older, crazier from the years with this ability piling on. Maybe now, I like the pain because I see it differently. It's no longer something that hurts me. It's something that confirms I'm not slipping away. That I'm here, just as real as anyone else.

I turn away from him. "Well, I don't know, Caleb. I've been in my room since we came home. Allergic reaction maybe? Besides, we don't know anyone here. Who do you think did it? Quinn?"

"No. I've been with her the whole time. She couldn't have."

So, she couldn't have because she was with him and not because she wouldn't? Those two are more unstable than I originally thought.

"It just doesn't make sense. I've never seen an allergic reaction like that."

I shrug, knowing he'll believe me due to there being no other way.

He eases up. "Does it hurt at least? 'Cause if it does—"

"No," I say flatly, waving my hand. "Besides, I already took some medicine. Now what were you saying about ghost investigators?"

He perks up. "They're here. They wanna talk to all of us. See what we've experienced."

I cross my arms. "And what exactly have you experienced?"

"Not shit," he admits. "You?"

"Not shit," I mimic.

With one last fleeting glance, I follow Caleb out into the hall. Ryne follows, floating a few feet behind us.

"I think I'm just going to fuck with them a bit." Caleb shrugs as he walks in front of us. "Be dramatic. I hang around my girlfriend enough to know how."

I lean against the wooden rail of one of the north wing staircases, watching below as Granna stands behind the front desk and talks to two people not much older than us. One is a boy with shaggy brown hair down to his shoulders wearing a too large tan baggy button up shirt over a stained white one. He holds out a mic in front of Granna's face which she politely pushes to the side. Behind the boy stands a girl with blonde hair pulled into a ponytail. She squeezes one eye shut as she peers into a small video camera lens and films.

"Caleb! Audrey!" Granna steps out from behind the desk, relief on her face as she hurries over to us as we come down. "This is Gavin and Leslie Peterson. They're ghost investigators. Gavin, Leslie, these are my grandchildren."

Granna squints her eyes as she gets a good look at my neck.

"Allergic reaction," Caleb supplies.

Moron.

Flustered from the new arrivals, Granna skims my neck, looking but not paying attention to what it really is. "Oh, are you alright, dear? Just take some Benadryl. You'll be fine."

"Way ahead of you, Granna."

Gavin gives a smug smile. "You guys should subscribe to our YouTube channel. It's called *Ghosted*."

Caleb snorts. "Sounds like some shitty show about confronting people who've blocked you on dating apps," he whispers.

"It really does."

"Yeah, we're pretty big on social media. We've just hit three-thousand followers," Gavin says, pulling out his phone to show his YouTube profile.

"Fifth most watched ghost investigator channel," Leslie says proudly.

At this moment, Quinn enters the room, standing beside Caleb, and directly next to Ryne, who pulls a face and side steps away from her. I fight the urge to laugh, shocked when I turn my focus back on the siblings to find Gavin staring at me.

"So, what's your name, beautiful?"

It takes me a second and a mocking laugh from Ryne to realize he's talking to me. "Audrey."

He holds out his hand for me to shake.

I take it tentatively, giving it a slight shake.

He shivers, releasing my hand. "Oh! Your hand is cold!"

It's because Ryne was touching me. Contact with ghosts will chill you to the bone.

"Audrey . . ."

"Woudstra."

"Gorgeous. You've got pretty eyes too. I love blue eyes with brown hair."

I sneer, flicking my ponytail over my shoulder.

"Quinn Simpson." Quinn holds out her hand. Gavin takes it and places a kiss on it.

Caleb glares at her before rolling his eyes, disliking her newfound friendliness. I can't blame him though. She didn't even go as far when introducing herself to Granna, so doing it now looks suspicious. I guess the breakup didn't stick. Can't say I'm surprised.

"And I'm Caleb Woudstra," he mocks, cursing under his breath. "Her boyfriend."

Pissing Caleb off must be how Quinn gets off. I swear his lifespan gets shorter every time she does, knocking off a couple of years at a time.

"Nice to meet you, Caleb," Leslie says shyly, which earns her daggers from Quinn.

"Yeah, you too," he mutters grumpily.

"They're going to be staying on the third floor of the east wing. Would you two please help them carry their luggage? I'm going to show them to their room."

"Yes, Granna," we both say.

"Thank you."

The six of us walk down the east wing's first floor to the end of the stairwell, the one secluded within the walls. Ryne is no longer with us at this point. Instead, I feel him materialize on the third floor alone, waiting for us at the top.

Quinn notes how the stairwell isn't as creepy in the daytime as it was that night and I remember unease settling in the middle of my chest on the stairs for reasons I don't understand. I'm not one who is usually afraid of the dark, but that night, for the first time, I was. Even the moonlight felt sinister.

We walk down the hall and immediately I know where we are. My heart drops into my stomach. Granna stops in front of one of the doors, her frame blocking me from seeing the number pinned to the door, but the presence envelopes me. I don't need to walk in to know I'm about to come face to face again with Aunt Rachel. I haven't had a chance to sneak a drink this time, so my senses track the manifestation like it does the ghosts. Then the door swings open and there she is, bruised skin and limp body. I quickly look away, a wave of emotion crashing into me.

"You gave them Aunt Rachel's room?" While it's not as much a shock as it was the first time, I still find myself wanting to crawl out of the room and vomit. She gives a solemn nod. I clamp my mouth shut.

I'm not supposed to *know* this is her room, considering Granna believes the last time I saw Aunt Rachel was ten years ago, not right now, standing right in front of her.

"I'm surprised you remember, dear. You were so young when you visited. I hope you're not upset," she whispers, pulling me aside as everyone else piles in. "Rachel's been gone for so long, I just felt I had no need to preserve the room when I have no trouble recalling our memories together."

I'm not upset. It's just going to make figuring out how Aunt Rachel died harder.

"Not at all." My own voice sounds foreign to me. Choked up. Broken. As if I haven't been that all along.

In the corner on the windowsill sits Ryne. He lacks the emotion pulsing through me as he watches the Trace replay. I focus on that, keep my eyes anchored on him.

Gavin and Leslie set their stuff down, Gavin taking one of his duffle bags from my hand before gesturing to the small sofa in the corner of the room. "Sit," he instructs. "I've got so much to ask you."

With Leslie recording, everyone takes a seat on the

couch. I drop into a lone chair as Gavin and Leslie take the bed.

"We're back with an episode of *Ghosted*." Gavin quickly waves his hands to the side for a dramatic flair. "We're at the Windhaven Hotel in Maine, where there have been ghost sightings and unexplained situations where guests have reported multiple paranormal phenomena occurring. Our research has concluded that there have in fact been a few deaths here and in one case, a suicide. With me here, I have Margaret Woudstra, the owner of this hotel, along with her grandchildren, Audrey and Caleb, and last but not least Quinn, who is . . ."

"My girlfriend." Caleb rubs his temple in irritation.

"Mrs. Margaret," Gavin addresses. "How many people have died here?"

"Five," she answers carefully, as if she knows where this conversation is going.

"Who were they?"

She shifts in her seat. "My husband Paul, my daughter Rachel, a young man named Bryce Turner, and a young girl named Caroline Philips."

She's missing two. Ryne and Judith, but Ryne said Judith has been here a long time. She may have been gone before Granna and Grandpa acquired the property. But Ryne? That confirms his suspicion. No one knows he's dead or that he died here.

It's funny. Ryne called me Melinda Gordon earlier, but I'm nothing like her. Where she helps ghosts move on, I keep to myself, allowing them to suffer for my own selfish reasons. Aside from Ryne and the little girl by the fountain, I've never gone out of my way to help a ghost. And after this, I don't think I ever will.

Ryne and I share a glance. He nods his head into the direction of something beyond me and when I turn around, I find Gavin staring directly into the same spot I was, searching for someone who to him, isn't there. He gives me a quizzical look, but I give him a 'what are you looking at?' face. Let someone else feel like the crazy one for once.

"Very interesting," Leslie comments, gaining the attention of her brother.

"Yes, very," he continues. "I did some research. Is it true you were the one to find your daughter's body?"

"Damn," Caleb says out loud.

Granna doesn't bother correcting him. "Excuse me?"

"Uh"—he gives the camera a nervous smile—"you were the one to find your daughter, weren't you?"

"Are these guys serious?" Caleb asks out loud, clutching the arm of the couch.

"Yes," Leslie answers. "It must have been very traumatic for you, Mrs. Margaret." She attempts to reach over and hold Granna's hand but Granna yanks it away.

She climbs to her feet. "This interview is over," she says sharply. "I told you two on the phone I would say their names, but not speak of circumstances. You have dishonored your word to me. Audrey, Caleb, see that these two get anything they need for their stay. I'm going to my study. Goodnight, Mr. and Miss Peterson."

Granna's pain is mine as she hurries out. It's the one thing left inside this hollowed out ribcage of mine. With that, she exits the room abruptly, leaving me, Caleb and Quinn with the siblings.

"Great," Caleb groans. "She left us with two weirdos."

"What was that, Caleb?" Gavin asks in excitement, pushing the mic towards him, completely unfazed by the stress he caused Granna.

"I said you two better leave my Granna alone or I won't tell you of how I felt a ghost grab my dick once," he lies.

Quinn laughs, but I stay zoned out, my mind racing back and forth between Granna and the Trace of Aunt Rachel.

"Cut," Leslie says. "Caleb, we're going to want a shot of you by yourself telling what happened, but before that . . ." She winks. "You get to see me in action for my segment. I sing to the spirits."

Quinn bristles, snuggling into Caleb's side as he stares blankly at Leslie with his mouth hanging open as if he's losing brain cells.

"Uh-huh," he hums. "Fun."

Gavin adjusts the ring light. "She's got a great voice."

"Ryne, what's going on?" Caroline and Bryce and float beside him, hovering while he leans against the wall, feet firmly planted to the floor.

He sighs and crosses his arms across his broad chest. "Don't know. I guess she's about to start singing to us."

"Why the hell would she do that?" Bryce questions.

"Ghost investigators," he supplies like it's a reasonable answer.

Leslie steps forward, bringing her hand to her chest. The room is silent as Gavin begins recording. She sings the intro of a song, her eyebrows pinching together in concentration.

Is she singing "Bring Me To Life" by Evanescence?

Caroline throws out her arms in exasperation. "You're telling me I'm dead while that bitch gets to live?"

Gavin belts out Paul McCoy's part from behind the camera, startling everyone with the sheer intensity of his screeching.

Leslie's voice rises a few octaves, quivering as she reaches towards Gavin, outstretched fingers closing into a fist as she yanks it back dramatically. She finishes the verse, tears pooling in the corners of her eyes as she steps to the edge of the room. A single tear runs down her cheek as she places her hand against the wall. "There's so much trauma here."

"Yeah, and you're causing it!" Caroline yells.

Ryne's face darkens. "I'm haunting her first." He cracks his neck side to side, smirking in my direction. "After all, this place *is* haunted."

"It's haunted?" Bryce glances around as if it's the first time he's hearing this.

Ryne's wicked smirk fades into a sneer. "You idiot. We're the ones haunting it."

Those Idiots Got Taken Out By Accidents And Furniture

June 10

Ryne soars across the land like he knows it and since his spiritual being is bound to the roots of Windhaven, I can't help but wonder to what degree they're connected—if the land speaks to him about what it's seen, if it's as ugly as what I have.

Due to his advantage of speed and lack of gravity, I've fallen behind. He continues to skim past the trees, dodging them with slight twists of his body. Whatever direction his shoulders move, the rest of his limbs follow. It's mesmerizing, how effortlessly he moves with the wind, how controlled and chaotic he is at the same time.

For a second, I almost think he's alive. It's hard to believe the muscles shifting in his back beneath his t-shirt belong to a dead man; that somewhere under the earth he's nothing but a pile of bones. At least, it's hard to believe until he turns back and gives me that wicked smile, the one that showcases his dimples and pinches the corners of his eyes.

How something so attractive can unnerve every fiber of my being I'll never know, but what I've always hung on to from Dad's religion is that the devil is not red horned and hideous. He is beautiful enough to lure you into temptation. Something tells me Ryne doesn't fall far from that.

Maybe I don't either. I've faced so many ghouls that sometimes when I peer into the mirror, I find them shrouding my being. It doesn't matter how well I put myself together—the clothes, the makeup—none of it matters. I can't mask the stress my abilities put on my mental state or stop it from swirling in the mirror of my eyes.

"You're thinking way too much." His tone is serious, any remnants of his wicked smile wiped away and contained.

"How can you tell?"

"You look like you're seconds away from floating up here with me."

The thought of my soul leaving my body makes my stomach flop, especially when I have an accurate picture of what that would look like. *Feel* like.

"You're observant," I decide, my face hardening.

Ryne lands silently in the grass. "There's nothing to do but watch people." He kicks at the dirt with the toe of his sneaker, head lowered and jaw clenched. I observe him as he stays in that position for a minute, then his head snaps up. "And you happen to be my favorite one, even before I knew you could see me. Convincing act by the way. The scream really sold it."

"Wish I could say the feeling was mutual. And thanks, it was fun making you look like an idiot."

He's not the least bit bothered as his lips curl into a smile, like I'm a caged animal, something meant for his entertainment. "So why did you pretend you couldn't see me?"

I stop in my tracks, not sure whether I'm following Ryne or walking straight off a cliff, but now that I think about it, the cliff seems like a safer option than being anywhere near this maniac. Until I remember there's a good chance I'd end up stuck here with him if I did. When I don't respond, he chooses not to press the issue. Instead, he waits for me to catch up before we continue on foot. I can't decide if it's out of habit or because it may be the only thing on this property that reminds him he used to be alive. I can guarantee being around Bryce and Caroline with their unhealed injuries isn't doing it. Maybe pretending he's taking a casual stroll with me does, but our walk is anything but casual. Every interaction has a motive.

"You better keep your promise to help me," I tell him, wary. Does he really want me to help him so he can move on? Or is this a ploy for something far more sinister?

"I'm down for the worse or the better."

More like 'for better or for worse.' His words are as twisted as he is.

"Down for the worse or the better?" I scoff. "You make it sound like we're married."

He shrugs. "Same thing. We're pretty much bound to each other. Just pretend it's a honeymoon."

I stiffen when he sounds way too happy about it. "But this *isn't* a honeymoon. It's a bunch of grisly murders."

"Oh, I'm well aware."

The bitterness in his tone takes me aback, but not for long because of course he is. He's one of them.

The trees loom ahead at the edge of the clearing, the Windhaven hotel further behind us with each step. A thin trail becomes evident as we near the woods, the grass under my shoes shifting to packed dirt and rock as we enter the cover of trees.

At the loss of light, I have no choice but to adjust to the darkness knowing the other three ghosts are lurking some-where in it and waiting for me. I don't want to converse with the ghosts. Hell, I don't even want to talk to Ryne, but right now, finding out who killed Aunt Rachel is the only thing keeping my grief from swallowing me whole.

Ryne glances over his shoulder, a smile once again split-ting his face. "Scared?"

"No."

"You should be. Where's your sense of self-preservation?"

Instead, I turn it back on him. "Where's yours?"

He lets out a low chuckle. "Sweetheart, I'm dead. My heart's not beating like yours, and you don't know how easy it would be to snuff that lil' heartbeat out." He does a pinching motion in the direction of my chest like he's extinguishing a flame with the tips of his fingers.

I can't even process the fact he called me Sweetheart instead of Melinda because I'm distancing myself from him, my skin prickling in a cold sweat as my distrust for him grows.

"I'm just saying, Melinda." He reverts back to his normal nickname. "Take care of it while you've got it. You don't know the things I've done to myself just to feel something." His eyes glaze over as soon as he says it, his thoughts going astray. "The things I'd do just to get some damn peace."

"Dead or alive, for me it's all the same. When I see ghosts like you flying around there's no peace for me either."

A strange noise erupts from behind me. When I turn, Ryne is lying in the grass consumed in a fit of laughter. He laughs so hard tears stream down his face, the boisterous sound like a slap to mine as it echoes through the woods.

My cheeks burn. "What?"

He climbs to his feet, stumbling through the trees as his giggles continue, then comes to a halt when his shoulder catches on a tree with a sickening crack. The smile slides right off his face as the pain registers. Even I can't stop the revulsion that rolls through me. I wince as his arm moves slightly in the breeze at an unnatural angle.

"I think"—his gaze slices into me as he braces his dislocated shoulder to his side—"you walk in front of your family pretending you're sane, but really, you're just as crazy as I am." He leans back before throwing himself forward, slamming his full weight into the tree. His shoulder pops back into place as he moans, his eyes rolling to the back of his head.

My mouth hangs open.

Ryne straightens up, testing movement in his arm before shoving his hands into the pockets of his jeans. "Alright," he admits. "Maybe I've got one up on you."

"Just one?"

He smirks.

I search deep in myself for the proximity to other ghosts. They're a constant presence, but if I concentrate hard enough, I'll know how close they really are. I turn swiftly to the right as a form begins to materialize.

"Boo," I quip in a sardonic manner.

Little Miss Ghoul—Caroline—lurches backward and falls onto her butt.

Behind her, Bryce's eyebrows hit his hairline. Even Ryne gives me a slow, drawn-out clap.

My message is clear: they're not the only ones who can haunt.

"My word, Bryce was right. You can see us." The voice is seasoned with age, but kind and distinctly female.

Judith moves from under the cover of shade provided by the leaves. Her long, tattered black dress billows in the wind, revealing her bare feet. Up close, I can tell she used to be beautiful, but age has weathered her as bad as Windhaven's sign. Unlike the other ghosts, she didn't die young. Her hair is stringy and gray strands outnumber her black ones, but despite it all, she has a genuine smile that reminds me of Granna's.

"You must be Judith."

I try not to stare at the bruises ringing her neck.

"And I'm Caroline." She waves her arms as if to remind us she's here.

"Of course." Judith smooths down Caroline's hair, causing her to frown and smack her hand away. "Do not forget our darling girl over here. She loves pretty things so I'm sure she'll take to you fast."

"You're pretty," Caroline concludes. "But you seem like a bitch."

"I can be," I admit. The word holds no offense for me. Bitch sounds better than bonkers.

"Your cousin is pretty too, but he walked through me." Anger simmers in her features and I understand why. Being walked through invalidates her existence, probably makes her think she doesn't matter and at fifteen, that's the worst thought in the world.

"Ryne's the prettiest though." She gives him a dreamy look.

He points to his throat and fake gags in her direction, cackling when doing so results in Bryce throwing up more water.

"What about me?" Bryce mutters from under his dark wet hair as he wipes his palm across his mouth. He pushes his hair over his shoulder as if to fix it.

Caroline curls her lip. "You look like the type of kid I made fun of when I was alive."

"You don't remember your life," Ryne deadpans.

"Nope, but just look at him." She throws out her arms, gesturing to his appearance. "I must've."

The conversation is hard to follow, because I'm struggling to process how alive they all seem. How Caroline acts like any other fifteen-year-old who believes the world revolves around them. How Bryce's feelings are most definitely hurt, but he refuses to say so. How Judith begins to quiet them like a mother while Ryne isn't the least bit interested by it all and yawns as if he's got something better to do.

But despite how alive they appear, their fate remains the same as Aunt Rachel's.

"Judith, what do you know about Aunt Rachel's Trace?"

Everyone falls silent, their expressions turning serious.

Her shoulders slump slightly as her expression falls. "Ah, yes. Ryne informed me about how you call them Traces. What would you like to know?"

"I know she didn't kill herself. Did you see who did?"

"No," Judith drawls. "But I felt it. Death has such an evident feel. It's easy to tell when it's in the air."

"Is there anything you can tell me?"

"I think whoever killed Rachel killed your grandfather, too. In his Trace, he looks as frightened as Rachel."

Grandpa was murdered? I hold out a hand to steady myself on the trunk of a tree.

Tension fills the air as the younger three ghosts surround us, all silent, their eyes shifting to Judith in question.

"Grandpa has a Trace too?"

Not all ghosts leave a manifestation and sometimes what is left is weak enough to fade. I don't know what factors determine whether they're long term or not, but I have a theory that it has to do with how people feel when they die. I think I'm the reason why Dad's remaining essence was so strong. Somewhere in the back of his mind he knew I wouldn't be okay, so even though he moved on, a little imprint of his soul stayed behind.

"Oh, yes. It's in the shed out back."

"In the shed?" How did it end up there?

Judith raises her eyebrows. "Your Grandmother never told you how he died?"

"No, and I never asked. Grandpa died before I was born. I never knew him."

"For the best indeed."

I penetrate her with my gaze. "What do you mean?"

"I mean your grandpa wasn't always the honorable man your grandmother portrayed him to be."

I furrow my brows. Granna always made him sound like a saint. I've always thought Dad inherited his kind nature from him, but I guess that's not always passed down. After all, I didn't get it.

"Granna kept secrets?"

"Oh, don't be so hurt, dear. Don't we all?"

I mean yeah, but I can't imagine what reasons Granna might have to keep such big secrets. As selfish as it is, I'm not ready to shatter the illusion just yet, so I opt to speak of something else instead. "You must've been around a long time. Seen a lot."

She inhales and softly lets it go. "That I have . . . and what I've seen? Wicked."

With a pang in my chest, I remember how Dad wasn't wicked. He was the purest this world had to offer. If religion works like how he always believed it did, then he should be waiting for me at the gates of heaven right now. He swore that's where he'd be if anything was to happen to him and I feel like I've let him down because I'm not sure if I believe in God enough to get there. Too many things don't make sense and I've never been one to have faith.

"Thank you, Judith."

She nods and smiles. "You're welcome, my darling. Ryne and I are here if you need any further assistance. I see he's offered to help you. Sweet boy, this one. Don't let him fool you."

"I appreciate that." But I doubt it. "Judith," I add. "Why haven't you moved on?"

Ryne makes sense since he's fairly new to ghosting, but Judith seems wise beyond her years, too self-aware not to have figured it out.

"Sometimes we have people we can't leave behind just yet and until my wish is fulfilled, I'm not going anywhere.

You are now one of those people, Audrey. You are part of us. We share a world no one else can."

While it's a nice gesture, I want no part of this fucked up family. They're still ghosts, and I'm still convinced they're all psychos. And yet, I can't help the admiration that courses through me as the other ghosts fly away, leaving me with Ryne.

"Well, if you ever want help—ouch!" I squeal as Ryne pinches the skin on my waist, hard. I yank away from him and rub the sore skin, glaring at him as a bruise forms. "What the hell is wrong with you? Again?"

Ryne's expression clouds. "Sorry about that, Sweetheart, but Judith and the others won't agree to you helping me. Don't offer to help Judith either."

"Why?" I challenge.

"Her death is a sore subject," he answers, getting in my face. "Leave. It. Alone."

"Fine." I sneer, pushing past him.

His brashness makes me wonder if the other ghosts have been pushing for him to move on faster, if they would approve of us searching for the answers surrounding Ryne's death if they knew. Would it be encouraged? Or deemed pointless and harrowing? I know the risk I'm taking with him. If it were so easy to pinpoint the exact regret that kept a soul from moving on, there wouldn't be so many spirits left here in the first place. With Ryne, it's so much more than failure; I'm risking his humanity and I'm not sure the emotional toll of that is something he can come back from.

Ryne catches up to me in an instant, appearing in front of me. I stop, not wanting to knock into him. "So, what's next?"

And none of that changes the fact he's still insufferable.

"Go to hell," I spit.

The corner of his mouth edges up. "Been there, but apparently I'm a little more depraved than they're used to."

I twirl my fingers around my temples. "You're fucked in the head."

"I am, but that doesn't change the fact I gave you a piece of your puzzle and now you owe me one of mine."

"Fine. Where do you want to start?"

"Those files. Can you get more of them?"

Accessing the morgue's database is easy when I have a crumpled sticky note in my pocket that contains the username and password. I'm sitting at the desk in my room, logging into my laptop as Ryne hovers behind me, his palm planted beside mine. I find myself staring at his hand, comparing how big it is to mine when he picks it up and slams it onto the dark wood, startling me.

I can't help it, I jump.

"When I slit my throat in front of you, I get nothing, but when I hit the wood, you're startled. You've got your priorities all wrong."

"The only thing that scares me is your smile."

"Ouch." He claws at his chest with both hands. "Straight in the heart." He drops his hands, reverting to his previous position above me. "At least it would be, if I had one." His voice takes on a rough edge.

"It really does scare me," I find myself telling him, but it's not because of how he looks.

"Why?"

"Because I don't know what you're thinking."

"So what? You don't know what anyone is thinking."

I concentrate on the screen to avoid his eyes. "But it's not hard to tell. Like Bryce? He was obviously hurt by what Caroline said, but he doesn't have the balls to say it."

"Yeah, his balls are shriveled up somewhere at the bottom of the ocean."

"And Caroline only cares about herself and superficial things."

"She does." He grabs the arm of my chair and turns it around, scraping it across the floor as he positions it to face him. He drops to his knees, so we're eye level, the contours of his face concealed in shadows. "And me?" There's a kind of desperation as he searches my eyes for the answer.

"That's what I'm saying," I whisper. "I don't know." The past few days I've spent scouring the property with him and questioning locals has failed to produce any reliable leads. In that time, I haven't obtained a clearer understanding of him either.

He pushes a stray brown curl off his forehead before climbing back to his feet. "Come on." His tone lightens as he steps away from me. "I don't have all night."

I turn back to my laptop. "Why? Is it past your bedtime?"

He swivels his head toward me. "No rest for the wicked."

"So, the saying is true?"

"Why else would I never get any? Besides, I've got some haunting to do. Someone's gotta live up to the local legends."

I conceal my smile behind my palm. "To start, we need to catalog who is here, figure out who died where and how so we can find any potential connections." I scan the screen. "Bryce was an accidental drowning eleven years ago. Stood too close to the edge of a cliff apparently. Caroline slipped and hit her head on a nightstand six years ago."

"Those idiots got taken out by accidents and furniture. My death was a whole lot cooler in comparison."

"Oh yeah, because you're just so cool for getting completely slaughtered," I say sarcastically.

"You would totally dig it if I had survived."

I ignore him and keep reading. "Aunt Rachel's claims suicide eight years ago . . ." My thoughts circle back around. "Bryce. He was already dead."

"What about it?"

I shake my head. "He never mentioned he was here during the time Aunt Rachel was alive."

"Because he doesn't know who did it either." Ryne says in a bored tone. "He was probably off puking his guts out."

"Maybe. Grandpa . . . was murdered. The killer was never found."

I slouch back into the seat. No. There's no way.

I scroll through the details of Grandpa's death, covering my mouth when the report shows a detailed drawing of a body, an 'x' on the back of his head where the fatal injury occurred. "With the trajectory and force, the injury couldn't have been sustained by accident. He was pushed."

Ryne leans down to read the screen.

"Granna never told me."

The light of the laptop screen reflects off his face. "So, Judith was right. If she's right about that, she might be right about whoever took your grandpa out getting Rachel too."

None of it makes any sense. Motives and everything attached to it. There's literally none.

Closing my eyes, I picture Aunt Rachel's Trace, the strange way she moved.

I sit up. "Speaking of Judith, there isn't one for her or you."

"No one knows she and I are dead."

"You're both considered missing then. It's also a possibility we've got a serial killer, which would explain not only my family's but yours and Judith's disappearances as well. It's a hotel, so it wouldn't be hard to come back over the years without looking suspicious."

"So, what's next?"

Since I'm not sure if the serial killer theory is even real, I see no option but to go to the source. I stand, pulling the curtains back to peek through the closed blinds. The sun lowers into the ocean, painting the water blood red. "Investigate the Traces. We'll find Grandpa's first."

My bed creaks as Ryne lounges in it, his arms folded behind his head. "You sure you can handle it, Sweetheart?"

"It's Audrey," I correct. "And what choice do I have?"

"That's the fun of it." A wolfish grin. "You don't."

This Must Count As Some Kind Of Necrophilia Textbooks Haven't Covered

June 13

The day my father died was like a million sunrises in one.

Today dulls in comparison to the sunrise of that one. It's not red, but a faint marigold orange, the colors so weak, the clouds barely take on a beige color. Gone are the cotton candy skies. He took those with him.

As the sun sinks into the ocean, Ryne and I sneak out of the hotel—well, *I* do at least. Ryne throws himself out the window before we can reach the stairs. His body results in a mangled and bloody mess, but he still manages to climb to his feet after popping a few bones back into place and spitting up the blood from his internal injuries into the grass.

"Are you done?" I remark.

His eyes flash in challenge. The curve of his mouth pulls up as he braces one hand against the side of his jaw and the other on the top of his head. With a sharp jerk to the left, it cracks. He rolls his neck to the side before leveling me with a triumphant look. "All done, Sweetheart." The words are sickeningly sweet, practically dripping in syrup.

I roll my eyes as the last trickle of sunlight vanishes. I don't prefer being out at night, but Caleb is nearly impossible to get away from now. After finding the bruises on my neck five days ago, he's followed my every move. I can't tell whether he's doing it because he's legitimately concerned or because he and Quinn are fighting again, and he's got nothing better to do. Either way, he's become a stalker and when I catch him trying to discreetly keep an eye on me, I can't help but think he looks like a complete nincompoop.

Like right now.

"Seriously, Caleb?"

He steps out from the shadows and smiles sheepishly.

I don't return his smile. "What are you doing?"

"Just happened to see you leave your room and decided to follow. What're you doing?"

I could slap him right now. Huffing out a breath, I pull my phone out of my pocket and flash him Hadley's contact information. "Not that I'm obligated to tell you, but I'm making a call," I lie through clenched teeth.

He squints at the screen. "How is my Sunshine?"

I yank my phone back. "*Your* Sunshine?"

Caleb blows a breath through his lips and winces. "Not my Sunshine," he corrects. "I did not mean to call her that. It's just—I'm the only one who calls her that so it kinda slipped—"

Ryne cocks his head to the side. "I thought he was dating that crazy bitch?"

"He is."

"He is what?" Caleb questions.

"What?" My voice raises an octave, frustration bleeding through my words. "I wasn't talking to you!"

"Then who—"

Pressing the phone to my ear, I shoo him off. "Shouldn't you go find your girlfriend? She's not going to be happy if she finds you trying to listen in on a call with *your* Sunshine."

He pulls a distressed face. "No, you're right. I gotta go before she comes looking for me." I raise an eyebrow when he leans in, as if afraid someone will hear us. "Can we keep the Sunshine thing between us?"

"Unless you've got a death wish, that would be wise." I pause. "Do you like Hadley or something?"

"Hadley? No. I mean, she's a great girl. I like her as a friend but . . . not like that. Besides, I'm with Quinn. I'll see you in the morning. Goodnight."

He rushes off and closes the doors shut behind him. I shove my phone back into my pocket. If I knew all it took was Hadley's name to get him flustered, I would've used it to my advantage ages ago. He totally likes her, but he's too dense and wrapped around Quinn's finger to see it.

Ryne crosses his arms and cocks his head to the side. "See, creeping like that is so much weirder when the person is living."

Strangely, he's not wrong. For good measure, I glance over my shoulder, paranoia lingering. What a bad time to be sober, especially with Caleb driving me nuts.

"You're losing it." Ryne's voice breaks through the air, deep and husky.

I whip around to face him. "What?" My nails dig into my palms as I clench my fists.

His lips twitch when his gaze flicks down to my fist, enjoying the fact he's unnerved me. "Oh, calm down. You know I'm not talking about your sanity."

I try to keep moving, but he suddenly materializes in front of me, smirking when I nearly crash into his chest. "You already lost that."

My shoulders involuntarily shake as I inhale sharply, his presence sending chills through my stomach like prickles of ice.

A dimple appears. "Wow. I like that reaction."

I step back before pivoting around him. "Do you ever stop talking? And don't be too flattered. Every ghost in Windhaven makes me feel the same way—uncomfortable."

He does feel different though, his presence distinct, like wading through lukewarm water and hitting a cool spot. None of the other ghosts feel like that.

His head swivels into the direction of the ocean. "You should've met me when I was alive. I was worse."

Ryne before he died? It's a strange thought. Was he charming? Did that dimple do the job? Death isn't just an ending, it's a beginning, a change that can morph you into something darker if not applied correctly—correctly meaning not being caught between worlds and wondering how the hell you ended up here.

"What"—I hesitate—"were you like?"

I fight the urge to facepalm. I shouldn't want to know anything about him. He's dead. Nothing will change that.

"As golden boy as they get."

"You?" I exhale out of my nose in disbelief. The boy before me doesn't ooze an ounce of golden boy. He's a chaotic neutral, with an affinity for pain and dark humor and psychopathic tendencies. I suppose he could've been charming, but the constant self-destruction and gore ruins it. Take all that away and maybe his smile would go straight to my stomach.

The said smile falters. "Uh yeah, I was." He runs a hand through his curls, focusing on anything but my face. "Everyone liked me. There was never a time when I wasn't the center of attention. Girls were always surrounding me, and I had a bad habit of making every last one of them feel special until they realized they weren't." He shoves his hands in his pockets. "I played football. I was good at it."

Not human, but *God* does he sound like one.

"I can see that."

He freezes. "You can?"

I shrug. "Sure. You've got the build." I eye the slopes of his shoulders, broad chest, and lean hips. His tall stature tops it off. Oh yeah. There's no question he was good at it.

Ryne lifts his gray shirt, revealing tanned abs. "Dead," he admits. "But I look fucking spectacular."

Heat shoots through my cheeks at his sculpted torso because *of course*. It's the equivalent of a sick joke. I've got the hots for a ghost. It couldn't have even been someone with a heartbeat. What is wrong with me? This must count as some kind of necrophilia textbooks haven't covered.

I school my face, turning on my heel and continuing my brisk stride. Better to keep walking then tell him he's giving my woman parts butterflies when no alive one could.

"I can hear your heartbeat from here."

"You cannot!"

His laugh is a slow drawl as he shakes his head. "Oh baby, you're so fucked in the head if you're finding me attractive right now."

My lips curl up. "Actually, that's you."

He runs his tongue across a sharp canine in his mouth. "That finds you attractive?"

I twirl my fingers around the side of my head. "No. Whose fucked in the head. You've splattered your brain on the ground too many times. Besides, I'm not the one who jumped out the window. Are you one of those freaks who has an unreasonable phobia of inanimate objects? Is that why you refuse to use the stairs?"

His eyebrows raise, but I'm not done yet.

"Yeah, don't think I haven't noticed? Who the fuck jumps out a window?"

Who kills themselves when they're already dead?

"Because I get bored, and pain is *not* boring." Before I can bite back, he speaks again, changing the subject. "You're so in tune with this world. Sometimes more than we are. Yet you had no idea your grandpa was here. You catch everything, so I'm kinda disappointed you're losing your edge."

"Then let me disappoint you more. I'm not worried about what a dead man thinks of me." I march toward the shed.

He grabs his chest in mock agony. "Low blow."

"What're you going to do? Haunt me?"

"Keep it coming, Sweetheart. I just might."

I don't respond. I simply do what I've done to nearly every other ghost I've encountered: I pretend he isn't even there.

The shed is a dark outline against the backdrop of the woods. The wood is cracked and painted baby blue. It chips and peels away from the boards like they're rotting away. Under further examination, I see they are. The burden of the

Trace's energy must stress its surroundings more than I thought.

I can't help but let my vision stray to the pond. It sits twenty feet away, its dark blue water rippling in the beam of the moonlight.

"You're not looking too good," Ryne says from beside me, his feet sliding through the dewy grass.

"I drowned there," I choke out.

"But you're right here, warm, with blood flowing through your veins. You didn't take an "L" that night. Come on." He covers my eyes with his hand and pulls me backward. My head gently bumps into his shoulder, my fingers digging into his forearm as I stumble. "Let's go."

We move, the sturdiness of his chest a comforting weight against my back and even though his hand is cold as death, it cools the burning behind my eyes. He guides me to the shed. Even when I fight for a glimpse of the pond, his fingers are unrelenting as he shields me from the darkness by shrouding me in his own. And the craziest thought forms in the front of my mind: Ryne's darkness doesn't frighten me a fraction, yet I'm terrified to be engulfed in the real world's.

He is so much taller than me, and I'm the Leaning Tower of Pisa against his chest, yet he still pushes us onward. When we stop, Ryne removes his hand. I let go of his forearm. I know I can make ghosts solid, but I never expected the touch to be indistinguishable from a human. It's fascinating and scary at the same time and my emotions are at an all-time high as I consider I'm about to see the Trace of my grandfather for the first time with the pond not far off.

I reach forward, my fingers flipping the latch. The door

squeals as the wind blows it wide open. I yank on the chain dangling for the ceiling, illuminating a single lightbulb.

The resemblance is uncanny.

I'm standing face-to-face with my grandpa, but I feel like I'm looking at an older version of Dad—the one I'd have if this was an alternate universe, one he didn't die in.

They have the same eyes, a shade so light it's been dubbed as the Woudstra blues. Every Woudstra born of Grandpa and Granna has them: me, Caleb, Aunt Rachel, Uncle Henry, Dad.

Dad didn't have lines in his face, but Grandpa's wrinkles give a clear indication of where they would've been on him, lines in his forehead and creases around his mouth from his smile. His hair is deep brown, but I bet in the sun the strands would've reflected a dark gold like the hair I used to wind my fingers in when I was toddler on his shoulders.

"Daddy," I sob quietly, my tears flowing like a busted dam into a dried-up creek that hasn't seen a drop in months. Finally, my tears are my own. I'm the tiniest bit more human.

I can barely tell this man isn't my dad, can barely comprehend this was a whole other person with a different life. I want it to not be a Trace, but most of all, I want my father alive. I want to see the breath rise in his chest and feel the warmth of his hand in mine.

I want, but it's never enough. It won't ever be. The past is gone and I'm living in a present and anticipating a future I can't be bothered to want. Without him, there's no such thing as the sun.

Dad was the only person who understood me and still loved me despite what I could see and how it became a part of me. Caleb and Granna can say they do, but they don't. No one will truly love me until they know the real me. And if my mom couldn't? Why should any of my other family members? Why should anyone?

Ryne tries to place his hand on my shoulder, but I knock it off. I don't want to feel anything. Besides, his touch? It's not real. Like Dad, he's gone.

"You don't have to do this right now," he tells me.

"I do." An aggressive swipe under my eyelids, and I'm ready.

I pace around Grandpa's Trace. How it begins seems sweet, like he had no idea what was to come. Carefree. He's fiddling with an old camera, the kind that you develop film for. He's smiling down at the camera when he's shoved backwards, his head cracking against the wood.

His face scrunches up in horror when he locks eyes with his attacker, and I can't help but think he knew who killed him and that's why he looked so horrified. I follow his line of vision, but when I peer over my shoulder, I find nothing but a vacant space. The blood spills and it reminds me all too well of the blood blooming from Dad's head.

I close my eyes and all I see are cotton candy skies.

When I open them again, it's already replaying. I look down at him as his attacker did, almost expecting to find his blood on my own hands. Revulsion and sorrow course through me. How can anyone do this and live with themselves?

Ryne is silent next to me.

"He really was murdered." I drop into a crouch.

Granna never told me. I don't think she told anyone.

"What an awful way to go," I whisper, the words ripping

open like a barely healed wound. One more and I might bleed out right here with Grandpa.

"It is," he agrees, with such intense focus on Grandpa, I swear he's gonna burn a hole right through his Trace. "But I can't help but think I would've preferred to go out like this."

The ghost himself is haunted, eyes full of fear as he wraps his own arms around his body and shivers.

With newfound concentration, I follow the movement of the Trace, this time with a special focus on the camera. When Grandpa falls, it stays clutched in his hand until he hits the ground. His fingers go limp, the camera skidding across the ground until it stops, teetering on the edge of a rotted board before falling into a hole in the floor.

Could the camera still be . . .?

I duck away from the Trace to the hole in the floor. I try to peer into it, but it's too dark. Taking a deep breath, I reach into the darkness, cringing when I feel dirt. I fumble about, until I hit cold metal. My fist closes around it as I pull it up, my wrist catching on the splintered wood and tearing my skin open. A line of blood slides down my wrist as I examine the dirty camera and cracked glass of the lens.

Extreme And Morbid, But Not Exactly A Surprise

June 16

My palms are coated in grime, my fingers full of splinters from the broken boards of the shed. The wood groans under my weight at the slightest movement, but there are no phantoms here, just me. Flask in hand, I'm a modern-day vampire as I shield away from the slivers of sunlight cutting through the rusted holes in the roof and suck up the remaining liquor like it's to quench a thirst for blood.

When I first saw Grandpa's Trace, the impact was like a drill to the cranium, leaving my mind so disrupted it took me three days to recover—three days for my soul to stop calling out to the Trace of someone who isn't my father. By now, I thought the tether would be broken, but here I am anyway, trapped by my own doing and huddled in the dirtiest corner of the floor in the shed even though I'm no longer able to see him.

Wiping the dirt onto the denim of my shorts, I reach for

the camera beside me, rolling it between my hands before squeezing it to my chest. The contents of the camera should entice me to move, yet I set the camera down to unscrew the cap of my flask instead. I flip it upside down. Not even a drop. I sigh, swiping at my damp forehead as the sweltering heat of the shed cooks me alive. That is, until my sweat is frozen over by an invisible wave of ice.

"Darling, what could you possibly be doing in here?" Judith's concerned words differ from the harsh, jagged sound of her voice, her vocal cords permanently shredded and swollen from being strangled. Fuchsia bruising contrasts against the paleness of her skin.

When I don't answer right away, she crouches to get a better look at me, taking in the streaks of grime across my arms from brushing up against the lawn equipment. At this angle, I can pick out every popped blood vessel in her brown eyes from the pressure exerted on her throat during the murder. Her ghostly form is the most unsettling of them all, but I've never been one to shy away from horror. I stare straight ahead. If there's anyone to be afraid of, it should be me, for being here, for finding more solace in a Trace than I ever will in people.

Judith's vision of me in the dark must be as clear as mine because she gasps before crowding into my side. It's like hell freezing over as frost begins to travel up my arm. It stings, but I don't care enough to voice she's hurting me and instead center on the pain exploding in my chest when the blurred edge of the Trace becomes visible again, sharpening as the effects of the alcohol subside.

"He looks just like him," I whisper, replacing the image of

Grandpa's irises with one of my father's, eyes so blue, they rival the waves of the ocean.

Judith rests a hand on my arm, but the sensation is lost to me. "Who?"

"Grandpa." My words slur as I throw my flask in the direction of his configuring Trace. Weaving my hands in my hair, I clench my fingers around the slick strands and pull my knees to my chest as a headache begins to form between my eyebrows. "I can't do this right now," I sob.

But I can't bring myself to leave either.

Taking a deep breath, Judith climbs to her feet. "We can't have that now, can we?" She disappears into thin air before taking shape in front of me moments later. She holds out one of my unopened bottles.

I eagerly pluck it from her grasp before breaking the seal. "How did you know?" I lower the bottle warily. "Were you spying on me?"

Judith shakes her head. "Margaret used to stash hers in the same place."

I tilt my head back for a drink, disturbing a dangling tool above me. I sputter as I swallow wrong, hacking my lungs out. I slam a fist into my chest a few times, before slumping into the wall. "Granna used to drink?"

"For a little while after Rachel died, but she stopped ages ago."

"Granna's a liar."

"I'm sorry I was the one to tell you. I assumed you already knew. Don't be so hard on her. She's been through a lot, much more than you," she reminds me gently.

And Judith's been there for every moment of it. I can't

fathom what sort of connection she must feel to her after all these years together. Alone in her room, has she unknowingly bared her heart to Judith in a way she couldn't in front of anyone else? Is that why Judith understands her while I struggle?

I slam the bottle down. "That doesn't change anything."

She chose to withhold what happened to Grandpa and the drinking from me and considering the range of secrets she's kept from me so far, anything and everything is on the table. I won't be blindsided again.

"Audrey—"

"She *lied*." I grit my teeth until my jaw aches as Grandpa looks like an older version of my dad—an age he'll never see. "I don't understand why she did."

Is this what Ryne felt when he was stabbed? Someone could kill me right now, and I don't think it would be enough to rival the needles of pain penetrating my heart. I'm caught between worlds with a curse I don't want that gives me the power to see. So why can't I go home and see my father waiting for me at the door?

It's such a selfish thought, I swear he frowns down at me from Heaven—if it's real—if he's really waiting for me at the gate like he says he is.

I purse my lips. Religion is like a constant thorn in my side. Like the ghosts, I can never quite tell if it's real and it's been a long time since I've let myself hope for anything.

Undertones of sadness create a fog in my mind. It's so dense I almost miss Judith saying, "I'm not sure. She may have wanted to protect the family, but instead she unknowingly planted a seed of mistrust."

I rack my brain for answers as to why Granna would lie. I

run my finger along the cracked lens of the camera next to me and picture the loop of Grandpa's Trace, his curled up fingers, body sprawled across the floor. Even the fall closely resembled my father's.

Fear ignites me, a fuse finally setting fire. What if Granna killed Grandpa?

It's a ridiculous thought, but grief has a funny way of misplacing blame and it's due time for another drink. When my fingers wrap around the bottle, I suddenly need Ryne here. I need him to tell me sanity is not wasted on me. Most of all, I need him to tell me I'm losing my fucking mind and for once, I hope I am.

And like a beacon, a spot of warmth forms despite the cold emanating from Judith's being, meaning one thing—Ryne is near.

I curse, rubbing at the spots of dirt on my knees but it's no use. There's nothing I can do to hide what a wreck I am. I brace myself, preparing for the ferocious laughter and mockery I'll have to endure from him.

Just as Ryne steps through the wall, Judith steps in front of me, the long tatters of her black dress hiding me from view as the rest of his apparition steps inside. "Judith," he says in surprise.

My breath is strained as it passes my lips, having inhaled the musty air for hours.

He scans the shed. "Have you seen Melinda?"

"My apologies, who?"

Ryne snorts and adverts his gaze. "Like you don't know."

Judith covers her mouth as she lets out a shrill laugh. "Just yanking your chain, dear. I'm not sure where Audrey went."

My lips twitch upwards. Mother Teresa, my ass.

"Well, let me know if you find her. We found something and I wanna see if she's okay."

"I'll send her your way if we cross paths."

Ryne nods and vanishes. I track his movement across the land until he's a good distance away before pulling myself up. "Worried about me? Yeah right." I flash Judith the bottle. "Thanks for this, but I've got to go clean up before someone sees me like this."

"If things get too hard on you, promise me you'll stop searching for answers."

I turn to face her, eyes narrowed. "Why would I do that?"

"For your health." She assesses me from head to toe, her face creased in worry. "Whatever you found, I don't like what it's doing to you or Ryne."

Or Ryne?

Once I'm cleaned up and contained, I head out to the patio, sliding the glass door shut behind me as I'm greeted by the heavy smell of chlorine. Guests linger on the beautiful limestone, adjusting their chairs for a better view of the sun while others splash around the built-in pool on the deck. Kids run past me as I step forward, leaning on the edge of the stone railing and peering down into the open clearing in search of Ryne. I spot him instantly, arms crossed, and one hand propped under his chin as he watches two young boys throw a football back and forth.

What does Judith think searching for answers is doing to Ryne?

"Not like that!" He bites down on his pointer finger as the ball torpedoes into the ground. He scoffs as he walks over, grabbing the football in the boy's grasp and pulling it back until his arm straightens with it.

"Who taught you kids how to play?"

Putting some force behind it, Ryne guides the ball as it's thrown, following through as it leaves the tips of the boy's fingers.

"Huh?" The boy is mesmerized as the football goes sailing, getting lost in the sun.

"Whoa!" The other kid jumps up and down as the ball flies over his head. "How did you do that?"

He retrieves the ball, rolling it over in his hands. "I don't know." He tests motion in his arm. "But I think I can do it again."

Copying Ryne's stance, he pulls his arm back before catapulting the ball into the air.

It's a perfect spiral.

Ryne smirks. "Atta boy."

"Mom! Dad! Look!" The two run off to find their parents.

"I never took you for a coach."

Ryne turns his head toward me as I walk down the stone stairs smiling. "Fine." He grins. "You caught me. I used to coach youth football when I was alive."

"You?" I point. "Good with kids?"

"The best," he corrects. "So, you've come back for more?"

I nod. "Just think about it. The camera had been sitting there for decades before we found it, and no one had even bothered to fix the hole in the floor. Imagine how many more clues there are around here that have been left untouched."

Ryne stuffs his hands into his pockets and focuses his

attention on the flowers. "Are you sure you're up for that right now?"

"Yes. Why?" I can't stop thinking about what Judith said back in the shed. "Are you not up for it?"

His eyes move back and forth over my cheeks, and I recall his face through the windshield when he told Caroline he was counting my freckles. I touch them, suddenly worried that's not what he's looking at all. What if I missed some dirt while I was in shower?

His teeth sink into his bottom lip as if he's having an internal debate with himself. Then, the side of his mouth curls up. Ryne strides into the direction of the hotel with purpose, his steps quick and calculated as if he knows exactly where he's going. It's a walk of confidence, I realize, and it doesn't matter if he knows where he's going or not. For someone like Ryne, there is no other way to walk.

I follow, but mine is nowhere near the same. I'm too cautious, my own steps sporadic as I take care to avoid knocking into guests on the patio. Why? Because I'm scared of bumping into someone and finding them sneering at me in contempt. I've been scared of this all my life. Thanks to my mother, I'm cursed to a life of teetering along the edge of every room, blending into every wall. If I can't blend, I make crass remarks, so that if I'm met with inevitable scorn, I can sleep at night knowing at least on my part, it was intentional. They think bad things of me, not because of who I am, but because I made them.

Despite my efforts, I still bump into someone, their arm clipping me as they pass by. I look down to where their hand brushed against my pants, shook to my core when I find a large smear of blood. I whip around to a girl heading in the opposite direction, a bucket hat covering her head, but that's not what stands out about her—it's the fact that behind her is a trail of blood.

Is she a ghost?

Forgetting Ryne, I tread on her heels, dodging incoming people.

"Nikita, is that you?" One of the guests breaks away from their group and makes a beeline to her just as I'm about to close in. I halt, Nikita now facing in my direction.

Definitely alive. Then, where is the blood coming from?

I peer elsewhere to not make my interest obvious, but it's useless as she still manages to meet my eye over the sea of bodies, so I retreat into the hotel.

"Ryne," I call out into the empty lobby.

"Took you long enough." Ryne floats above me, legs crossed with arms behind his head. "I was starting to think you were getting bored of me."

"Psychopaths are rarely boring."

"Neither are pretty, unhinged girls like you."

"Pretty?"

"Huh, that *would* be the part you question me on."

I shake my head as if to rid myself of the conversation. "We're getting distracted. Let's focus." I run my hand along the empty front desk as we pass it, wincing slightly when it irritates the splinters in my fingers.

"What's wrong?"

I rub at the sore spots. "Just a few splinters."

"Let me see."

Before I can say anything, he grabs my hand and flips it over to examine it. "These aren't bad. One time I impaled myself on a branch if you really wanna talk about splinters."

Extreme and morbid, but not exactly a surprise.

"Of course, you did. Ouch!" I yank my hand back as he prods at one.

"Sorry," he says mischievously. "I'll get them out." He catches my wrist in his grip. I hone in on the bones of his knuckles, intrigued by how strong they look. I have never seen anyone as comfortable in their skin as he is. Murdered, but he looks untouched by it all, on the outside at least. Inside he's wrangling a monster, one whose sinews are wrapped in infectious memory and teeth sharp enough to rip into his fragile state of mind.

"It's fine—"

His lips brush my skin as he leans down, his teeth grazing me as he pulls one slightly sticking out with his teeth. Instead of pain, I'm greeted with a pleasant shock of nerves that dip deep into my stomach. I clasp my mouth shut as my cheeks turn rosy because that's not normal. Teeth skimming my palm shouldn't feel this good.

Turning his head sideways, he spits it out. "How does that feel?" He bites at the edge of another one before I can answer. "Tell me if it hurts." He pauses when he sees the distrust tightening the corners of my mouth.

He slowly releases my hand, chuckling softly as he dips his head down. "Contrary to what you're probably thinking, I don't enjoy causing physical pain to anyone but myself. I mean it, how does that feel?"

Better than I'd like to admit. "Okay . . . I guess."

"Are you sure?" He swipes a finger across his own cheek to indicate the blush laid beneath my freckles. "You look a little *feverish*."

My jaw ticks. "If I look feverish," I seethe, "it's because

you make me sick!" I explode, my voice booming. In the rare moments I am honest with myself it's only to accept that I *do* experience some kind of thrill when I'm with him. I hate how casually he throws it in my face.

Hadley would call it flirting, but to me? It's an attack and I have no qualms about fighting back.

"Me-ow. Do you bite too? I hope so."

"Ryne—"

"Put the claws away, Sweetheart," he interrupts. "We've got an impending investigation, remember?" Ryne lands next to the door of the stairwell. "Ever been in the lighthouse?"

"No, it's been blocked off for decades."

"Better hope you've got a strong stomach, then. Shits about to get Tarantino."

Considering the body-horror he subjects me to on the daily, it can't get much worse.

A knowing smile tugs at his lips as he saunters inside, walking beneath the metal stairs to double doors safeguarded by a lock and chain.

Stepping foot into the room triggers what feels like an earthquake and the buzzing in my head from that night Caleb, Quinn, and I were on these stairs creeps into my head. At first, it's muffled, so faint I barely sense the shift, but the closer I get, the more distorted it becomes, the air wavering around me.

Ryne grabs the lock, giving it a hard yank. The chain binding the door rattles as it hits the ground.

"You ready?" Ryne's expression is all hard lines and tired eyes as the humor leaves his features. The burden of his death has never been more obvious; it hides in every shadow of his face, the dark circles beneath his eyes.

"I was told it's bricked in."

"It's not."

"How do you know?"

Ryne's Adam's apple slides up and down his throat as he swallows. "Because"—his voice takes on an edge as he plants both hands on the handles, throwing them open to reveal a spiral of wooden stairs—"This is where I was killed."

I spin, taking in the circular walls surrounding me and reaching high. They're made of brick, coated in a layer of white paint except in a few places where the red shows through.

I raise my foot to the first step and stop. It's speckled with brown stains. I follow the spots, stumbling back when it turns to splatters.

It's dried blood.

Ryne floats behind me, like he's scared of this place blemishing him anymore than it already has. I avoid the blood to climb further, maneuvering around the patches like I did to the blood of Dad's Trace on my kitchen floor.

"I can remember what the knife felt like." His fingers find his throat as he traces the line, his features slackening as his eyes take on a faraway look.

"What . . ." I trail off, wetting my dry lips. "Was it like?"

"Agony. I had a knife in my chest, but I thought the fear would kill me before the knife did. You were right when you said I'm fucked in the head. You would be too if you saw walls covered in your own blood and wondered how the hell you were still alive as you choked on your own blood."

The statement is spoken into the atmosphere, the temperature around us dropping as his voice chills the air. I must not be as desensitized as I thought, because when I see the dried blood on the walls I'm back in the asylum, the taste on my tongue, my limbs sticky and stained with it. And that smell. It never leaves and I used to fight the urge to sniff something stronger to rid myself of it.

Maybe that's why Mom left. What're you supposed to do with a child who keeps crying because she can't stop smelling blood? I wasn't given a chance. Completely screwed from the start.

"A knife went through your chest?" I've only known about the scar circling his throat.

"My chest, my hands, my stomach. My—throat. Everywhere."

"Show me your scars." I need to know I'm not the only one who bares them, even if mine aren't physical.

His tone takes on a threatening edge. "Some scars are meant to stay hidden, right? You ever gonna tell Caleb why you're always wearing thick socks like we're in the dead of winter?"

He knows. The socks are suddenly constricting my ankles, too hot against my skin. I scratch at my ankle with the tip of my white sneaker, lowering it slightly, but not enough to reveal the blood that won't wash off my skin.

"How did you get it?"

Silence.

But that doesn't deter him from following with, "I bet it's exhausting to see murderers with blood on their hands from their last victims and know there's nothing you can do to prove it. Plenty of them come through here."

It is. Sometimes, alive people are stained with the same blood I am. Not because they're dead but because they killed someone. I've lost count of how many murderers I've let walk past me because while I know they've killed someone, I have no way to prove it or help.

"You get used to it," I say, not willing to put any more of my emotions on display for him.

His laugh is bitter. "That's the thing. We shouldn't have had to."

A look of understanding passes between us as we trudge on. At the top, I'm given the entire expanse of Windhaven. The ocean is bright, the sun catching on ripples in the water as waves crash into the cliffs and the pine trees rattle from the wind. The gravel road winds down the property, surrounded by a variety of colorful wildflowers. Sometimes I forget, but without all the murder and gore, Windhaven can be really beautiful.

Ryne is silent beside me, rocking back and forth on his heels as he stares off blankly. The stairs have affected him more than I thought.

"Are you okay?"

No answer. It appears I'm not the only one not up for answering questions today.

Assuming he needs a minute, I pace around the room, glancing over the rusted controls of the lighthouse and old filing cabinet. I move on to find a chalkboard littered with sticky notes arranged in perfect lines. I pull one off the board. There it is again, the color purple. I read the writing and gasp. It's Aunt Rachel's handwriting. The tiny letters in impossibly neat lines are unmistakable.

Dad, is it really you?

I move onto the next note, examine the unfamiliar messy scrawl.

Yes, Rachel. It's me.

How are you here right now?

I had to come back for you.

I tear off note after note, gathering them all in my hands to make sense of them. Backing away, I shake my head. Impossible. Grandpa has been dead since before I was born and since he has a Trace, how the hell was he writing notes to Rachel?

I knew it was you. The signs you left for me around the hotel. No one could've known what those things meant but you.

It was the only way I could let you know I was still here.

Unless it wasn't him writing the notes, but the person who murdered her. What kind of elaborate sick game is this?

"Ryne, come here."

It's the kind of a game a serial killer would contrive. Granna said Aunt Rachel was acting erratic before she died—this has to be why. I'd go crazy if I thought Dad was still alive too. If this cursed ability is good for anything, it's that it gives me confirmation my father isn't suffering.

I search through all the loose papers, searching for something, anything to confirm my find. When there's nothing left to be found, I slam it shut and flop forward onto a twin sized mattress sitting in the corner of the room. Propping my chin on my hand, I think, fingers clenching around the sheets on the mattress. I pause when I realize what I'm doing. "Oh, ew. What's that doing here?" I scrunch up my nose when a musty smell infiltrates my nostrils.

I toss a quick glance over my shoulder and do a double take when Ryne's in the same spot.

"Hey," I rush over, grabbing him by the shoulder. "I called your name—" He rips his shoulder from my grip, panicking as ragged breaths leave his lungs, eyes looking through me as if I'm transparent, as if . . .

I'm the ghost.

Bryce materializes in front of me in an instant. His wet hands shoot out as Ryne lunges forward into the air.

PTSD

June 16

Guilt over Ryne is like a heavy rock tossed down the well of my stomach as soon as we're back in my room, overshadowed by the fact that someone was communicating with Rachel, pretending to be Grandpa before she died. It's a mess.

"Come on, buddy." Wet handprints soak through the cotton threads of Ryne's shirt as Bryce holds him steady. "You're safe."

Ryne hyperventilates, his shoes squeaking against the hardwood floor as he backs up into the wall. As soon as his back is against it, he jumps away as if scalded. It's like we didn't leave the lighthouse. "I thought I was back, I was—" His eyes snap open in realization. He looks down at Bryce's hands on his shirt and then to me, his face slipping into a blank expression. A callous laugh sounds as Ryne processes Bryce's words.

"I'm not safe!" Ryne exclaims manically. "I'm dead."

A wry smile forms on Bryce's face. "You know what I mean. You're not *there*."

"I know," he replies dryly. "Now get your soggy ass off me. I'm good."

Bryce drops his hands and heaves out the window before wiping his mouth with his sleeve.

"Ew." Caroline's head pops up from under it, barely avoiding the vomit.

"Ryne?" I say, my voice small.

He doesn't bother glancing in my direction, the glossed wood of the floor piquing his interest. I've inflicted some damage and I don't know whether to blame it on the fact I asked him for answers or for knowing he wasn't okay and not saying anything sooner.

Caroline floats through the window, opening my closet as the show begins. "Audrey, why did you touch him? I know he's told you not to. He's told us *all* not to. You never know when he's lost in a memory."

He hasn't told me, but judging by the corded muscles in his neck, he should've.

"PTSD," Bryce supplies. "It takes him back to the night he was killed."

Even ghosts can be diagnosed with PTSD. Yet another thing blurring the lines that distinguish them from humans.

"It's why he won't let me touch him," Caroline says, glancing into the mirror as she holds up one of my shirts to her chest.

"Us," Bryce whispers.

"Yeah, yeah." She heads into the closet, claiming she's going to try on a pair of my jeans. She shuts the door. "Ryne," she calls out.

He cocks his head to the side, a scowl etched into the hard lines of his face as his full lips thin.

"What?" he spits out in a dangerously low voice.

She throws the door open, before turning around to look at her butt in the mirror. She bends a knee. "Do these pants make my ass look good?"

"You're dead, Caroline. It doesn't fucking matter."

"That doesn't answer my question," she drawls.

"No. They don't."

"You're so mean!" she whines.

All he does is shrug. "You asked for it," he says without a hint of sympathy. Without another word, he runs forward, diving out the window.

My heart gets lodged in my throat as I pitch myself forward.

"Ryne!" I cry out.

I press my cheek to my palm as I lean onto the windowsill, chipped white paint sticking to my elbows. The grass is bloody, but he's gone, and even though logically I know he can't die again, unease is restless in me at the thought of him being hurt.

"Don't be too hard on yourself," Bryce says. "You couldn't have known, but yeah, that's why he hurts himself. If he's the one inflicting the pain, he takes back the power that was taken away when someone else did. And . . ."

I gesture for him to go on.

Bryce leans back and forth on his heels. "And it's why we don't think he should be helping you. All of this? It's too much of a strain on him. Everyday, you risk him fading away."

"What do you me—"

A gust of wind rushes by. When I turn around, Judith is behind me.

"Judith!" Caroline and Bryce are quick to surround her, adoration in their eyes.

I slide down to the floor, my head hanging. "I didn't even feel your presence," I admit out loud, surprised something slipped past me when I usually feel everything around me like a second skin.

She waves me off, the gesture reminding me of Granna. "Is Ryne okay, darling? He was emitting some kind of dark wave."

My cheeks flame. I cover my face to prevent her from seeing the emotion flickering across it. "I don't know."

Her face softens as she walks to my side, the wind stirring her coarse hair. "Ryne may seem like the toughest, but he's the most sensitive of us all."

I snort. "I don't know about that."

"Bryce and Caroline have accepted their fates and choose not to dwell on them. Ryne does, even though it's been a year. It makes him vulnerable. A couple months is usually all it takes for us to accept what's happened."

Vulnerable to what? Acceptance takes time. They can't rush that.

My eyebrows scrunch together as I tilt my head to the side. "If they've accepted their fate, then why haven't they moved on?"

They, because Ryne told me to steer clear of Judith's death. She talks of acceptance, but has she done it herself?

"Acceptance isn't the same as closure."

The power of her words surges through me, and I swear I've never heard anything so true.

"Were you there?"

"I'm not sure I understand the question, darling."

"When Ryne died."

She nods as she processes my question before answering. "No. I felt his death, but I didn't witness it myself."

"He told me he was stabbed multiple times and that his throat was slit."

Yet he doesn't bleed like the rest of them. Why is that? Just when I think I've figured out the rules to this spiritual plane, I'm proven wrong.

"Oh?" Judging by her surprised tone, this is news to her. Ryne may be careless with his body, but not with information. God, I should've kept my mouth shut.

"Yeah. He remembers."

"Poor boy. Did he know the person who killed him?"

"No. He can't remember faces."

"For the best. He's been through enough. He doesn't need to be tortured by that, especially if it was someone close to him."

I want to ask what she means by that, but Ryne's words are still on a loop in my head, so I choose not to just in case she's referencing her death. I run a hand through my hair, blowing out a breath.

I always spill. Like a faucet filling up a sink. Like a girl with too many damn secrets and not enough places in my mind to keep them. I'm tired of watching my words because I never know what I'm supposed to say.

I'm tired of pretending to be the girl I'm supposed to be.

Ryne is off somewhere doing God knows what to himself, so I'm left with Judith trying to pick up the mess that's me. And while I appreciate the gesture, she can't offer what I'm looking for. I don't even know what that is, or since when Ryne has been the only one who has it.

Ryne doesn't pretend. Ryne makes me feel *seen*.

"Have a good night."

Before I have the chance to respond, there's a sweep of breeze and Judith, Bryce, and Caroline are gone. I watch as they follow her through the trees, their presence whisked away. She really is like a mother to them. Mine left when I was so young, I can't help but envy their bond.

Knuckles rap against my door in a steady rhythm and I'm teleported back to the world of the living. It's Caleb. Quinn's are always off beat and Granna's are nearly too soft to hear with the delicate bones in her fingers.

"What?" I demand when he opens the door. My mood's been foul ever since I found out about Granna keeping secrets and has grown even worse after finding the sticky notes. Did Granna know about Aunt Rachel thinking Grandpa was alive? Is that another secret she's keeping from me? I keep mine for my own good and to save my family from thinking I'm a lunatic, but Granna is *normal*. So, what could possibly be the reason for hers?

He frowns, physically taken aback by my response as he peers around the room as if I'm talking to someone other than him. I'd find it funny if I was, but after the past few days, I'm not in the mood to laugh, and I'm not currently being subjected to any haunting.

When he doesn't answer, my patience wears thin. "What do you want?"

"Nothing," he says nonchalantly, trying to keep his tone even. The annoyance is there though, and I'm just waiting for it to rear its head. I almost want to egg him on for it. "Did—uh Quinn apologize to you?"

"Why should she? She'll make another snide comment before nightfall." I give him a pointed look. "You know that."

He scratches the back of his neck. "I'm sorry for her then. She was out of line. I told her if I ever hear those words out of her mouth again, I'm gonna end it. She can't treat my family like shit."

"While I appreciate the gesture, I don't care what your girlfriend thinks of me."

He clenches his jaw and nods. "Granna wanted me to tell you dinner is ready. Quinn's down there already. We're just waiting for you."

"I'll be down in a minute."

"Alright."

With that, he turns on his heel, retreating from the scene —from me. I take a few gulps of liquor and follow, keeping my pace slow enough to stay behind him as he stalks down the stairs to the library. The door in the back leads to a small private dining room on the edge of the kitchen. While the guests dine in the big hall, we eat our meals here for a more intimate gathering.

I take a seat in the cushioned part of the wooden chair, the arches stretching a little past the top of my head. The chair is so straight, my back stiffens. Slouching isn't an option unless I want wood digging into a couple of my vertebrae.

Granna's not sitting at the table with Caleb and Quinn, but I can hear her scuffling around in the kitchen with the cook.

"Audrey," Quinn says across from me.

"What?"

"I'm sorry about last week . . . and how long it's taken me to apologize. I haven't seen you around lately."

Fighting the urge to snort, I stuff a bread roll into my mouth, chewing around the mocking smile making its way onto my lips. She'll always be sorry until she does it again, so I'm not convinced. Besides, our rooms aren't far apart. She could've said something days ago.

I finish chewing and swallow, the room so quiet I can hear it slide down my throat. I set the roll down, facing her. "How about we just call it a day? You keep your distance, I'll keep mine."

Caleb slams his glass down, rattling our silverware. "Audrey . . ."

Act normal. I don't need to read minds to know he thought it. It's all over his face, to keep the fragile peace for his sake, for his rude ass girlfriend.

"Say it," I dare him. "Whatever you're holding back. You're obviously thinking it."

He huffs out harsh breaths, trying to reign in his temper, but one thing is certain: I'm done trying to control mine. Resentment bubbles up in me.

"I'm sick of tearing myself into pieces small enough for you to swallow." I climb to my feet, grabbing my half-finished dinner roll and ripping off another bite. "You two can fucking choke. Your apology doesn't mean shit."

"What the hell does that mean?" Caleb demands, following me into the library.

A chill and blip of warmth, and I know who's decided to drop in to watch the show.

I whip around on Caleb. "You're the worst one," I yell. "You act like you care so fucking much for me, but when someone says anything about me? You pretend to be mad and smooth it over. You don't really care what they say, just that you can be good with Quinn. Your threats to her mean nothing. *She* knows they mean nothing."

"That's—"

"The truth and you know it. You pretend with me every day. You act like you don't know that I'm—that I'm sad. I pretend I'm not." My voice breaks as I wrap my arms around myself, realization a cruel, mean bitch. "And you let me."

We used to be so close. I even considered telling him my secret until Quinn came along. Then I couldn't trust him with anything.

Caleb is speechless, his mouth slightly open as his eyes pinch together in pain.

Movement behind him catches my attention. I expect to see Ryne loitering around, witnessing my devastation, but it's not him. It's Granna.

A full plate of steaming food rests in her hands. Her eyes are glassy, the pale skin around her nose and cheeks pink. Maybe it's perfect timing. Maybe it's God, like Dad would say, but my outburst at Caleb has left my emotions wrung out, and I'm ready to go to my room so I can hang them to dry. I don't have it in me to say anything else. I slam the door behind me in case anyone thinks they have an invitation to follow.

A good thing too. A second sooner and I would've blurted out that I've got a sickening gut feeling she may have had something to do with Grandpa and Aunt Rachel's death.

And if she did, who's to say she isn't covering something up about Aunt Rachel's.

I simply look away, shaking my head. This would've broken Dad's heart like it's breaking mine now.

"Hey there, Sweetheart."

I freeze in place, my body automatically unwinding at his presence once I hear his voice. I survey the room, desperate to find him. There's something unnerving at feeling him but being unable to spot him. His floating form comes to view in the foyer. He lingers on Granna's crystal chandelier, leaning back into the ring of it, legs crossed and his arms resting behind his head as if he's sprawled out on a bed.

Hearing the relieved sigh come from my own mouth causes me to clamp it shut. I mentally put my guard back up. I can't rely on a ghost for anything, even relief.

"Where have you been?" I demand.

He shrugs, cocking an eyebrow. "What's it to you?"

I ignore the sting from his words and proceed to walk up the stairs slowly, making sure my shoes squeak against each step. He hisses at the sound, covering his ears.

"Using my trauma against me? That's petty, even for you, Melinda." He cocks his head to the side, the corner of his mouth lifting up. "Is this retaliation for going M.I.A?"

"Audrey," I correct.

His eyes latch onto mine in disbelief as he brushes a finger over my alcohol flushed cheek. "You aren't in your right mind right now, are you? I never took you for a mean drunk."

I bristle, falling back into my normal stride with my face ablaze.

"You didn't answer my question."

"Mmm," he hums, smiling as he disappears from view.

When I reach my room, he opens the door for me, giving me a mock salute as he steps aside for me.

"Ryne," I growl.

He smirks, glancing down. "You're so taut all the time." His finger outlines the clench of my fingers without actually touching skin. He bites his lip as his fingers move up my arm, until they hover over my shoulder. "I loved seeing you"—a swift tug on my bra strap—"snap."

I jerk away from him. "So, you get off on my suffering now, you sick fuck?"

"Did you not just get off on mine?" he demands with a jerk of his head.

When I recoil, his posture relaxes. "But no. I get off on the fact you know you deserve better, so put the claws away, alright?" He smirks, making a clawing motion in my direction.

I cough to squash down the butterflies. "Whatever, Danny Phantom." I step away from him, plopping down onto the edge of my bed, my back sore from the chair. My skin still burns on the part of my shoulder where Ryne didn't touch me, not really. "I'm sorry," I say, disgusted with myself. "That was really fucked up to do." And so unlike me. I've *never* exploited someone else's trauma like that before.

I glance over at Dad's picture. It's wishful thinking to believe I could even resemble the kind of girl Dad would be proud of. I picture him rolling in his casket as I practically stomp on his grave.

"I'm sorry too. For a moment I thought—" He cringes, kicking back into the chair on the other side of my room, abruptly changing the conversation. "You should know I've taken it upon myself to haunt that girl for you. She's in denial right now but give me another night or two and I'll have her batshit crazy."

I smile. It's a completely unhinged but flattering thought. I switch positions and lay on my stomach on the edge of the bed. "Quinn? And how do you haunt, exactly? You can't touch her." None of them can. I'm the only exception.

"I may not have this ghosting thing down as good as Bryce, Caroline, and Judith, but I have been getting better at picking up inanimate objects."

"And how's that working out for you?" I kick my legs back and forth in the air.

He gives a half-hearted shrug. "It takes some skill to master, and it's a hell of a lot harder than football, but you'd be surprised how terrified people get when you toss some shit across a room."

I laugh, my anger fading as I recall what happened between us. "I'm sorry about earlier too. In the lighthouse."

Recognition flashes in his expression, before his face falls into a passive mask and he turns toward the window. "Nothing to be sorry about, not after what I did to you."

I prod at my neck, lightly applying pressure to the bruises, but they don't hurt. They never really did.

Ryne clenches his teeth.

"Why did you do it?"

"I didn't think I could."

I grab the camera on my bedside and run my fingers along the rusted metal. "Hurt me?"

He snorts and brushes me off. "No offense, Melinda, but discussing my violent tendencies isn't exactly what I'm here for."

"Full offense, you mean." I snuff out the hurt in my chest. I'm the one who wanted everyone to stop pretending. "Spit it out. What're you here for then?"

A wicked smile. "You owe me."

I look down. "I couldn't find anything on you. You know that." When I search for his face, his eyes are locked on the camera as I fidget with it.

Noticing I've caught him, he runs an aggravated hand through his hair. "I've helped you twice. You found something didn't you?"

"Yes, but—"

"Fuck!" he howls, so loud it echoes off the walls, through the barriers between his world and mine. He scrubs a hand down his face, his facial features creased in anguish as a dark aura emits from his figure.

It's the most emotion I've ever seen out of him. A crazy Ryne? I can handle that. A vulnerable Ryne? I don't know where to start.

He drops onto the floor, the back of his head knocking into the wall. I gasp as something starts to happen. His figure flickers in and out, his body becoming transparent until he begins floating a few feet off the ground.

"Ryne!" I outstretch my hands, willing to go against everything I stand for just to make sure he's okay. His hands remain, obscuring his face from view.

My own hands go right through his form. A strangled gasp leaves my throat as I'm unable to touch him the first time I try. I claw at his form as his body sinks through the wall, but it's not just sinking—it's fusing into the wall. He's not going into another room; he's becoming a part of it.

"Ryne," I cry out, as the wall ripples around him. "Come back. You're gonna disappear. You're gonna—"

Become a Shut-Eye. Sleep for an eternity if not woken. *Never* move on.

This is what everyone was trying to tell me. This is what makes Ryne vulnerable, the fact he can become a Shut-Eye at any time.

"I'm not giving up on you," I promise. "I just need to find another way. We need to find another way."

I can't stop now. What will become of me if I do? What about Ryne? Will giving up be something he can't come back from?

He flickers as his eyes slide open. "How? You're just a girl who's nearly lost her mind. What are you gonna do?" His voice cuts like razors along my skin.

"Lose what's left of it with you. I told you I'd help you."

I'll do anything to ground him.

He inhales a shaky breath, his form dissipating once more before he finally becomes solid. Then, without a word, he spirits away.

Throughout the night, I keep tabs on Ryne as he desperately clings to his humanity. His presence has gone haywire, but every time I try to locate him, he's gone. The movement disorients me, various cold spots sprouting in different places along my body. I twist in the blanket so it's a cocoon, heat gradually consuming me. I want to stay awake in the chaos but keeping track of Ryne is the equivalent of counting sheep and eventually when I feel him and Judith's beings collide, I'm lulled into a slumber.

Get Naked, Live Your Best Undead Life

June 19

My arm is frozen to my side. I try to gain feeling back into my hand by working it back and forth, but my joints protest, each of my fingers cracking like they're coated in ice. Eyes sealed shut in sleep, I rub at my arm blindly, willing the friction to warm me up when the worst realization slams into me.

I shouldn't be this cold.

I shoot straight up, the blanket pooling around my waist. A silhouette lingers by my bedside, the camera cradled against their torso. I flick on the lamp in a quick motion, my head too cloudy from sleep to sense whose presence is here with me. The harsh light illuminates the room and Ryne's face.

His hazel eyes widen a fraction, clearly not expecting to be caught.

"Ryne?" I cover my chest with the blanket, hoping he doesn't notice I'm braless. "Why do you have the camera?"

Why is he here at all? All the ghosts typically leave me alone once I've gone to bed.

His mouth opens, but no words come. Tightening his grip around the camera, he takes a single step back before whisking away.

"Ryne!" I throw the blankets off me and run out the door to follow him. I stumble through the dark hallway, my feet thudding against the carpeted floor. All guests are sleeping in their rooms, so there's no one to see me as I sprint through the hotel in nothing but a tank top and shorts, my hair whipping behind me as sweat gathers along my hairline.

I nearly slip on the polished floor when I make it downstairs, catching myself on the banister. Pulling myself up, I trudge forward, heaving in copious amounts of air as my lungs beg for it. My heart has been kicked into overdrive, like the equilibrium of my entire being relies on the intactness of the camera. And it *does*. Without that camera, I am nothing. This investigation is nothing.

I throw open the double paneled doors, yanking them closed behind me as I hit the clearing. I twist around, the woods in the distance on nearly every side of me. The lighthouse towers above me in the night and for once, I wish it still worked, that it could light my way into this uncharted darkness.

When I spot the part of the woods where Ryne disappeared, I make my way to it, trusting my ability enough to lead me there blindly, even though getting lost in the woods at night is a real concern. I concentrate on his energy, my arms shielding my face from twigs and leaves as I break through the vegetation. A sharp sting, and the cut on my arm from the shed reopens. Droplets of blood run down my skin.

A little way in, I stop when I near him, his back facing me. I slowly crouch out of view, resting my elbows on the tops of my knees behind a bush.

Son of a ghoul. He's doing way too much. I was trying to fucking sleep.

I hold my breath as I peek up from behind the bush, careful not to rustle the leaves. I flinch when something howls out into the night and hug myself. Ryne stands on the edge of the woods that overlook the sea, his head swiveling toward the direction of the sound. He stills until the sound fades, turning back to the depths of the murky water. He extends his arm out, the camera dangling over the edge. When he shows the first sign of dropping it, I lunge forward.

"No!" My scream pierces the air as I dive for the camera. He's so startled by my appearance, he releases it. I snatch it out of the air, my eyes widening as the momentum throws me forward. My feet scrape against the edge of the cliff. I plummet through the air, Ryne's horrified face getting further by the second. The waves crash against the cliff, roaring in my ears along with the wind. Ryne disappears off the ledge, materializing in front of me as he wraps his arms around my waist. Then the world spins, everything in my vision breaking apart and reforming.

A rush of nausea hits my gut and I'm no longer falling. Instead, I'm lying flat on my back in the sand. Rolling over, I cover my mouth as I fight off the urge to hurl all over the beach, the other hand holding the camera in a death grip.

"What the fuck, Audrey?"

I flinch at his use of my name, how the syllables roll off his tongue.

"You can't just go diving off cliffs." He waves his hands

up and down in front of his body, as if the brisk movement of his arms will convey just how much I can't.

"Really, Ryne?" I curse and flop onto my back, guarding the camera to prevent him from getting anywhere near it. "It's your fault I fell in the first place."

"You're *alive*." His eyes are wild, pleading, and desperate in a way I've never seen before.

My lips curl up as I shake my head. "So what? You were gonna throw the camera off the cliff. Why did you do that?"

Still on his feet, he considers the question, his brow hardening as he glares down into the sand at his feet. "You wouldn't get it." He turns away, looking out into the vast ocean. "You'd have to be dead to understand."

"Try me."

But the unrelenting set of his jaw warns me I'm not going to get anywhere with this, so I focus on the churning of my stomach instead.

I moan and close my eyes. "Why do I feel so sick? Is it because you spirited away with me?" God, I feel as dead as he is.

When he doesn't answer, I throw my arms out to my sides, sand sticking to my skin. "At least look at me when I talk to you!"

He finally meets my eyes, anger simmering in his features until he sees me sprawled out in the sand, my mouth pinched as I send him a glare of my own. His jaw slackens. Ryne opens his mouth and pauses before closing it again, the anger vanishing instantly.

He rolls my words over in his mind. When he finally uses his voice, it's husky. "Spirited away? I teleported with you."

He cringes. "Not everything's gotta sound so damn ghostly, Melinda."

"Like, I get that you're used to throwing yourself off the cliff, but don't throw my things too!" I huff out a breath, my chest rising and falling rapidly.

Ryne's dark eyes slide over my form, the green flecks hidden in the dark, a sliver of moon in distress as it tries to shine.

"If you're mad we haven't found more on your death or even about earlier just say that. Don't apologize if you don't mean it and don't throw a fit and steal my shit. You *know* how important this is to me." My voice cracks as emotion clogs my throat.

"I do." Like he's in a trance, Ryne walks over, his strides slow and even. There it is, that slow prowl.

I hold my ground by refusing to move a muscle. I keep my position defenseless, because I want him to know he can't scare me. "Try to take this camera from me again and our deal is off." If I wasn't selfish, I'd have called it off the moment I realized he was at risk of disappearing because of *me*. I could do it right now, send him away to save him, but as Ryne steps between my spread legs and drops onto his knees, telling him to leave becomes the furthest thing from my mind.

Swiping the camera from me, he tosses it to the side. Letting out a growl of frustration, I lift my head off the ground and turn it to the side as I reach over a couple inches for it. When I've got it, I turn back to find Ryne's arms caged around me. My head falls back when I see the yearning in his eyes and how he licks his lips when he runs them over my body.

I shift. Bad idea, especially when the inside of my thighs

touches both of his. I know the warmth of them must seep into his being because he clenches his jaw, sand crunching between his fingers as they clench into fists in the sand. When his eyes open, something feral in them has been unleashed on me. My grip loosens, the camera slipping to the ground.

He leans down, his mouth brushing the shell of my ear. "I want you. I want you so bad it's all I can think about."

His words send a lick of fire through my body, my face overheating until I can feel the warmth gather in the center of my cheeks.

Is this what all those heated looks have meant until now? The slow once overs and even slower smiles? I swallow. This isn't some proclamation of love. It's something entirely different that I'll never understand. This has nothing to do with me and everything to do with his animalistic nature and a tiny bit of his sociopathic one that will always view me as some kind of toy for him.

Threaten my life, spill his blood in front of me—it's all the same and none of it, not even the prospect of death, frightens me. But this intense wanting? I'm fucking terrified. Why would anyone want me? What kind of joke is this? If I wasn't the only one who could see him, I wouldn't be in this position with him. Instead of me, it would be a girl who is high on life, who throws her head back to laugh and has a glorious smile.

"Ryne," I whisper, searching his eyes. "You're scaring me."

He's off me in an instant.

I sit up and bring my knees to my chest. His back is to me

as he tosses a quick smile over his shoulder. "Sorry. I'm just horny and it's amplified when you're around."

But it's more than that.

"You're not just horny, though. Right? You like the warmth I give off."

"I do, but—"

"You can touch me," I blurt out without thinking. "I—I mean appropriately of course."

Once I'm out of his system, he'll want nothing to do with me. We'll be strictly business, to haunt and to hold until we aren't.

Without warning, Ryne scoops me out of the sand and dumps me into the ocean. I squeal as cold water laps over my body, my head and the tops of my knees the only parts of me that have yet to be submerged.

"What did you do that for?" The ocean cleanses me of dark thoughts, the current carrying them off to sea.

"Because you need to cool off." He runs a hand through his curls, giving me a feverish look. "I am the last person you should be giving access to your body. You should know by now I'll take it without hesitation."

"Without hesitation?"

"Without hesitation," he emphasizes darkly.

"Maybe you should cool off too, then." I pull his legs out from under him, giggling as he loses his balance and splashes into the water beside me, fully clothed.

Ryne shakes water from his curls, the drops flying around us.

We splash around for a bit, my tank top and shorts completely drenched. Ryne remains fully clothed, peeling his wet t-shirt away from his chest as if it's sticking to him uncomfortably. I take in his jeans, the material darkened from the dampness as it constricts his legs.

"Why don't you take your clothes off? I'm uncomfortable *for* you."

Ryne narrows his eyes as if he's trying to figure out if I'm joking. "And why the hell would I do that?"

"You'll do anything to feel alive, won't you? So, prance around the ocean in your underwear. It doesn't get any more alive than that."

Get naked, live your best undead life.

"You going to join me, Sweetheart?"

"This *is* my underwear."

My chest surges at my boldness. What is happening?

Ryne lets out a low whistle.

He falls silent after that. I take my attention off the handful of sand and seashells I scooped up from the bottom of the ocean floor to see what he's doing, quickly averting my eyes when I catch the muscles in his stomach rippling as he yanks his gray t-shirt up and over his head before flinging it onto the shore. A few faint scars are etched into his chest from the blade that killed him, completed by the thin scar circling his throat. I examine them, taking a moment to consider what that must have felt like and how much pain he went through, and most of all why on him, they healed, but my thoughts are cut short. His pants come down next, those black designer Calvin Klein briefs I saw peeking out of his waistband so many times now on full display.

And as we splash water at each other, the drops are like tiny crystals that fly through the air as they land in the ocean. We dunk each other into the water, laughing as we surface before tackling each other into the soft waves once more. We swim and swim, until my muscles ache from laughter and sleep tugs at my mind. Ryne walks me back to the hotel, each of us wringing out our clothes before he bids me goodnight, twisting on his heel and heading down the hall. And with the blood pouring into my cheeks and the warmth spreading through my body, I feel something I've never felt before. The alcohol fog has lifted from my mind and for the first time in forever, I'm completely my own. I am more alive than ever.

I go to close the door, but it catches on something. I pull it open to find Ryne on the other side, an apprehensive look on his face. He's come back and the air around him is measured with an unsureness so unlike the persona he wears during the day.

"Can I come in?"

We both know he can, but the fact he doesn't electrifies the space between us because he wants me to know I'm the one in control here and it's such a kind, human gesture I want to throw all my reservations about ghosts out the window and let him. I want to break down the wall, but breaking it means it won't be able to go up again.

"You can."

I step aside for him, even though there's no need. He must appreciate the gesture because he lightly brushes a wet strand of hair out of my face. He can walk through the wall if he wants, but he doesn't and it's a new side of his character I've had yet to witness till this moment.

Ryne stands in the middle of my room with his back straight and hands shoved deep into his pockets. He gazes around the room as if he's seeing it for the first time, taking in the makeup sitting in a messy pile on the dresser, courtesy of Caroline. Without moving, he says, "You said I could touch you." He clears his throat when his voice carries the note of a slight tremor.

Sucking in a breath, I walk past him, gently sitting on the edge of the bed. I fear if I move too fast or am too rough, I'll break this fragile bubble we've created.

Ryne lifts his hands as I sit in anticipation. What is he going to explore first? My money is on hips simply because he seems like the type who likes a handful of ass.

To my complete and utter surprise, he cradles my face, his thumb pressing against my bottom lip. His fingertips brush against my cheeks. I close my eyes, scared to see what might be swirling in his own.

In the dark behind my eyelids, I rely on touch to know what he's doing. His hands move down my arms, shifting to only the skim of his pointer finger when he outlines my ribs over my shirt. Once he's past my waist, his hands fully envelope my hips, moving down until he's squeezing along the edges of my thighs right below the hem of my shorts.

I open my eyes as a smile teases my lips. *I knew it.*

His fingers pause, slightly inching beneath the thin fabric. His eyes pose a question when they meet mine. I know what he wants, to feel the skin of my hips without the fabric in the way. I nod, placing my hands over his and giving him an encouraging push.

He bites down on his lip. "Shit."

His eyebrows shoot up as soon as he slides them higher, the tips of his fingers peeking out of the waistband of my shorts on each side "I forgot you weren't wearing underwear."

I can't help it; a laugh bursts out of me as he retracts his hands.

I open my eyes, ready to see his face once the seriousness

and vulnerability of the situation has passed, only to find Ryne looking pained instead. His eyebrows are pinched together, his mouth pulled down in sadness if I've ever seen it.

I blink and he's gone.

I sit in the bed, feeling a mixture of emotions: horror, embarrassment, hurt, and anger. Sighing, I fish for the bottle beneath the bed, taking a large drink before falling backward into the heap of sheets and blankets.

Hard Pass, Ghostbuster

June 22

When most people are avoiding someone, they tend to take different routes, keep their head down, and avoid eye contact.

Ryne appears to prefer jumping out of fucking windows.

"Ryne," I call, following the dab of warmth in his presence that distinguishes him from the full-fledged ice storm of the rest.

Around the corner, his head jerks to the sound of his name, a soft sigh escaping his mouth when he finds me standing at the opposite end of the hallway from him. A guest exits their room as we face off, locking the door behind them and whistling a tune as they take a casual stroll, a beach towel tucked under one arm.

"Excuse me," they say.

I tear my eyes off Ryne for a moment and find them giving me an expectant look, but I stay rooted in place, scared the slightest movement will send Ryne, arms outstretched and flying through the window. The beachgoer mumbles under their breath and brushes past me as I concentrate on Ryne, who is like a scared animal ready to flee at any given time. I plead with him internally to talk, to vanquish this weird tension between us he summoned by running off on me with no explanation.

It's no use. He moves in a swift motion, prying the window open and crouching onto it like a cat before dropping down.

Phantom of the assholes.

I lean over the edge, nearly toppling out of it myself when the tips of my toes leave the floor. Ryne stares back up at me from below, blood soaking the grass around his head, arms and legs sprawled out as if he is in the process of making a snow angel of blood.

I can't read his expression. It's neutral; not something from him I've grown familiar with. I'm used to that deranged smile of his. My lips part at the complexity of it all. I straighten my spine, loosen my grip on the edge of the window.

He must sense my resolve. Sitting up, he pops the bone of his arm back into place before climbing to his feet. He rolls his neck to the side, prodding the wound on the back of his head. I cringe when it appears to be mushy, like the back of his skull is broken. As the scent of blood permeates the air, I cover my nose with my shirt, the scent sending my memories into a downward spiral I can't escape.

After a quick examination of the red substance, he shrugs, wiping his stained fingers onto his dark washed jeans. Without a spare glance, he shoves his hands into his pockets and saunters away, his long legs eating up the distance as he heads off to do God knows what.

Huffing out a breath, I push down a twinge of hurt. It's easy to write off people avoiding me when they know nothing about me and see the mask I show to the world. But being avoided by someone that *sees me*? I can't lie, that one hurts and even telling myself over and over that I shouldn't care what a dead man thinks doesn't do the trick of squashing it.

I push stray pieces of golden-brown hair out of my face and navigate the land, stopping at the raised limestone patio overlooking the sea. Caleb and Quinn lounge in the sun, each clad in bathing suits as they mingle with a few of the other hotel guests. Their faces appear oily in the sun from the forming beads of sweat.

It's summertime, but the proximity to the ghosts leaves me chilled to the bone. Soaking in the sun wouldn't even be enough to melt the ice that resides in my core, so deep down that sometimes my limbs go completely numb. So, there's no point in going into the sun for me. But when Caleb waves me down and hollers my name from below, I think maybe a trip out of the town will give me a little bit of time to unwind.

And give Ryne the space to sort himself out.

I head downstairs and climb the block stairs to the patio, shielding my eyes as the sun beats down on my face.

"Hey," I say, squinting.

"Hey, cuz," Caleb says carefully, lowering his glasses and gingerly sitting up, one leg on either side of the lounge chair.

"Audrey," Quinn greets, putting on some sunglasses.

The conversation dies, the chirping of the cicadas heightening around us.

"So, I'm in the mood to leave." I rock back and forth on

my heels, ignoring the words still unsaid between us, but that's not my main concern. I'm more worried about getting the hell off this property.

Caleb nods slowly. "Wanna go back to the shops in town? I planned to take Quinn since she couldn't go last time."

Couldn't go? More like they were fighting so he didn't want her to.

I watch as Quinn twirls her fingers through Caleb's curls, commenting on how she'd love to see his hair in braids again soon. He places a hand on her thigh and gives her a big smile. I take in the peace surrounding them. They do seem a little more mellowed out lately though, but maybe that's just because I haven't been around to witness the dramatics of the relationship.

"Sounds good."

"I was kind of hoping we could go out alone," Quinn grumbles.

"I'm sure you were," I say, so sweetly it hurts.

She pushes her sunglasses further up her nose.

"Quinn," Caleb's voice deepens in warning.

She lowers her chin. "Sorry, babe."

He runs a hand down her back in acknowledgment before aiming a pointed look and upward tilt of his chin toward me. "Audrey, me and you need to talk."

As the engine roars to life, it attracts the presence of those who cannot. Last time the three teenage ghosts surrounded Caleb's Ford Focus, I peeked into the side mirror and pretended I couldn't see them. Now I meet their curious eyes openly as they speak to me.

"Where are you going?" Caroline demands, stomping her foot into the dirt road like the fifteen-year-old Little Miss Ghoul she is.

"Into town," I supply. "I'll be back later tonight."

She slings her arms around my waist and lays her head against my chest. I lift my arms up in surprise and look to Bryce for help.

He grins, taking a step back. "You're on your own," he mouths, so Caroline can't hear.

I narrow my eyes at him before awkwardly patting her back, my lips pressed in a tight line.

"I'll miss you." Caroline sniffs. "Audrey?"

"Yes?" I answer, my voice pained from the physical contact.

"Can you bring me back a tube of lip gloss?"

"I can."

She lets go of me and jumps around, squealing in delight. I blink. I never realized she liked me so much, let alone at all. People rarely do.

Bryce slouches forward, water droplets cascading from his long, black, hair. "Does Ryne know you're leaving?"

"No," I say slowly. "Besides, he's been avoiding me for the past few days. I don't think he'll care."

"That's what you think?"

What I *know*. It's obvious. "He's been in a mood." I shrug it off, so he won't get wind that something actually happened. I won't be caught dead telling a ghoul that I let another ghoul get handsy with me. "Me being gone will give him some time to get out of it."

For the first time since I met him, Bryce straightens his back and gives me a strange expression, like he knows something I don't. "Do you think Ryne is avoiding you because of something *you* did?"

"What else would it be?"

"Nothing. I thought you'd know Ryne better than that by now. You've spent more time with him in mere weeks than we have in the whole year he's been here."

I watch the water drops slide down his face, looking for a sign to confirm he resents me for continuously flaunting my humanity to Ryne, thoroughly causing him to ache more for his own, but there's nothing but kindness reflecting in Bryce's waterlogged face.

Caroline crosses her arms across her chest. "Yeah," she admits begrudgingly. "I kind of hate you for it."

"Because he wants something from me." I use him, he uses me.

Down for the worse or the better.

But even I'm starting to doubt it's that simple.

Bryce gives me a quick once over. "I have a pretty good idea of what that is."

I wonder what they'd think if they heard Ryne say he forgot I wasn't wearing underwear.

"No," I grit dryly. "You really don't."

Bryce stays quiet. Caroline and him share a glance.

"What?" I ask, self-consciousness manifesting as the urge to push Bryce back into the ocean where he belongs so a turtle can gnaw off his other pinky toe.

Caroline twists towards him. "Do you think it's the eyes or the hair?"

"Both. I'm pretty sure if he had an ideal type, it'd be her.

He's said before, he's a sucker for brunettes. The freckles though . . . I don't think he even knew how much he liked them until he saw hers."

"Again with the freckles." Caroline grabs a piece of her dirty blonde hair and touches her freckle free face. "Well, shit. This sucks." She pins her gaze on my chest. "I bet Ryne likes her boobs too. Ugh." She circles me and pokes at my butt. "I bet he likes her whole body!" She gropes her own chest. "I am as flat as a board!" She screeches to the sky. "I have nothing!"

"I don't think chest matters," Bryce assures her, nudging her shoulder with his own. "I think what really gets Ryne about her is her personality."

I laugh because it's *Ryne*. He's not capable of liking anyone. Not in the way they're thinking, at least. A flash of him hovering above my body, eyes feverish with want invades my mind. I push it back far into the recesses of my brain and shake my head. His interest in me doesn't go beyond his fascination with my heartbeat and how warm my skin is because I'm alive.

"Well, he's stupid then. Mine is *so* much better."

"Can't argue with you there." I'm bad for his soul.

"About which part?"

Both. I smile. "Ryne being stupid, obviously."

They both begin to laugh, and the sound detangles a bit of tension in my chest and stops me from wanting to shove Bryce off the cliff. It's so easy with them. Why can't it be this easy with everyone?

Warmth blooms within me at the same moment Bryce and Caroline swivel their heads around.

"You feel him too?" I question.

"No," Bryce admits. "But the wind got stronger. Usually means one of us is near, but I can't tell if it's Ryne or Judith."

"It's Ryne," I muse. "His presence feels a bit different from yours."

"What does it feel like?" Caroline leans forward.

"Ice being poured down my spine."

She frowns.

I'd normally panic at her reaction, but with these two there's nothing to take personal. They always treat me the same.

"It's not a bad feeling," I amend, smiling. "Just cold. Ryne's feels almost the same, but it's got a warm spot to it."

"Maybe you should tell him that," Caroline offers.

Bryce nods. "Out of us all, he really needs to hear it."

Before I can come up with a response, footsteps crunch through the gravel of the dirt road.

I pivot on my heel.

"Not so fucking fast, Audrey," a sing-song voice chimes.

Caleb hitting me with his Ford Focus sounds real good right about now.

The ghost investigator, Gavin, rushes over, a megawatt smile on his face as his camera bounces against his chest. "Quinn offered to give us a ride to town."

Oh, I bet she did. If I couldn't see ghosts and risk her coming back as one, I'd probably be contemplating murder.

Gavin's sister, Leslie, comes up behind him, followed by Caleb and Quinn.

"Hi, Audrey." Her shoulder knocks into mine as she moves past me without apologizing.

I pin Caleb with a glare, raising an eyebrow. "You agreed to this?"

He scoffs, offended I even asked. "Hell no, but you know Granna—"

Actually, I don't. She's practically a stranger.

"—she overheard and made the decision for me."

"After what they said?"

"Something about keeping Windhaven on the map." He shrugs. "I can't really blame her. She says she keeps this place running for us, so we can sell it someday or make it a home."

"I'd sell it."

He gives me a strange look. "Why? It's paradise."

I wrap my arms around my torso. "You conveniently forget there's a graveyard here."

Graveyard, because I don't like the word cemetery. Seems like too normal of a term to describe a place where corpses are buried, and 'burial grounds' seems too spiritual and makes me think about things I can't even begin to comprehend. Things Dad would've wanted me to know.

Anxiety becomes carnivorous as it begins to eat me alive. I don't want Dad buried there. I hate the thought of him being six feet under, even if it's only his body, the shell of who he used to be. But most of all, I hate the thought of letting him rot because I'm scared the rest of my memories will decay with him. I'm scared I'll never get another cotton candy sky. Undertones of sadness color me, and these days even my sadness seems more vibrant than the sun.

"Maybe try to focus on the good parts," he offers gently.

There it is. Insinuation I'm dwelling over something I shouldn't be. I leave the conversation at that, sliding into the back seat and setting my backpack on top of my lap. Next to Leslie, I avoid conversation by preoccupying myself with the scenery as we drive down the road.

I clench my teeth as we pass the graveyard, fighting the cold tendrils that reach for my body like fingers.

One last turn onto the main road and we've left the property.

Something in the side mirror catches my attention. On the edge of the property, a figure stands on the end of the dirt road. I roll down the window, sticking my head out. The wind whips my hair into my face, obscuring my view as I fight for a glimpse, but when I finally get one, they're gone.

The drive is long and being stuck in a car of four people, three of them I don't exactly care for, initiates a deafening silence. The silence is so loud, I wonder if I've accidentally stumbled into a graveyard again and lost all my senses, the ghosts blowing a fuse in my circuit.

"So where are y'all going?" Quinn meets Gavin's eyes through the rear-view mirror.

"We wanna check out the voodoo shops, chat with some residents and ask if they've got any local legends about Windhaven."

"You think Windhaven is popular enough for local legends?" She quirks an eyebrow in disbelief.

"It is! You haven't heard them?"

Caleb shoots her a sideways glare as Gavin starts going on a tangent, no doubt mad Quinn is being so friendly with them despite the fact they're actively trying to exploit our families' deaths for views.

"Oh yeah!" Gavin exclaims. "Did you know a woman disappeared in 1979? Nearly forty-two years ago? They never found her body or who killed her, but they said she frequented Windhaven so much, they searched the grounds but found nothing."

Black and gray hair fills my mind. I think of her pale skin, the purple bruises on her throat, the blood in her eyes.

Judith.

What if the same person who killed off my family killed her too? 1979 was a few years before Grandpa died.

Goosebumps rise from my flesh like the dead rising out of their graves. "Granna knew her."

Caleb slams on the breaks, throwing us forward as he parks. "You don't know that," he chides.

Yes, I do. I know Granna knew Judith. She must have. It all makes sense now: Judith's insinuation of Granna keeping secrets. How could she assume such a thing if she didn't know her? If she frequented Windhaven when she was alive, then Granna *must* have. There's no way she didn't.

Is she keeping secrets about Judith too? And who killed Aunt Rachel? Why is my family dying here? Why did Ryne?

Granna knows more than she's letting on. She's more than connected in this, she's almost pinpoint in the center of it all. It's like I'm in a fog, suffocating and dense. The more information I find, the more questions I have and the harder it is to find my way.

We pile out of the car once we arrive at the destination Gavin and Leslie have selected. The shop's name is Cauldron Corner. The logo of a voodoo shop hanging above the door of the shop is—surprise—a caldron with smoke coming out of it. Instead of staying back with Caleb and Quinn, I follow Gavin and Leslie inside.

Putting the voodoo aside, maybe I can get some information out of these two.

"Why are you going in there?" Caleb demands, his voice

taking on a worried edge. Quinn adds fuel to the fire by giving the shop a disgusted look.

Right. He's as religious as Dad was. I recall Sunday mornings, Caleb showing up at eight thirty in order to attend a nine a.m. service with him. He'd always ask if I wanted to come, but never forced me or ever made me feel bad for not going. He'd just say it would be there for me if I needed it. I still don't understand what he meant by that, but I wish I did.

"Does it matter?" I tilt my head and feign innocence. "Or are you scared I might buy a voodoo doll and put your name on it?"

"Haha," Caleb says dryly. "Not even you would go that far. You're too iffy on religion to think you'd get anywhere by stabbing dolls."

"Pretty accurate. Gold star for you." I pretend to flick one his way, an uneasiness settling in my stomach. Iffy on religion, huh? Is that how he perceives me? I frown, more bothered by his statement than I expected.

He fake catches it. "Thanks. I thought you might be going inside just to avoid talking to me."

"Interesting analysis, but no." I cast a glance over my shoulder as I turn away. "We'll talk when I come out."

"Fair enough. Quinn and I will be at the next shop over."

Quinn wraps her arm around Caleb's as they walk away, pointing things out in the windows as they do.

I enter the shop, a small bell above the door announcing my arrival. The walls are covered in masks, trinkets, totems, and jewelry. Cabinets are lined with crystals and books.

A woman glances up, and the word "demon" courses through my mind as I remember what she called me—screamed at me. She drops the crystal in her hand. It clatters onto the floor. Eyes wild, she slowly backs up, turning her back to me once she's close enough to the door before she rushes out of the shop, the bell ringing in urgency this time.

It's her—the woman who saw the ghosts.

One of the shop employees sighs and plucks the crystal off the floor and glances at the door in disdain. Shaking her head, she sets the crystal up on the shelf and faces it a few times until she's satisfied.

"Who was that?" I ask.

"Ida Morales. She's a psychic with a tent a few blocks over. Her business cards are right there if you want one." She points to a card holder on the counter.

I swipe one and shove it in my pocket.

"Gavin," I call out, when I find him interviewing the cashier, a notebook in his hand.

"What's up, Aud? I'm just talking to Marsha here about the people who have come here in an attempt to cleanse Windhaven."

Cleansing is such a load of bullshit. It never works. At least the rituals I've seen haven't.

"Never call me that again."

"Oops." He gives me a sheepish smile. "What's up, Audrey?"

"What else do you know about that woman? The one who died."

"Next to nothing. Marsha doesn't know about that, which is why we're going to talk to more people and see what they know."

I nod. "Okay. Tell me anything you find out."

A goofy grin is aimed at me, but I don't like goofy smiles.

I like wicked ones with sharp teeth and a little bit of blood in them. I like Ryne's smile.

"Why?" he asks.

Frustration prickles me. Oh my gosh, he thinks I'm flirting with him. I shrug. "I like true crime."

"So, you've watched Ghosted?"

"No," I deadpan.

He shrugs and falls into pace with me as I begin to exit the store. "I've been wondering, are you into the narcs?"

I wrinkle my nose. "What?"

"Narcotics. Drugs." He waves a hand as if willing me to pick it up faster.

"I'm not." But I have been tempted. I'm curious as to what will be strong enough to drown out the ghosts.

"Well, if you ever want to . . ." He leaves it open for interpretation.

"Got it. I'm good, though."

"Or if you just wanna hang, come to my room anytime." He bites his lip in anticipation.

I roll my eyes. "Hard pass, Ghostbuster."

I push ahead into the shop where Caleb and Quinn went.

"Ask me how I did it," Caleb says from across the table.

I take a sip of my lemonade, my finger sliding up the side of the glass and gathering condensation. "Ask you how you did what?"

"How I got my girlfriend not to bother us."

My eyes flit up to find him wearing a mischievous expression, but I'm not in the mood to humor him. "You killed her?"

His eyebrows furrow. "What? No. I gave her some money."

Instead of putting in my two cents on the situation like he wants me too, I cut to the chase. "What did you want to talk about?"

He leans forward in the chair, bracing his elbows on the table. "I'm sorry."

"Why?"

I'm not going to let him brush me off this time.

"Because you're right. I've known how sad you are, but I didn't know how to deal with it, so it was easier to let you convince me you're okay than to question it. I . . . feel awful I put you in the position where you felt like you had to."

"Okay." It's not the response he's looking for, but I don't know what else to say. There's no big emotional statement, not because I don't want to, but because I don't have one. It's like Caleb said, I'm not the most religious being, but forgiveness always came simple. No grudges here. Not from me. Just disappointment, because out of everyone I felt like Caleb was the one who viewed me as normal.

"Answer this." I speak up before he can get a word in. "Do you think I'm crazy too?"

"No!" Caleb raises his voice, cursing under his breath when he accidentally catches the attention of the whole restaurant. He leans forward. "No." His tone is softer this time. "This isn't something I've done to you for any reason. I do the same thing to Quinn when we're fighting. I do it to *everyone*."

I think back to Granna's words the first night we arrived

at Windhaven, how she said she saw Aunt Rachel's erratic behavior and did nothing.

Nothing. Maybe that's the problem.

Nothing could have stopped all the victims of Windhaven from dying, but after discovering Aunt Rachel's Trace, I want to make sure I'm doing *something,* so why not put this burden of an ability to use? The weight of my resolution presses into my shoulder blades. My spine straightens as I sit taller.

I push my plate back and rise from my seat. Caleb copies my movement. "Come with me?"

"Where?"

I pull the camera out of my backpack. "I've got some film that needs developing."

It's A Sanity Thing

June 22

Climbing out of the car, I stretch my limbs and listen to the mindless drone of conversation between Gavin, Leslie, and Quinn. Caleb, like me, stays silent, shooting me a knowing look when the time calls for it. It's cousin telepathy or some shit, because I swear, sometimes I read his mind and he reads mine—neither of us likes these so-called ghost investigators.

Gravel crunches under the sole of my sneakers, the sun outlining a shadow beside me. I expect to see another shadow cross its way to mine when I hear footsteps behind me, but it never appears, so I turn, faltering in my steps.

"You left."

Ryne.

Warmth spreads through my chest, but I'm not sure if it's because of him or the alcohol I consumed in the privacy of the bathroom before we left town. He towers above me, hands shoved in his pockets, brows slightly pinched as he pouts.

I sober up, trying to smother the buzz in my head. "I did." I do a quick survey of the property. Everyone is so lost in their conversation, they haven't noticed I failed to follow. I cross my arms and lean in towards him in case anyone might hear me. "It's not like you wanted me here."

He sighs, running a hand through his deep brown locks, a single curl falling into the middle of his forehead. "I didn't know if you would come back." His voice is a mixture of relief and exhaustion.

I laugh, because if that was an option, I would've been gone a long time ago. "I live here. I'm stuck, just like you."

His eyes flash as he drops his hand. "It's not the same. You can get away when it's too much. I can't step foot off the property line. I tried when you left. Bryce and Caroline did too." He swallows. "You . . . make them want things they haven't wanted in a long time. Things I didn't know they were capable of wanting till now. Ever since I got here, I've felt like the only one who hasn't moved on is me."

He forgets that if they moved on like he thinks, they wouldn't still be there. Yet here they are, haunting these halls alongside him.

"What about you?" *What do you want?*

A cruel laugh. "I never stopped wanting things, but you make me want things *badly*."

I lick my lips. "Like?"

His mouth curves into a smile. "Can't tell you." He points to his temple and twirls his finger. "It's a sanity thing."

I step back at the mention of my fragile mind, always

seeming like it's on the verge of collapse. "Why?" I challenge. "Afraid I'll lose it or something?"

"Afraid that *I*," he amends, "might lose what's left of my mind if I let *you* in on my carefully guarded secrets."

My eyebrows rise, my mouth opening at a loss for words as my face burns, the blood under my skin making an appearance in my cheeks.

His eyes widen slightly when he sees my expression, like it's something he didn't expect. Ryne reaches forward, his fingers digging into my cheeks and squeezing till my lips are smushed together. A faint pink dusts his cheeks as he angles his head, giving me a view of his side profile.

"I didn't know ghosts could blush."

"Stop looking so surprised," he says gruffly, lacking his usual maniacal laughter and devil-may-care personality. He lets go of my face and turns toward the direction of the sun, the light enveloping him. "Come on. I decided to stop being difficult. Let's focus on you so we can focus on me."

I narrow an eyebrow. "Meaning?"

"Let's go investigate Rachel's Trace. Figure out who the hell was communicating with her through those notes."

And not talk about what happened between us, apparently. Another issue amongst everything else threatening to break the surface.

He saunters ahead of me, heading towards the steps of the hotel. Unlike everyone else, he notices right away when I don't follow and proceeds to vanish before appearing right in front of me, the outline of him blurring before he comes into focus.

"Something wrong?"

I stumble back, almost losing my balance as the alcohol

impairs it. I concentrate on my white sneakers, the earth of the property caked onto the sides. "No."

I can't investigate Aunt Rachel's Trace right now. I won't be able to see it.

"How about later?" I ask, my voice raising an octave. "I'm worn out from today."

"Yeah, and I'm dead." He barks out in laughter before coming to a halt. "What about it?"

I roll my eyes, bringing my fingers up in a wave. "Bye, Ryne. I'll see you in a bit."

Back in my room I drag the near-empty bottle of Malibu out of its hiding place. It's surreal to think the other day I still had half a bottle left, and that my tolerance is to the point where I need to drink at least a quarter of it a day to function. There are barely three sips left.

It's not going to be enough to drown out the Traces. But by the time we go investigate, I'll be sober, so why not drown out the world a little longer?

Not bothering with a cup, I throw my head back and chug it, dropping the bottle, the glass clanking on the hardwood floor. I fall back onto my bed, turning away from the open window to avoid the sunlight.

Nothing in my life is right.

Right now, I belong to a cold cover of darkness. I want to submerge myself in the shadows, but other things—evil things—lurk in them and if I step into the light, I'm going to get burned. So really, there's nowhere for me to go.

A sudden gust of wind and Ryne appears, his presence pulsating through my body. I flip over to find him lifting the empty bottle, examining its contents. "Ah," Ryne hums, meeting my gaze. "So, you're a liar now. You just don't want to investigate Rachel's Trace again because you're intoxicated."

A dizzying sensation washes over me from the movement. "It's just a minor substance disorder," I protest. "I could quit anytime. Aside from now, I've literally lived my whole life dealing with this ability sober."

But I lost my dad. I saw his Trace, and after Grandpa's, it's like getting my heart ripped out for the second time. And because I'm unlucky as fuck, I had to see Aunt Rachel get murdered. I had to watch her hang right above me.

I've seen my entire family *die*.

Ryne tosses the bottle aside and snorts. "Minor substance disorder, huh? Sounds like a nice way to say raging alcoholic."

He's that voice in my head I always try to silence, resurrecting thoughts I don't dare to give life to. You know you're fucked when a ghost is telling you you've got issues.

"I'm not." My words are as weak as I am, each one collapsing after a syllable. "You're insensitive," I spit venomously.

"Duh, you'd be too if you were dead. No heart, no soul, remember?"

"If that's the case, being around me wouldn't hurt." I huff out a breath. "Who's the liar now?"

We both are. All I know is that when I see a Trace, I still see the blood on the kitchen floor, the same color as the sunrises my dad loved so much. And when Ryne sees me, he remembers flickers of the life he didn't fully get to live.

"Alright, then why are you drinking? You know we need to investigate Rachel's Trace."

"I'll be sober later."

"That's not the point. If you drink to drown out Traces, why are you drinking now?"

My ears begin to ring. Sweat breaks out across my skin. "I don't know."

When did drinking stop being about the Traces? When did it become about living?

The world distorts around me, the humming in my head turning into a distant headache.

"I can't do this right now." I flee the room, fingers fumbling as I lock the door behind me.

With nowhere to run, I take refuge in the shed, howling at Ryne to leave me alone when he knocks from the outside. "Go away!"

"Sweetheart . . ."

It's like I'm in a grave, walls of dirt caving in around me, crushing my body, my lungs, until I'm unable to breathe. It's suffocating. One wrong move is fatal, and I've been using Ryne and the death of Aunt Rachel to block it out. To block out Dad because it hurts to feel him.

Death to block out death. I've finally done it. I've lost it.

When I wake up, I can't remember where I am. My head is brimming with what feels like cotton, my throat parched and in need of water. I groan as I lift myself off the hard floor, aching on the side I laid on.

Grogginess distorts the world around me, the presences too muffled to track as I pick myself off the floor.

I make my way through the hotel, ducking my head down to avoid anyone from honing in on me and the glassiness of my eyes and slackening of my face I've seen in the mirror so many times. At my room, I fish the key out of my pocket, attempting to push it into the lock, but instead of sliding in, the door opens a fraction instead.

My heart thuds violently against my ribs. I know I locked the door. There's no questioning my sanity on that one.

I slowly push the door open, a gasp ripping out of my throat when I find Caleb holding up an empty bottle. He brings it to his face and sniffs the lip of the bottle, his nose scrunching as he inhales the fumes of alcohol. His eyes flit to mine in a searing accusation.

Silence stretches out between us, the air devoured by tension so thick it makes inhaling harder.

"Why are you in here?" The words are raspy, further evidence of the alcohol burning the back of my throat. "Who let you in?"

"I did."

I jerk my head toward the window as Ryne's form emerges.

I shake my head, a single tear slipping down my cheek as betrayal rears its ugly head.

Ryne looks away, as if it pains him as much as me.

"The door was open," Caleb trails off, lowering the bottle. "I . . . was looking for you."

"You found me." I try to lighten the conversation, but it just results in me sounding even more pathetic.

I drop my head into my hands, squeezing my eyes shut to prevent the tears from coming. I thought the tears were gone and my tear ducts had finally hardened to nothing, but maybe they had just been backed up and I wanted to cry so bad that there were just too many at once to shed.

"How long?" Caleb asks as tears gather in his own eyes.

But something in my gut tells me he can figure it out, so I wait, watch his expression morph as he pieces everything together. Horror flickers across his face. It's funny, I always thought if he ever looked at me like that, it would be from discovering the curse I had no say in, not from something I did to myself.

"Since Uncle Peter di—"

"Yes," I cut him off. "Since Dad died. It—it helps."

But lately it consumes me, and I can't stop from collapsing in on myself when I admit it. My knees buckle, my arms caging around myself as if they'll be enough to hold up my frame. But I don't hit the ground—I can't, not when Caleb throws his arms around me, grounding me in a way I didn't know he was capable of, because he always pretends. Caleb always pretends everything is okay so all *his* worries go away. So maybe this time he'll pretend again. I want, no—*need* him to.

But the hard set of a jaw is unrelenting, his eyes like sparked flint as a fire is lit in them.

"I'm here, cuz. Always. Let me help you get through this."

How?

I freeze, making a move to push him away and hesitating, my hands shaking mid-air as I contemplate my decision.

"You're not alone," he assures me. "We can do it together and I swear on my life I'll stay 'till you're through it."

I ball my hands into fists. If I wrap my arms around him, it's over. I accept the help he's offering and get clean. Or I push him away because the process is tedious and something I'm not willing to go through.

Willing to go through? I mouth to myself. Ha. It's just another way of saying I'm not going to change. And to win this fight? I *have* to.

I turn my face up to the sky as if I'll spot my father in it. I don't, but I sense him nonetheless and it's not the spine-tingling sensations I feel when in proximity to all the ghouls orbiting the hotel. This time, it's the breeze that passes through the window that smells like him for a few seconds, crisp and clean in a way that makes me remember being a child.

I close my eyes and breathe in, peace washing over me in gentle ripples as the sun warms my skin and my fingers clench the soft fabric of Caleb's shirt, like I would to the hem of my father's. The breeze doubles as a whisper of encourage-ment, the rustling of the pine trees an applause, all my senses lighting up as my resolution is made.

"I want to be sober," I decide, my arms closing around Caleb's waist as I rest against him, no longer having to carry this burden on my own. Let someone else bear a bit of weight for once.

I leave my eyes shut a moment longer, my head swiveling toward the window, allowing Ryne a view of my face. As I let him, I contemplate what face he's making. Is he wearing the wicked smirk? When I open my eyes, he is not smirking. He's not wearing any expression at all, but his eyes are soft, the corners of his mouth relaxed.

Then, I'm given the most dazzling smile. It steals my breath, makes me hold onto Caleb tighter.

"So, we're really doing this?" Caleb asks in awe.

I pull away enough to see his hopeful face. "We are."

As Caleb steps out to gather some essentials for this

endeavor, the sweeping of the wind blows in the other three ghosts. My room has become a party and I'm starting to believe someone has hung a warning sign outside my door indicating 'ghosts only' because my room is full of them now that Caleb is gone.

Bryce, Caroline, and Judith gather in the middle of the room, each floating as they begin talking—at least Caroline does. I don't think she knows how to stop, her whole face becoming animated as she makes all these wild hand-gestures to Bryce, who watches with more patience than you'd think anyone would be capable of.

She pauses when she notices me watching her. "Did you and Caleb's talk go okay?" Caroline questions. "Ryne kept waving us away anytime we tried to come in."

I nod, smiling as she gives me a thumbs up before going back to her conversation.

It's moments like this when I can observe them in a natural environment, figure out things about them I otherwise wouldn't. Like the way Bryce watches Caroline. At first glance, it can be assumed he's being creepy, but there's a lot of reasons for this. He's soaking wet and his hair is never not in his face, and he slouches so bad that with his tall lanky structure, it seems like he's constantly hovering. It's just his appearance, and I've picked up that the way he looks at Caroline is because he's a protective older brother.

I lay on my bed as Ryne perches on the edge of the windowsill, one leg dangling off the side just as it was the day we first met. It makes me contemplate whether he's going to throw himself out of it or not.

I've observed ghosts for so long that now their telltale signs are a no-brainer for me. If I watch one long enough, I can usually figure out behavior patterns—and more importantly, motives. What pushes the dead to continue to operate like the living? There's always something and that's what makes it easy to tell them apart from those who become a Shut-Eye, forever lost between worlds because they've forgotten their purpose and what kept them from moving on in the first place.

Ryne is different. The behavior he exhibits is the most bizarre out of any ghost I've come across and despite it all, he's the one who's the most human of all.

He meets my eye. "How do you feel?"

Stone cold sober.

I grab a pillow, curling my body around it. "Do you think I've been erratic lately?" I ask, because out of anyone, Ryne is going to be the one to tell me the truth. I need answers. I need a million reasons to convince myself I should do this.

No hesitation. "Yes."

The truth is like a bee sting injecting venom into my veins, swelling until I'm suffocating on it.

"But some of it is justified. Caleb wasn't really there for you." He refers to my outburst from dinner.

I know. It's the strangest phenomenon. I communicate with the dead better than I can with my living cousin. I understand them better than I'll ever understand anyone else.

"But this time?" he finally says. "He's here to stay."

"And Granna? You can't tell me I'm wrong."

She could be a killer.

Ryne hesitates on his words, opening his mouth to speak before shutting it, his cheekbones becoming more defined as he clenches his jaw. He glances at the other ghosts before meeting my gaze head on.

"I think that one is a delusion. I think Judith said something and you, being intoxicated, thought more about it than you should've."

I'm such an idiot. Of course, Granna didn't kill Grandpa, Aunt Rachel, or anyone. Then who was writing Aunt Rachel those notes?

"Ryne?"

He urges me on.

"I want to be sober, but I need your help." I glance into the corner at Bryce, Caroline, and Judith. "I need all of you."

Judith's smile is warm and encouraging. "We're here for you, darling."

I smile back, my heart soaring.

We're quick to discuss a plan. It's going to be messy and there's going to be a lot of kicking and screaming, but I need to do it. I need to start living in the world around me instead of half in and out of both in a third dimension of intoxication, not knowing what's real and what's in my head. My world is real and so is theirs and it's time to stop moving like I'm dead and walk like I'm alive. I need to live like my dad always wanted me to. No more searching for his blood in the sunrise of the sky. No more faded, colorless sunrises.

I'm ready for the cotton candy ones.

I Won't Let You Be Here Alone

June 23

The first few hours are the easiest. While I crave a drink, I have an effortless control I didn't know I yearned for and since power over myself is something I've never felt, I get drunk off that instead. But it doesn't last. Good things never do.

I'm crying as I throw up, permanently hunched over the toilet. My head is pounding, and my mouth is dry. The air is full of sickness. Ryne rubs my back in circles, his fingers cold against my sweat slicked back as Caleb tries to convince me to drink more fluids.

I don't recognize myself in the full-length mirror. My skin around my eyes are blotchy from crying while the rest of my face is pale and sallow. I brace my hands on the edge of the counter on either side of the sink. My eyes are rimmed red, hair in a messy bun on top of my head with strands spilling out of it much like my emotions and addiction are spilling out of me.

Since when have I been like this? How did it just sneak up on me?

Caleb has more help than he realizes as he empties my last bottle down the sink, encouraging me to keep going.

Outside the bathroom, Bryce is rooted in front of the doorway. If I try to escape, he threatens to heave water onto me, but even that threat isn't enough to keep me from trying. It takes Ryne restraining me. No matter how long I scream for, he refuses to let me go and Caleb is forced to sit there and watch me struggle against invisible restraints. He is at a loss for what to do with me and keeps a distance as if he's afraid he'll make the fragile bubble around me pop by entering it.

But Ryne has no reservations on doing just that. The darkness in each of us is uncharted territory but neither of us is afraid to dive in. Ryne is wading through mine right now, but he's not ruined for it like I thought anyone who discovered the corruption in me would be. It's our dynamic. Equal footing in ways I'll never truly understand.

My wrists and arms are covered in bruises from my own doing, of constantly trying to struggle out of his grip. Even when I tell him he's hurting me, in a devious attempt to garner enough guilt to make him release me, he doesn't, because he knows if he does, I'm a goner.

"Manipulation tactics don't work on me," he tells me. "Not when I've used all of them myself."

It's those words that force me to confront how ugly this whole thing is. The pain is severe, but there's a brutal promise that it's better than the alternative.

As Caleb watches helplessly, there's nothing he can do but dismiss me talking to Ryne as hallucinations, since according to the internet, I'm bound to experience them sooner or later, but we aren't there yet. If we do get there, will Caleb, like Mom, decide he's better off without me?

Caroline has taken up residence on Ryne's perch of the window. Just in case I try to jump and since we're only mere hours into this rehab, I fear what the next twenty-four hours will bring me and if there's something within me that'll make me want to.

At twenty-four hours, I have yet to sleep. Judith smooths my hair as I try to, and for the smallest moment, I wish she were my mother. But I can't let myself get attached to someone who's already gone. Besides, her touch doesn't do the trick anyway, so I push her hand away and begin pacing back and forth around the room instead.

Caleb covers for me with Granna when she comes knocking, wondering where I have been and if I'm okay. I'm not, and while I want to leave the room desperately, the thought of seeing the disappointment on her face instills fear in me, although what really terrifies me is being sent away again. It's this thought that keeps me sane, because sent away would no doubt wreak havoc on my mind. I just know if it were to happen, there will be no repairing the damage this time, not when the damage from the first time is an open wound that hasn't healed yet. One that may even be infected.

Caleb tells her I'm sick and that I'll be going to the doctor. It's not a lie. I will go for continuous treatment once I get through withdrawal symptoms. I'll manage it with medication, but that won't be enough. The core of it is grief and I'm still not sure how to navigate it.

At forty-eight hours, my heart begins to race out of control. It beats so hard, I'm scared it'll stop. I'm plagued by shaky hands and short breath. The ghosts' presences are stronger than they've ever been. Every movement is like a dagger of ice into my skin.

"Don't move!" I cry out, trying to soothe my stinging skin.

Bryce takes a step back without meaning to, and when he does, I scream. Ryne covers my mouth to muffle it and in my thrashing, I bite into his palm, drawing blood.

He hisses and wraps it in his shirt. "God, you're lucky that felt good."

I feel them everywhere, so much their presence sensitizes my skin and hurts. I think I'm going to die. But I don't. I'm still alive and I can't tell if I'm relieved or devastated.

Even seventy-two hours later when I begin hallucinating.

I'm in the shower when I begin crying. The blood stain on my ankle is no longer covered with a thick sock and now it's like an ailment latched onto my skin. The blood crawls, spiraling up my skin in vein-like patterns it never has before. A reminder, a plea to never forget. I scratch at it, scratch until my skin is peeling off.

Caleb is pounding on the door, but I'm too fixated on stopping the blood from consuming me to answer. As my wailing gets worse, Ryne yanks back the shower curtain, not even processing the fact I'm naked. When he climbs in the tub, I collapse into his arms, shaking in the hot water, mumbling about ghosts and blood smeared across the walls as I try to climb out of my own skin. He's fully clothed, water cascading down his face.

"What's wrong?" His eyes search my face for a sign, for anything because I'm a shell of a person. I don't even remember who I am, only who I've become and I despise her.

I twist in his grip, my back against his clothed chest as I point a wavering finger to my ankle. "The blood, it's moving."

"It's not." His arm wraps around my stomach to keep me in place.

"It is! It's crawling up my leg!"

"The blood stain, where is it from?"

"The asylum," I finally spill. "I asked a ghost to help me escape and he killed everyone. One person became a Trace, and their blood got onto me."

Mom took me there without Dad's consent when I kept telling her about the ghosts. When he came to get me out, she left. And in response, he divorced her. I don't think I'll ever stop hating myself for causing her to leave. It put him through so much pain.

Ryne reaches forward and slides his hand under my thigh, fingers slick against my skin and lifts it up, wiping the blood off my ankle. All of it disappears.

"How?" I whisper, dropping my head backward so I can see his face.

Am I hallucinating this too?

I expect to find his eyes all over my vulnerable naked body, but they're attached to the tiles of the shower, continuously reading my shampoo label over and over. "If blood from a Trace can stain you, there's no reason a ghost can't wash it off. It's incorporeal."

"Incorporeal?" I whisper.

"Not made of matter. No material existence." Ryne cradles my head. "I may not be anchored enough to this earth to hold you down, but I won't let you be here alone."

Phantom Of The Assholes

July 9

A week later, the withdrawal symptoms are gone, and I've somehow managed to hide it from Granna and even sneak off to a doctor. I'm left tired, my steps faltering with the weight of embarrassment over my head. Ryne, Caleb, Bryce, Caroline, and Judith saw me in my worst moments, but it's not how I succumbed to addiction that has me hanging my head, it's the fact that Ryne saw me naked that's horrifying me. He may have been averting his eyes, but I know ghost boy saw more than he's letting on and it's a little unnerving for him to be so quiet instead of speaking on it since he *loves* putting his two cents in on everything.

Quiet Ryne is a figment I can't begin to comprehend. It's unnatural, even for him. I'd rather hear something provocative than not know what he's thinking at all.

Caroline sits on my bed, holding a compact mirror up to her face as she applies some lip gloss from the tube I bought for her while I was in town the other week. She has yet to leave my side and I wonder if it's because she likes having complete access to my clothes and makeup or because she's genuinely worried about me.

The others are off elsewhere, doing whatever the hell ghosts do after being locked in a room used as a rehabilitation center for what Ryne calls a "raging alcoholic." It's harsh, but maybe it's what I need to hear to remain this way. While the physical battle has come to an end, the internal battlefield in my mind is far from over. It's like a landmine, one wrong step and I'll go up in flames and pieces. Sobriety is something I'm going to have to work at every day.

I sit beside Caroline, biting back a smile as she overlines her lips.

"What?" She demands, lowering the compact.

"You over lined them."

She frowns, her eyebrows drawing together as she pouts. "I have thin lips, though."

I pull a tissue out of the box on my nightstand and wipe the gloss off her mouth. She sighs and allows me to keep dabbing until it's all gone.

"What's wrong with thin lips?" I ask her.

"You're alive and you don't know? Fillers are the trend, and they look awesome, but obviously, I can't get fillers."

"You're pretty without them."

"Do you think I could pull off fillers, though?"

"I think you could pull off whatever you want."

I reach into my makeup bag for some lip liner to match the red gloss. I over line slightly, but not enough to be noticed. I fill in the rest of her lips with the lip liner before applying the gloss. When I'm finished, she raises the mirror up, angling her jaw upward and side to side for a better view.

She looks to me for approval. I notice her cheeks and the rest of her face lack the color to match. The red stands out against her pale skin and ghostly gray eyes. Remembering the sweet blush that dusted across Ryne's face, I lean in and pinch the apples of her cheeks, hoping for the same effect.

Caroline squeals and pushes my hands away.

I pin her with an intense stare, waiting for color to form. It never does.

"What was that for?" She rubs at her sore cheeks.

High pain tolerance must be more of a Ryne thing then a ghost one.

I shrug. "I thought it might give some color to your cheeks."

"I like to avoid being as repetitive as Ryne, but you know I'm dead, right?" she asks as a drop of her blood runs down the side of her face from the gash on her temple and drips onto the spaghetti strap of her tank top. She wipes her face self-consciously, frowning at the red staining her palm.

How can I forget?

Sadness cradles her face, her shoulders hunching forward. "My cheeks can't naturally gain color. Blush please." She closes her eyes and sticks out her chin, waiting for me to apply some.

I dig into my makeup bag for some blush before rubbing some onto the bridge of her nose and cheeks. "I swear Ryne's did."

"It was probably left-over blood from one of his torture sessions. He's the definition of cute but psycho."

Ryne comes back when I finish Caroline's full face. The makeup makes her look more human and adds a couple years onto her age. If I didn't know better, I might think she was around my age.

"Do I look pretty?" she asks him. "Audrey thinks so."

Ryne shoots me a glare, shaking his head in a 'you're really entertaining this delusion?' way.

I give him a look that is equally as hard.

A helpless sigh, but the corner of his lips lift up in my direction. He drops it before turning back to Caroline. "Well, you don't look *that* terrible."

"From you that almost sounds like a compliment." Caroline claps her hands in glee and tackles me in a hug. "Thank you! Thank you! Thank you!"

I pat her back. "You're welcome."

"I'm going to show Bryce." She hesitates and turns back to me. "You should stay here with us forever. It could be like this every day." Without another word, she spirits away.

I frown at her words, hoping she understands that since I'm alive, I cannot. Forever here is no life for me, and the more she gets attached, the harder it's going to be for her to let go.

"I'm worried about her," I tell Ryne as we're left alone. "She knows I can't stay here forever, right? She can't either. Will you talk to her?"

Ryne waves his hand in dismissal and shakes his head. "She'll be fine. Don't worry about it."

We lapse in silence. He stands there motionless and as soon as he makes a move to shove his hands into his pocket, I groan.

"Oh my god," I exasperate, covering my face. "Just say it."

He glances around the room, cocking an eyebrow. "The *fuck?* Say what?"

I glare at him from between my fingers. "Something about how you saw me naked. I know you saw *something,* and I know you're just waiting to shove it in my face."

His mouth hardens. "Aside from a lot of leg and some thigh, I saw nothing."

I'm a burning ember as I drop my hands down to the side, my fingers curling into fists. "You're lying. I know you looked. Why wouldn't you?"

"I didn't. What's the point if you're not into it? I may be a complete bastard, but I'm not enough of one to take a peak while you're hallucinating from withdrawal."

He pins me in place with a glare of his own. It's the most serious I've ever seen him and everything he's suddenly opening up to me is scary. I thought this world was the most terrifying thing I'd encounter, but human emotion seems to be what has me wanting to run away in fear.

"Oh."

Ryne reverts to his normal persona and runs a hand down his face. "You're pretty concerned about what I think about your body." He smiles in disbelief. "I don't know how I feel about that."

Heat runs through me as his tongue darts across his bottom lip. "I'm not," I say, still fixated on his mouth.

A smirk. "You're such a liar. If you're that worried about what I think, Melinda, I'll give you an honest opinion." He plops down in the cushioned chair in the corner of the room and leans back, stretching out one of his long legs as if waiting for a show.

"Hard pass, Ghosty."

"Ghosty?" His smirk completely dissolves into a beautiful, small smile, one he tries to hide with the palm of his hand, like he doesn't want to be caught dead with it because it makes him vulnerable. And it does, because I do this to him. I make him feel human. Something warm blossoms in my chest.

And then we're both smiling. It has such an unnatural feel after these past few months that it makes my cheeks sore.

Ryne waits for his smile to vanish before letting his hand fall from his face. "You up for the investigation now?"

My own smile widens, but unlike him I don't hide it. "Stop changing the subject," I joke. "Let me make you feel human."

I pause mid laugh, realizing what I've just said. Ryne stares at me, calmly sitting there with his fist clenched in front of his mouth, eyes swirling with an emotion I'm not ready to identify. I remember what transpired at the ocean, in my *room*.

"Um," I stammer. "I—" *Am an idiot.*

"Rachel's room?"

Is he propositioning me or? "To investigate the Trace?"

"Yep."

I head upstairs while Ryne flies through the wall, avoiding the stairs. I enter the guest wing of the hotel, stopping in front of what used to be Aunt Rachel's door. I knock, hoping Gavin and Leslie are gone.

Ryne opens the door from within, stepping aside for me. He slams the door behind him, snickering when it causes me to jump. It fades when he finds Aunt Rachel strung up from the ceiling. The sound of the rope creaking under her weight has me grinding my teeth.

I swallow, fighting the invisible noose making its way onto my neck.

"What was she like?" Ryne questions.

"Obsessed with movies. She was always quoting them and taking this small portable projector with her everywhere. She used it for everything. She'd even project her homework onto the wall to solve it. Granna and Grandpa were older when they had her. She was twenty when she died."

The Trace replays. Aunt Rachel disappears from the ceiling and appears on top of the mattress by the headboard of her bed, her hands forming a triangle as they zigzag across the wall. The motion washes up a sense of nostalgia, but I can't place it.

The crumpling of a foil wrapper draws my attention. I turn to find Ryne holding up a strand of condoms. "And not even one is missing from the box." He shakes his head. "Thought he was going to get laid as he filmed his own Ghost Adventures for his ten followers. What a loser."

"You watch Ghost Adventures?"

Ryne gives me a pointed look. "I'm dead, not stupid. Besides, it's one of the only channels Margaret has on cable."

I laugh, feeling as if some third dimensional wall has been broken. "That's probably all that's available too. Granna's TVs are ancient."

"Because death wasn't enough for me, I'm cursed to go out without streaming services too. Unfortunate as fuck and I'm wondering if the man upstairs hates me."

"You're a believer?"

"I am. My faith has faltered since then, but I can't let it go."

Dad's past words surface in the front of my mind. "Sometimes, I hear my dad's words in my mind. It's like"—I struggle to convey my thoughts—"I know what he would say right now even if I wouldn't."

"Okay. What would he tell me that you wouldn't?"

I shrug a single shoulder. "I'm not sure I believe this, but he'd say God doesn't hate you and that thinking that way is the devil trying to deceive you."

"Pretty bold thinking for someone who claims not to believe it themselves. Religion is ingrained in you more than you realize. I think we all have times where we struggle with our faith. Where's your mom?"

"Gone." The memories form. "When she took me to the asylum thirteen years ago, I woke up one of the Shut-Eyes. Only it wasn't a normal Shut-Eye. It was a Bygone."

"What's a Bygone?" Ryne asks as he peers beneath the bed.

I rummage through drawers that have gone unused for years. Guests must predominately live out their suitcases, because there's a thick layer of dust on top of each perfectly cut sheet of wallpaper placed at the bottom of them.

"Just a word I use to describe an ancient spirit, basically. They're the ones who've become more powerful and evil with time. They can bend the spiritual plane to their will and even touch living people if they're strong enough."

I pull open the last drawer and there is it: Aunt Rachel's projector, something I never thought to consider a clue till now. I turn around to call Ryne over, but my words get caught in my throat, the image of him holding the camera over the cliff surfacing. In a hasty decision, I stuff the projector into my back pocket, strategically pulling my t-shirt over it to hide the bulge. When I turn again, he still hasn't noticed.

"Anyway, I asked him to get me out, but he went and killed everyone before holding my hand and walking out. After the massacre and being the only survivor, Dad couldn't get over how Mom put me in a situation like that without his consent, so he was done with her, but she was going to leave anyway because of me."

Ryne bites his lip and nods. "So, that's why."

"Why what?"

"Why you pretended you couldn't see us. Why you were so freaked when we knew you could."

I close the now empty dresser drawer. "It is." I swivel around the room. "We're missing something. I know it has to do with that wall, but out of all the times I went into Aunt Rachel's room as a child I can't remember anything ever being there." I examine the behavior of her Trace. "What is she doing?" I think out loud. "Why was her behavior so erratic?"

What did she see before she died?

I expect to find Ryne following my line of vision, but instead he's concentrating on the door. "They're coming."

Panic invades my body like an unwanted entity. "What do I do?"

Ryne places one leg on the edge of the window and pries it open, the curtains billowing around him when it cracks open, white paint chipping from where it was painted shut.

"Ryne," I drawl out in warning. "Don't . . ."

He leans forward, casually folding his arms.

"Don't you dare."

His smirk widens, reflecting a level of crazy even my twisted mind can't compete with.

The doorknob twists. I jerk my head to the side.

"Later, Sweetheart."

Son of a ghoul. Phantom of the Assholes. The ghost on motherfucking dumbass street winks at me before free-falling out the window. Maybe he should keep trying to kill himself, because if he can't I will.

"I'm going to kill you, Ryne," I hiss to myself as I take refuge in the closet, burrowing deep into clothes that reek of Axe.

Ryne materializes next to me, using his finger to make a popping sound with his mouth. "Sorry, Sweetheart, my cherry's already been popped for that one."

"I'll still kill you," I whisper, my lips brushing his ear.

"Like *how* would you kill me?"

"That was the fakest psychic I've ever seen," Leslie deadpans.

Out of sheer panic, I wrap my arms around Ryne, forcing his head beneath my chin, my fingers buried in his soft hair. A single curl winds around my finger like a ring.

"Hell yeah she was, but damn. Our views are going to be popping."

I roll my eyes at Gavin's boyish voice and squeeze Ryne tighter against me. A harsh grunt sounds from him, his cold breath blowing down the middle of my chest all the way down to my stomach.

Oh God.

I glance down, my eyes adjusted to the dark enough to find Ryne's face between my boobs, eyebrows pinched, the blood beneath his cheeks blooming once again. Caroline was wrong. It's not the blood from one of his torture sessions. It's too pink to be blood and not only is it stamped across each cheek, but it glows over the bridge of his nose too.

"Don't stare too much," he murmurs weakly. "You're making it worse."

So Caroline was right. He likes boobs.

Instead of being completely embarrassed and pushing him away like I usually would, his blush gives me confidence. I summon the boldness I displayed in the ocean.

"If I knew putting my boobs in your face would shut you up, I would've done it a long time ago."

I'm met with revenge when his fingers trail up my ribcage. "Careful," he warns. "I am not the one you should be playing with." Half of his mouth turns up, revealing his sharp incisor.

His hand lands beside me, his arm grazing my waist.

The projector.

I push him away from me only to fall backwards. Ryne swoops forward to catch me, but it doesn't stop me from toppling over a stack of shoeboxes.

"Did you hear that?"

Shit. I look at Ryne. "Can't you like, spirit us away?" I whisper, urgently.

"Outside, yeah. I can't teleport you through a wall!"

Light floods in as Gavin throws the door open, but before he has the chance to spot me, someone speaks from the doorway. "My Granna wants to see you downstairs to discuss payment."

Gavin raises an eyebrow. "We already paid."

"Yeah, well . . ." Caleb trails off. "Your card declined."

Gavin is taken aback. "It did?"

"You may want to get that fixed before your fans find out. That's just embarrassing."

Gavin curses as he rushes out the door, Leslie behind him.

I let out a shaky breath, but a pair of shoes step in front of me. Keeping a hold of Ryne's head, I peek through the rack of clothing to find Caleb standing there with a rigid posture and crossed arms.

"Audrey, what the hell is going on?"

I reveal myself, pulling Ryne with me.

"How did you know I was in here?" I question, knowing what the answer is going to be.

"I followed you."

"Why?" I hate being watched over. I hate being treated like I'm going to spontaneously combust if I'm not, but most of all I hate how him showing up proves he thinks I'm weak for succumbing to addiction in the first place. If the roles were reversed, *he's* the one who would crack under pressure if he had to bear the burden of this ability everyday like I do.

"Because I'm worried! You've been shutting everyone out and sneaking off and I thought it was going to stop after we got you sober, but you're still doing it. I thought you were seeing someone behind me and Granna's back, but now that I saw you literally break into Gavin's room, I don't fucking know what you're doing now. Is this robbery? Did I just become your accomplice? Are we thieves now? You know I just lied to him, right? I've got to get out of here." He panics.

Addiction is such a fickle, human thing. But my abilities? Either he'll think I'm crazy or a monster and I can't decide which is worse.

"You really want to know what's going on?"

Only there is another possibility that stampedes over the two.

"Yes."

I lose him to secrecy. What's worse than that?

"Well, to start, I see ghosts."

To my surprise, I don't even have to convince him. Caleb and I sit on the edge of the peninsula, basking in the sunlight as I explain everything to him.

"It just makes so much sense!" Caleb exclaims as we discuss my ability. "Why you always secluded yourself and always seemed like you were occupied by something that wasn't there."

I pick a dandelion, tearing at the stem and running my finger across the soft top. The seeds spread in the wind off the edge of the cliff. They're like a million tiny souls in the breeze, searching for heaven, a few of them getting snagged on the grass along the way as if condemning themselves here forever.

Ryne lays on his back beside me, cracking open an eye occasionally during the conversation. I thought he'd take to Caleb like he did to me when we first met, but he doesn't have the slightest interest in my cousin. He couldn't care less. His nonchalance—I kind of like it because somewhere in the back of my mind I thought the attention he paid me was because I was the only one around with breath in my lungs who knew he existed. As bad as it sounds, knowing he doesn't share the same fascination for Caleb as he does for me makes me feel special and I can't remember a time I ever felt this way before. It's nice and I swear the warmth that spreads from my chest combats the shield of ice coating my heart. For the first time, I'm gradually beginning to thaw.

Caroline sits on my other side, watching Caleb, but keeping silent. Despite being a ghost, she's a little shy of strangers when they become aware of her, which I know now that I've seen her meet someone living aside from me.

"Tell him I think he's cute," Caroline whispers as if Caleb can hear her.

"You know he has a girlfriend."

Ryne snorts. "And you're dead."

"Ugh," Caroline whines. "Why do you always have to remind me? I can't stand you sometimes, Ryne. Where's Bryce?"

"Off with Judith."

Caroline frowns and crosses her arms. "She always spends more time with him than me." The lines of her frown deepen.

"Quinn," Caleb trails off at the mention of girlfriend. "Fuck. She's not going to believe this."

I lean forward, my fingers wrapping around his wrist. He flinches, the cold of the ghosts inside me chilling his skin. "You cannot tell her."

"But she's my girlfriend. If she knew the truth, she wouldn't say all that nasty shit."

I shouldn't have to prove myself to earn kindness and basic human respect.

"No. She's going to think you're as crazy as me. Trust me, Caleb. You don't want to spend any more time in my world. It does something to you. Changes the way you move and operate."

"But—"

"No," I say firmly. "You haven't seen Ryne die or anyone else for that matter and that shit changes you. You know blood doesn't faze me now? Not blood, not gore, not violence, not anything. You wouldn't survive a day in it. Imagine every day you watch somebody *die.* Imagine seeing our entire family die in front of your eyes. Not once, not twice, but multiple times."

He inhales a sharp breath. "Audrey . . . that's awful."

"If you ever try to tell anyone, I will deny it. You understand?"

He throws his hands up in surrender. "I won't," he promises. "You're right. Besides, I know how she is. She won't believe me anyway. She'll write it off as me acting out to hide the fact I'm cheating behind her back."

"Are you?"

"Obviously not, but she's convinced I am." He places a closed fist under his chin. "Which in turn makes me wonder if she's up to something. Do you think she'd cheat on me with that idiot Gavin? I hope not. That shit would be embarrassing. Not for me, but for her. A downgrade if I've ever seen one."

I sigh, a migraine forcing itself into the space behind my eyes. "This is a nightmare." Who would've thought someone finally finding out I'm not crazy would be this stressful?

"It's not though," Caleb says softly. "I can finally be there for you in a way that matters. I don't have to wonder if there's something I'm missing. We're all a team now."

"Don't you get it?" Ryne drops a hand onto my leg and shoots Caleb a pointed look even though he can't see it. "Ghosts only."

Caleb's awareness seems to be nothing but a nuisance to him now.

Caleb continues his speech, having no clue Ryne is speaking to him. "I'm here for you, Audrey. I want to help solve Aunt Rachel's death, Grandpa's, Ryne's, everything. Granna deserves to know what happened, especially after how messed up she is about Uncle Pete."

"She is?" She seems fine, more concerned about the hotel than anything else.

"Well, yeah. You didn't really believe she was fine, did you?"

I don't know. I've never considered it. "She . . . never mentioned him."

"It's the things people aren't saying that are eating them up."

No wonder Dad hasn't been a topic of conversation between us. Why did it take Caleb mentioning it for me to notice?

"Oh." I hug my knees to my chest.

"She's worried about you, but she's not going to talk to you about it until you're ready to approach her first. Said she's been through this enough to be okay, but that she fears being insensitive to you."

I know the feeling. Sometimes I think I'm insensitive to the world.

"Fine," I agree to his previous proposition. "You can help me solve the murders. Just don't ask me every five seconds if ghosts are here with us."

He agrees before pulling me in for a side hug. "You aren't alone anymore. I'll do what I can to be here for you, carry the extra weight of that world for you if it's ever too much."

When the weight of Ryne's hand leaves my thigh, I realize he's right.

I'm not alone, and I haven't been for a while.

GHOUL AND GIRL

July 9

When I was a kid, I remember telling Dad I wanted to live forever, but he said what we wanted wasn't the same thing, so I asked him why. He said he didn't need millions of years to be happy because if happiness was how we measured forever, then he already got his forever when he got me.

As I stand here, fist poised just inches from Granna's door, I wonder if she's gotten hers or if she's been deprived of it like I have. The breath that leaves my lungs is heavy with sadness, but it's been a minute since I felt like that sadness would kill me.

I've always been caught between worlds, but I've been so wrapped up in myself that I never considered that someone else could be hurting more than I am. I'm the one who sees ghosts, but that doesn't mean she hasn't felt them clinging to her fragile frame this whole time. My ghosts have always been visible while she's probably driven herself mad questioning if her own were real and I can't believe I ever considered for a second that she killed anyone when she's the one who has lost the most.

With what's left of my courage, I knock.

A faint "coming" sounds through the door a moment before it's opened, revealing Granna's exhausted face. I look at her—really look at her. Her hair is not pulled into the tight low bun it was on the day Caleb and I came to Windhaven. Instead, it's loose, her silvery strands framing her face, the wrinkles more evident around her mouth and eyes.

"Hi, Granna."

"Audrey," she greets, leaning in for a hug. "How're you feeling?"

"Better."

"What a relief! I was worried when you refused to leave your room and let anyone in."

Caleb's words course through my mind, what he said about Granna not being the type to speak first. Then I get it. We're saying things, but nothing that matters. If I *want* things to matter, I need to take that first step. Dad's gone. I have no parent responsible for it anymore. From now on, I've got to do it for myself. It's a step in the dark and I don't know if we're landing on solid ground or falling straight into an abyss neither of us can escape.

"Granna," I say, vulnerability seeping into my words.

I hate how I sound. It gives way to how cracked I really am. All my demons are becoming visible. Will one look at them send her running?

"Yes, Audrey?" She angles her head towards me and gives me an encouraging nod when I falter, because I don't do this. I don't tell anyone what's in my heart, let alone my head because I'm already drowning in it. I've been at the bottom of that pond since the day I died.

"I don't want to bury Dad," I admit, the words catching in my throat as they're spoken into the world for the first time ever. I flex my fingers, as if doing so will help me work through my thoughts faster. "I hate the thought of him being in the ground when I look for him in every sunrise. I hate the thought of going somewhere else to find him." The knot in my chest unravels slowly as the words uncoil themselves from the steel bands of my heart.

"I can't lie to you, Sweet One. I wanted to bury him right between your grandfather and Rachel. I wanted him right there so I could rest knowing he was surrounded by the rest of his family."

"He's already resting." I'd promise her the truth if it didn't make me sound insane. What was left of Dad was a Trace, his remaining essence. There was no ghost. He's crossed over, as did Aunt Rachel and Grandpa.

"He is," she assures me, like I'm not the only one who really knows. What propels a belief so strong? "And don't worry yourself, Sweet One. I couldn't bury him if I wanted to."

I blink. "Why?"

"Because he didn't want to be buried. He wants to be scattered, across the grass, in the ocean and the wind, and when you do it Audrey, he wants you to have a clear view of the sky, right at sunrise."

My heart fills, becoming so full it threatens to overflow. *Finally*, something I don't mind drowning in. He's been here with me the whole time. He taught me how believing wasn't seeing. He believed in what I saw when I couldn't.

Faith is what he left for me and it's up to me whether I live up to that or not. He believed in what I saw, so shouldn't I take a leap and trust in what he saw too? My vision burns, the blues and grays I've been seeing suddenly becoming the most vibrant of colors as my world swivels on its axis and becomes just right.

"And with your permission, I'd like to have a bonfire on the edge of the property, not to mourn your father's life, but to celebrate it."

Granna cried when I told her she could keep the urn that holds Dad's ashes after I scatter them. She was so happy, and for once I'm grateful I've got this strange ability. When you see death everywhere, there's no need to keep it as a reminder.

Once I let him become a part of the earth, I hope I'm able to see him in every sunrise, gust of wind, wave of the ocean, and blades of grass around my feet instead of his bloody Trace I left behind in a kitchen in Texas.

I'm preparing for the night ahead as Ryne tells me what he refers to as his own horror stories of guests he's caught doing disturbing acts when they thought they were alone.

Caroline sits beside me, reading the labels of the makeup bottles before swatching it onto her skin, smiling at herself when she is able to use concealer to cover up the stream of blood running down the side of her face and dripping onto her chest.

Ryne smirks at my scrunched-up face. "I'm just saying it

was nasty." He lounges on my bed. "You wouldn't believe half the shit I've seen."

"Maybe you shouldn't spy on guests."

I cringe, imagining the number of times he's probably watched me unknowingly.

"That's insensitive to say when you know there's not a damn thing for me to do on this god-forsaken property."

"Hence the constant suicide attempts," Caroline adds, dabbing some eyeshadow onto her face.

Bryce chuckles from the chair in the corner.

My hair rises on my arms when a dwelling presence on the property rapidly switches locations, landing here in this room.

"Hey kiddos," Judith greets. "What're you all getting ready for?" Her gaze latches onto Caroline, who struggles to put on false eyelashes in the vanity mirror.

She shrugs. "Margaret is throwing some kind of party for Audrey's dad." Caroline stands, her chair scraping across the floor. "I'm going to try to put these on in the bathroom. I think I need more light." She closes the door behind her.

Sometimes I find it strange when the ghosts call Granna by her name like they know her, but in reality, they kind of do. They've all been watching her for ages and have probably spent more time with her than I have in all my time combined. Walls can talk when ghosts are constantly lingering in them, catching every whisper and secret and having nowhere to spread them but amongst themselves.

Judith smooths down her tattered dress as she takes a seat on the edge of my bed. "Ah, right in time for the full moon. It's going to be a lovely night."

"It is. I've never been to a . . . wake? Is that what they call it?" I glance to Ryne for confirmation.

"Don't know, Sweetheart. I'm—"

"Dead. I know. But it doesn't mean you're stupid," I shoot back with a smile when his smirk widens, revealing the edge of his white teeth. I love how the banter has gone back to normal between us. I didn't think we'd ever get out of the woods after we went and got all vulnerable on each other like we were any other humans on this earth and not a girl caught between worlds and a boy plagued by his dormant heart.

"Be careful, darling," Judith warns, gripping my hand with her icy fingers. "Please."

The smirk slides right off Ryne's face.

"Careful about what?"

An expression doused in sympathy crosses her face as she locks eyes with Ryne, who stares back expressionless, like he's peering right through her into the past.

"For whatever the hell lurks in the night," Ryne says gruffly, dropping his eyes to the polished wooden floor. "Because a night like this is fun, but full of chaos. There's going to be so much going on, you won't notice things."

"What kind of things?"

He shrugs a single shoulder and paces around the room. "Lots of them, I guess. Couples hooking up behind bushes. People popping pills when they think no one's watching. A teenage guy like me getting completely slaughtered by a girl with a pretty face and killer smile."

No.

"You were killed here during a party?"

He didn't mention that part when he first told me about it.

He nods. "I couldn't remember the night, but when Judith found me wandering around asking where everyone was and why my neck and body wouldn't stop bleeding. She told me there had been a party here and I remembered it. I remembered everything in so much detail I thought it was happening to me all over again, but Judith told me she saw my body before she found me wandering around." A maniacal laugh. "I felt like I was dying but I was already dead."

Bryce lowers his head in respect while Caroline is silent behind the bathroom door, but I know she hears him. The energy in the room has shifted and the tension radiating off each of the ghosts' presence would be off the charts if I had one. But I don't and I'm left with my abilities screaming at me that something in the air is not right.

"You wanna know the worst part? Her face isn't blurred like the rest of them. I can't remember my own family, the people who loved me most in the world, but I can remember the bitch who killed me."

His expression shatters, his emotions laid out in pieces. "Thanks for that by the way, Judith. I guess whoever killed me isn't the only one who twisted the knife in my gut."

"Ryne!"

But it's too late. He's already gone.

Bryce and Judith are gone in the next instant as well and I'm left nearly deserted by everyone except for Caroline who finally exits the comfort of the bathroom.

"Where have you been?" I demand.

She carefully sits back down in her chair and gently pulls it forward. She chooses her words with care, pausing before speaking. "Bad vibes," she answers before grabbing the brush and running it through her hair like she doesn't have a care in the world for what just happened.

And there it is, one nasty truth about these wandering spirits. They're so detached from the earth; they struggle to hold onto their humanity.

I frown as Caroline turns toward me. "I'll catch you later. The hottie with the body is on his way over." Her form disappears through the wall.

"Knock, knock," a lighthearted voice says.

"Come in."

Caleb pushes the door open but doesn't cross the threshold. I grimace. *He's* the hottie with the body? Gross. I was hoping she meant Ryne.

"They aren't here."

"Even Ryne?"

I roll my eyes. "Obviously."

"Huh."

"What?"

"That dead motherfucker is always with you." He takes a seat on my bed. "I've been waking up lately and sometimes it takes me a second to remember what happened."

"It's scary for you, isn't it?"

He rubs the back of his neck. "I'm not going to be watching horror movies anytime soon."

"Me either," I admit. "I get enough of one watching Ryne."

"You and Ryne."

I get up and toe my foot into my sneaker, wiggling it around until it's on right. "What does that mean?"

"Nothing, just trying to wrap my head around the fact I'm pretty sure you're in love with a dead man."

I laugh, clutching my middle as I hunch over. "Love Ryne? Oh Caleb, you're going as mad as the rest of us. What rabbit hole did you fall into?"

"Ha. Ha. Ha. Joke about me losing my mind then. Anything to cover up the fact you want to get freaky with Casper."

"Casper," I sound out, trying out the nickname. "That's a good one. I haven't called him that yet."

"Is that some kind of kinky ghost shit y'all do or—"

I cut him off with a scathing look.

He throws his arms up in defense, struggling to contain his smile.

We begin walking downstairs to the foyer where a couple of people have already shown up. Granna talks to a man in his late thirties about when they're going to start the bonfire and a couple teenagers pick at the snacks set out. They must be from around here. Dad grew up here. I wonder if their parents knew him.

Someone else catches my eye: Linda Harper. At the last second, I decide to try to avoid her in case she hasn't forgotten Granna volunteered me to go visit her grandson in the hospital. It doesn't matter how much time passes or how much progress I make, graveyards and hospitals are a no-go, and I don't feel like walking around with my senses being shot out again anytime soon when I'm still reeling from the last time.

"Audrey!"

She waves a hand at me. I catch Granna's eye in sheer panic, but she shakes her head at me and urges me on.

"What in the world does that old bat want?" Ryne appears beside me, as if she's about to come greet us both.

"I don't know," I admit, a little too happily. He seems less stressed than he was before the party. "She's grieving. Her grandson is in the hospital."

He knocks his shoulder with mine. "What's she complaining about then? He's not dead."

"I guess she's afraid he will be."

I plaster a fake smile on my face as Linda approaches, rubbing her eyes and squinting at me for a second before smiling.

"How are you?" she asks, pulling me into a hug.

Ryne laughs at my obvious discomfort as her hug overwhelms me. I lightly pat her back, not used to people initiating physical contact with me.

"Mrs. Linda, who is this?"

A tall boy steps up beside Linda, placing his arm out for her to take.

She takes it graciously. "This is Audrey Woudstra, Margaret's granddaughter. Peter's daughter."

He holds out a hand and shakes my own. "I've heard about you. Our dads were friends when they were younger. Linda's son too."

"Really?"

"Oh yeah." He picks up a cup of soda from the table and takes a swig. "They go way back. My name's Teo."

"Nice to meet you."

"Likewise, Audrey."

Linda beams up at him. "She's going to come to the hospital to visit my grandson."

Mouthful of Sprite, Teo cringes, swallowing before setting his cup back down on the table. "I mean," he recovers. "Don't get me wrong, she's definitely his type."

His eyes slowly pass over my figure.

"What a fucking tool," Ryne says.

"—but come on, Mrs. Linda. She doesn't know the guy."

Linda waves him off. "Nonsense." Before Teo can say anything else, Mrs. Linda is making her way over to Granna.

Teo falls into step with me as we enter the nighttime air. Smoke fills the cool evening breeze as the wood splinters from the fire. A few families have already gathered around it, helping their younger children roast marshmallows from a safe distance. The property is full of laughter so radiant I almost forget Windhaven is a place full of sorrow and not something that lives up to its name.

"Sorry about Mrs. Linda. She's . . ."

"Grieving?"

He blinks a couple times. "I guess you'd know about that. I'm sorry about your dad."

I don't know what to say. I am too? I settle on, "Thanks."

He dips his head slightly. "But yeah, Mrs. Linda is grieving someone who hasn't died. Someone who is not going to."

"How are you so sure? Oh . . . I mean how do you have so much"—I think of my father—"faith."

"Because he's my best friend. He has to live."

I want to snort at his ignorance, but my own heart is too hopeful to be mocking his. Besides, I want to keep it this way, the lightness of my limbs and the lack of weight on my mind is refreshing. But it doesn't change the painful awareness that once you've thrown out your hope to be squashed, it's not something you'll always be able to get back intact.

Teo's smile radiates a hope that blinds me as he tells me about his best friend. His friend was loved by everyone, and he loved everyone back just as much, even though according to Teo, he could be completely self-absorbed at times and didn't realize what was going on around him.

Hope must be contagious because I remind him, he doesn't need to use past tense just yet.

Somewhere along the way, I find myself breaking away from Teo and telling him I'll see him later before making my way beside Caleb and Quinn, who sit in lawn chairs side by side laughing at things that don't matter and intently discussing things that do. The moon shines brighter and the waves in the distance rap against the shore as if they're knocking on a door. It's peaceful and chaotic at the same time and like most things, it reminds me of Ryne. His speck of warmth in the cold, the mania of his laughter, and face full of vulnerability and emotion. Ryne, who I don't have to look for because he's right beside me.

"Can you feel it?" I whisper so no one around us hears me.

He holds his hands out, the light of the fire like twin flames dancing in his hazel eyes. "Kind of," he says softly. "It's muted." He sighs and drops his head before lifting it up to me. "You know how when you're freezing cold you put on a blanket?"

I nod.

He drops his face and angles his body toward me. "And how sometimes you're so cold you can't warm up, but you feel the softness of the blanket and know how it should feel?"

"I do."

"That's what it feels like." He drops his head into his hands, scrubbing his face. "It feels weird to remember being human. That's something I don't know how to be anymore."

"Ryne?"

207

He cracks open an eye and stares at me sideways. "What?"

"You're the only one who makes me feel human. Sometimes I don't feel real unless I'm with you." Warmth snakes through my stomach as I reach over and grab his hand. Music softly thrums in my ears, people around us sway, some talking in groups while others stay seated. "Dance with me?"

His face pulls down in concern. "I can't. People will think you're insane—if they don't already."

I yank out of his grasp before his finger can close over mine. "Wow. Thanks."

"What? Nobody can gauge it as accurately as I can."

He's not wrong. "Fuck you, Casper."

A sexy tilt of his lips as he interlocks his finger with mine and slowly steps backwards, pulling me with him.

"Where are we going?" I ask as his arm slides around my waist.

"Woods. We can dance there."

An unsure smile crosses my face. "Really?"

Instead of answering, he lets go of my waist but keeps my hand in his before outstretching our laced limbs. The wicked smile fades, the softer one I've come to know as his most vulnerable face taking over like a full-blown possession, one not even the strongest exorcist could dispel. He takes in my outfit, the tank top tucked into my faded blue shorts, the short socks I've paired with sneakers because there is no longer a need to hide my ankle. The evidence of the horror I witnessed, gone thanks to his touch.

"You've got some killer legs, Melinda. If I wasn't a ghost, just seeing you in those shorts"—his gaze lifts—"would've dropped me *dead.*"

"You wouldn't be a ghost then," I say, out of breath. "Because you'd know exactly what killed you."

He shakes his head. "I'd come back as a ghost." He says it with certainty.

"Why?"

"I'd regret that I couldn't look at you a little longer. Moments like this make me think I don't mind being stuck here as long as you're here."

I squeeze his hand, hoping the warmth from my body can somehow transfer to his, so he knows the heat is completely because of him. The numbness, the coldness that has resided in me for ages, slowly exits my body as I melt.

The light of the fire dims from his face the further we go. We exit the fire to be bathed in the moonlight as it streams through the branches and leaves of the trees. Ryne sways us back and forth, his breath light against my ear. I lean my head against his still chest, the absence of his heart lulling me into a safety net I didn't know I needed. Suddenly, I'm weightless, my feet in the air and when I open my eyes, all I see is the moon, large and beautiful, emitting light and showing off its craters.

When I glance down, I see the trees in the distance and the bonfire so far, it's a speck in the night.

"You could drop me," I say out loud, realizing how high we really are.

"You're scared, huh?" he says against my ear, his teeth slightly grazing my earlobe.

I pull away to glance up into his shining, moonlit eyes. "I should be."

"But you're not."

"No."

"*God*, I want you to be mine forever."

The hand splayed across the small of my back gently traces up my spine, his fingers moving over each vertebra like he wants to outline every part of me. I bite down on my bottom lip at the sensation, the slight sting underwhelming in comparison to the feel of his hands on my back. I gasp when the pad of his finger hits my bare skin on the edge of my tank top and keeps traveling. When his finger reaches my neck, it draws a line across my jaw and back up before he finally cups my cheek. Eyes on my mouth, I watch in anticipation as his lips part, his tongue darting over them in a quick motion like all his control has snapped. What hasn't changed is the fact he's still a predator and I'm prey that he desires. The only difference in this dynamic is I don't just mind being devoured, I crave to be.

"Beg me not to." He closes the gap between us. "Tell me no and we'll call it a night. We'll go back to being ghoul and girl or whatever the hell you want to be aside from this."

This. Like the word causes physical pain for him because it's something neither of us can afford to want, especially not from each other. We can't stay locked down at the Windhaven Hotel together forever. But I've never cared much for forever, and I'm not going to start caring for it now. Not now. Not with him.

I turn my head side to side, not once leaving his eyes.

"Are you drunk?" he asks incredulously when I can't stop staring into his eyes.

A slow smile. "On you."

"Audrey," he scolds, but with the yearning in his tone and desire caught in his throat, it sounds more like a praise. My name on his tongue flips my stomach and folds my heart in half. "Fuck."

The rest of the tension drains from his body as he leans forward and presses his lips to mine. The kiss is magnetic, full of so much life I feel as if he's breathing it into me. For the first time, I'm not caught between worlds. I'm in the world of the living and I've dragged him across the threshold with me, because under my hands, he's alive as well and I'm no longer sure who's keeping who tethered here.

The warm movement of his mouth is real, so real every part of his body against mine generates a reaction. Electricity passes through our hands, into our skin, across our mouths. He maps my body with the palm of his hands as mine wrap around his soft curls before returning to the curve of his cheekbone. Ryne kisses me so much, my lips tingle from it and at the first trace of pulling back, Ryne bites down onto my lower one, tugging it slightly before releasing it. I drag a soft sound out of him, one he coaxes from me in return. When we pull back a few inches from each other I'm surprised to find his lips are swollen and pulled back in satisfaction.

Ryne lowers us to the ground, my feet barely brushing the tip of the grass. He lifts a hand between us and places it on top of his hollow chest. "If I were alive—" He breathes out. "My heart would be slamming out of my chest."

And even his words aren't enough of a warning for when it does.

Ryne's dormant heart beats once, causing a faint red glow in his chest. His heart is like a lit match, all his ribs and veins visible through the fading light before it falls silent to the world once again. Ryne falls to his knees at the sensation, the side of his face in the grass as he fists his shirt where his heart lies. He shakes violently, the sensation foreign after a year without it.

"You saw that." It's not a question. "I felt it." He falls back, his fingers digging into his chest.

"Ryne—" I reach out to him, knowing he's about to spiral, but he moves out of my grasp, the sensations becoming too much for him.

"Margaret's calling you."

I peer through the trees to the clearing to find Granna standing at the bonfire. Ryne told me once he heard everything, but I never realized ghosts had hypersensitive ears to this degree.

"Go on," he encourages me. "Spread your dad's ashes. I'm just . . ." He inhales a harsh breath. "Shocked. But I'm fine." He climbs to his feet, brushing grass off his shirt.

I hesitate, but he recovers, shooting me a wicked smile. "Race you to the fire."

I mirror his expression to cover my worry. "Try not to burn in it."

His tongue slides across his teeth. "You know I can't promise that." He dissipates from view.

I run to the edge of the woods, discreetly maneuvering my way into the rest of the crowd. "Here!" I push my way toward the front of the fire where Granna stands.

She gathers all the guests around the bonfire and asks that everyone walk down to the edge of the cliff with us for the spreading of Dad's ashes. She gives me the small silver urn. I slide my fingers along the rounded object, coming across the engraving in the middle. I lift it to my face. *Peter*

Woudstra, it reads. A lump forms in my throat as his name crashes like waves around my mind.

I lower the urn to my chest and cradle it carefully, the coldness of the metal rivaling my own as we walk toward the cliff. As we near the edge, I notice the footsteps behind me recede as everyone gathers in a crowd behind me, offering some space. My breath is caught in my throat when the first rays of the sun peak from the ocean, the red glow burning so bright that tears form in my eyes. Yet, I can't tear my eyes from the sun. I stare until it hurts and blue spots form in my vision. The more the sun rises, the warmer I get. It starts as a stream flowing above my skin, until the heat has no choice but to flow within.

When the sun is three quarters out of the ocean, I teeter closer to the edge, dislodging rocks and kicking them off the cliff into the ocean. But I'm not afraid, even when a short breeze ruffles the hair on my head and the frayed strings of my shorts. Seconds feel like minutes as I carefully lift the lid, my hand shaky as I clasp onto it, squeezing because I'm scared of letting go.

As if sensing my fear, a cold hand covers mine, gently raising it to rest on the side of the urn, the top still buried in my palm. Another hand follows, until both my hands are enveloped by larger ones on both sides of the urn. A small ball of warmth flares in my stomach, but it's not from the sun. Ryne stands behind me, his chest against my back and his head hanging above mine. Slowly, together we tip the urn forward, the ashes spreading in the wind, getting lost in the gleam of the sun. I let my head fall backward until it's resting on Ryne's shoulder, his support the only thing keeping me standing. As the urn empties, it becomes lighter. So does my heart.

"I miss you, Daddy," I whisper to the heavens. "I'll love you forever."

I'll see you in every sunrise.

Even when the urn is empty, I remain filled but it's not some unfathomable, gut-wrenching feeling. What's filling me to the brim is peace.

Space and time are irrelevant as I stand here and become a part of the world around me, Ryne keeping the promise he made to me in the bathtub when he said he wouldn't let me be here alone. He holds me down, lifts me up, keeps me grounded when I can't figure out how to do it myself. And while I've never cared about forever, I wouldn't mind if this was it.

Ghosts Only

July 12

When people tell me he's in a better place, I believe it, because someone like my dad has no place to go but heaven.

Ryne stays by my side through it all, steadying me every time raw emotion threatens to knock me off my feet. When people say the phrase 'let your emotions loose,' they always talk of the catharsis you'll feel afterward, but what they fail to mention is that when you've been suppressing them for so long, letting them out is like re-breaking bones that have mended wrong so they can heal right this time.

"Sorry," I mumble when he grabs my elbow to stop me from collapsing.

He shakes his head. "For the worse or the better."

My fingers rest atop his hand. "For the worse or the better."

The number of condolences and prayers are on the rise as

people I don't know take turns hugging me and whispering words of kindness and wisdom that align with verses from Dad's religion. Those who are non-religious in turn offer me good vibes and tell me my father lived a lifetime of happiness thanks to me. It's flattering, and while I wish I was a girl my daddy could be proud of, I'm not. But I'll get there eventually if life permits it and for once, picturing myself past twenty is easy. Something in my heart tells me I got a long life ahead of me so maybe I should prepare myself to enjoy it.

Once the party dies down and a couple people begin to head out, Ryne grows agitated, his body spasming, and he loses control of his limbs in what appears to be an aftereffect of that one erratic heartbeat. When he can't control the movement, his form begins to blur at the edges as his mind falls into shambles.

I pull him into the cover of the trees so I can speak freely. When no one can see me, I latch onto him, not ready to let go of the peace I've found. "Don't go."

He gently unwraps my arms from his body and steps back. "Sorry, Melinda. You feel too good right now, and that's not exactly what I'm looking for."

He doesn't just want to feel *good*. He wants to feel *alive*. I nod, knowing what he's going through is so much bigger than me, and while it's something I can comprehend, it's something I'll never truly understand until I die and am caught on this earth with him wondering why I can't just let shit go and move on.

I give a reluctant nod, refusing to meet his eye.

Leaning down, he places a swift, hard kiss into my lips. "I'll see you around."

And with that, he spirits away.

Heart in my throat, I take in the darkness around me. Fear of what lurks in the night creeps up on me as I remember Ryne's words and Judith's pleas. I don't remember the trees being so looming and the path being so obscured when Ryne was here. When did we get so deep into the woods? How did I forget that pine smells like poison? Even though the sun has risen, the trees shade the area until I can't tell the difference between day and night. All I remember is Ryne and how his eyes twinkled in the moonlight.

An overwhelming anxiety grabs onto me like the spirits in the cemetery. It's a combination of things—my worry for Ryne inducing the most stress while the rest remains due to the horror story I heard earlier.

The grass shifts beneath my feet, the wind picking up and causing the trees to lash out like monsters with claws made of branches. I surge forward, cautious of my surroundings. Thanks to the wind, I can't follow the smell of smoke, but I can follow the slight glow of the fire between the trees.

As I'm about to enter the clearing, I spot something a little unusual—a girl in the woods, but instead of trying to make her way out of it, she stays creeping along the edge, hidden behind the trunk of a tree.

Warning bells sound in my head. She's not a ghost. There's a pulse jumping out of her throat and sweat slicking her skin. I almost wish she were one though. Then I could explain what she was doing in this secluded area while the few lingering guests remain in the open, but since she's not, I dread the answer.

I sneak up behind her, my footsteps as silent as the ghosts who move around Windhaven Hotel.

"Hey," I say, narrowing my eyes as she whips around to

face me, her hair catching in the wind to reveal her frightened face. It's the girl with the bucket hat, who bumped into me and left blood. Nikita.

She stumbles back, but no noise leaves her mouth.

"What're you doing out here?" I cross my arms and lean on one hip.

"I—Where did you come from?" Recognition flashes in her face. "You were here a few weeks ago."

"I live here."

"Oh . . . You're Margaret's granddaughter then?"

I raise an eyebrow. "I am. You still haven't told me who you are."

"I'm a local."

"So why are you here then?"

She wraps her hands in the hem of her t-shirt, a red ring of something coating her wrists. "I needed some answers."

This piques my interest. "To what?"

"A boy. He . . . I . . ." Her breathing picks up and she recollects events, her eyes filling with tears. "I can't. You won't believe me. No one will."

She runs off into the clearing, past the dying flames of the bonfire.

"Did you see it?"

My skin grows cold on one side as Judith appears beside me, her face shadowed by the trees. She watches the flailing girl, her mouth set in a grim line.

"See what?"

"The blood on her hands."

I seek her out again. People move out of the way as she runs through the crowd, cries of outrage sounding as she bumps into people and causes a few to spill their drinks. She picks up an empty glass and hands it to its owner and that's when I see it: both her hands are coated in bright red blood that snakes past her wrists and dribbles down the tips of her fingers.

I tilt my head slightly to see the world at a different angle.

No one around her reacts to the blood on her hands, even as she's handing them back cups smeared with it. The gears in my mind shift, clicking into place. No one is reacting because they can't see it. It's not an accidental trace of blood like what stained me. Blood is on her hands because she murdered someone.

"Bryce!" I leave the cover of the woods and begin making my way down to Bryce's spot on the edge of the peninsula. He heaves into the ocean one last time before turning to me, his sternum cracking as he pushes his bones back into place.

"Everything okay?" he asks as I stop in front of him, like he wasn't the one who just cracked at least five bones in his body.

"Where's Ryne?"

"He's not with you?" A water droplet runs down his cheek.

"No. He ran away. He was upset."

"Why?"

"He thought his heart beat. I saw it too, but . . ."

"Shit," he curses, throwing his soaked locks over his shoulder. "His power as a ghost is probably getting stronger.

Phantom kicks like that—I've experienced them before. Our power manifests itself in different ways and is often disguised by human-like gestures. We're dead, but our body's muscle memory and mentality function like we're human, so it's the shittiest disguise ever."

"I need to find him." I pivot on my heel, preparing to break into a sprint, but Bryce does something out of character. He reaches for my shoulder. He's *never* touched me before.

He clenches his teeth as if it pains him. "You can't feel him?"

"No," I hang my head in defeat. "I'm too anxious. When my anxiety spikes like this, it smothers it." I inhale a breath before releasing it. "I'm going to keep looking for him."

"Audrey."

"What?" I demand, noticing how sick he's become just from touching me. It's too much for him, the sensations. He's been a ghost for far longer than Ryne and his pain tolerance is nowhere as high.

"Don't."

I jerk my shoulder back. "Why? What did you do to Ryne?"

He holds up his hands. "Nothing, Audrey. Nothing he wouldn't have done to *himself*."

His meaning catches onto me.

"That doesn't mean much considering Ryne is always trying to kill himself!"

"That's what I'm trying to tell you. You don't know what kind of state you're going to find him in. Do you remember that day he lunged at you? He's got trauma, and sometimes it takes him back to that day and he's not in his right mind."

"I know," I hiss.

"Look, I'm not just worried about him becoming a Shut-Eye. It goes both ways. As much as I like you, the dead and the living should not be together. He could seriously hurt you."

"He won't."

I head towards the hotel to find people clearing out as the day goes on, the sunrise now gone as the sun has risen to the highest peak, a sky of blue circling it. I search everywhere for Ryne, in rooms, on window ledges, and the grounds of the property but I can't find him.

Pausing, I search for his energy from deep within myself, but it's useless. My heart rate is elevated and the thrumming in my ears blocks out the sounds and the presences against my skin. At some point, Caroline tags along with me, flying beside me as I run through the flower field, my mind racing.

I stop short in my tracks when I find blood splatters on a few flowers, their pink petals stained red. Near the blood trail is a pile of—oh my god.

I turn away, fighting off nausea as Caroline drops to her knees to get a better look.

"Are those Ryne's intestines?" she asks, glancing back at me. "What're they doing here?" She prods it with the edge of her flip flop. "False alarm! Someone must've dropped some hot dog links for the barbecue and Ryne bled on them."

"Like that makes it any better? How did you even get that confused?"

"How am I supposed to know the difference between cow remains and human ones?"

I follow the trail out of the flower field down to the gravel road until I'm in front of the graveyard. The black fence is before me, the word "cemetery" spelled out in jagged metal letters on a sign above the walkway. The tips of the fence are sharp enough to cut and I fear Ryne has taken advantage of it.

I stare inside at the green and yellow patches of grass, some of it dead, some of it alive, the ground having been neglected along with the gravestones. Most of them are covered in moss and weathered beyond belief. A chill goes through me at the thought of walking in and my anxiety awakening Shut-Eyes and conjuring forth spirits. I think of the bodies and bones six feet under, how Grandpa and Aunt Rachel are among them. Dad not being in the graveyard is the only solace I get, but even that doesn't stop me from recoiling.

I step forward, prepared to go through the open gate and freeze.

"Aren't you going?" Caroline asks.

"I can't," I whisper.

"You have to! Ryne won't listen to anyone but you and I know you've seen him begin to fade away. He's going to become a Shut-Eye if you don't stop him."

"I'm scared."

"You can't be! Ryne's in there. He may be a mess, but with him there, you're going to be okay, and he needs you just as bad. Pinky promise." She holds out her pinky to me.

Mustering a smile, I intertwine my pinky with hers and hold it for a second, give it a slight tug before letting it go.

Stepping forward, I enter the graveyard.

The grass has a slight dew on it and the dirt is packed into the earth. I walk around the headstones, full of names, dates, and R.I.Ps that mean nothing when you come back as a ghost.

I follow Ryne's blood. The further I go, the more blood

paints the grass, a contrast of green, red and yellow. I want to stop in my tracks, look the other way and run, but I can't stop —not 'till I get to Ryne.

The ground would swallow me whole if it could. I'm still not convinced it won't open at any moment and take me. I walk beside the blood, avoiding stepping over graves. I hear it's bad luck and while I've made it clear I'm not superstitious, I know the dead are vengeful and have no qualms about haunting forever.

It's like with every step my feet dig deeper into the ground, legs heavy as if I'm trudging through it. One wrong step and I might hit someone's casket and find myself buried in it. Untethered spirits are probably trying to latch onto me, but I keep myself from checking because I need to keep going.

Ryne lays against a Woudstra marked grave, and I'm blown away to find it's the new headstone of my father. He slouches into it with his back to me, his head hanging low. Blood is everywhere, coloring him and burning my vision red. I step around him, covering my mouth when he sits there, drenched in blood from head-to-toe. There's a gaping hole in the middle of his chest, the skin beneath his shirt raw as if it's been gouged out of him.

But that's not the worst of it.

In the middle of his cradled hands is his heart, covered in blood and still not beating.

Ryne stares into oblivion, his eyes looking past what's there and into a distant space only he knows. "You saw it too, right?" He repeats the same line from earlier.

He doesn't bother meeting my teary eyes or see when my tears begin to fall and course down my cheeks in silent agony.

I drop down, planting myself into his lap before closing my clean hands around his stained ones, effectively protecting his small broken heart.

"You shouldn't be here," Ryne speaks, his voice monotone as he finally meets my gaze. "Ghosts only."

I Want His Heart, Whole In His Chest Whether It's Beating Or Not

July 12

"Ryne, please get into the bath," I beg.

He shakes his head and stares at the tiled floor of the bathroom, his blood a muddy red against the milky white in a way that reminds me too much of my father on the kitchen floor. He's been slumped against the wall all morning, immobile since Bryce helped me drag him here. The hole in his chest still hasn't closed and oozes so much blood that I swear his soul drains out with it.

"Fuck." I lift my hand to run it through my hair, pausing mid motion as I remember it's coated in blood. "Where is Judith?"

Ryne needs a parental figure right now, not me.

Bryce talks in a soothing tone. "Calm down, Audrey. Caleb's knocked a few times now. You should go downstairs and eat."

"No! What about Ryne? What about you and Caroline?

You can't possibly expect me to let you two handle this alone. Besides, you two need to eat too—" I cut myself off. I am so stupid.

Bryce gives me a sad smile. "There's nothing you can do for us at this point. Caroline and I are fine."

"Of course we're fine." Caroline rolls her eyes. "We don't drop dead if we don't eat a few bites like you. Your skin looks horrible. Go eat and get some color. I can't want to be you if you don't look as pretty as you always do."

"We can't drop dead, because we are," Ryne mumbles, covering his face as he lets out maniacal laughter, his shoulders quaking.

"See?" Caroline throws out her arms. "He's fine."

While I'm not convinced, I'm left with no choice as Caroline pushes me out of the room. Downstairs, I pull out my seat at the dining table. The breakfast plate sits in front of me, mocking me with its sunny-side eggs and bacon smile. Everyone else around me eats their breakfast in silence, Caleb piling eggs into his mouth while Quinn sips on a chilled glass of orange juice. Granna offers Caleb another plate, which he accepts gratefully.

"Aren't you going to eat, darling?"

I look at the stainless-steel utensils on either side of me, the glint of their metal. I carefully pick them up, stars swimming in my vision as I take in my own hands, a near replica to the girls from last night. Fingers tightening on the fork, I stab at the eggs, carefully placing the bite into my mouth, chewing, fighting back another fresh wave of tears.

After breakfast is done, I hurry up to my room, sniffling as I throw the bathroom door open to find it empty, the dried blood the only remnant of what happened. I begin running the sink, a sob racking through my body.

A shift in the air and I sense him before his hands land on my waist from behind. I pause, my bloody hands still covered in soap, despite how washing them last night didn't rid me of the blood either.

"Sweetheart."

"Ryne." I try to keep my tone even, but all I remember is the hole in his chest and his heart between his hands.

He doesn't say more, just reaches forward, clasping my hands in his and washing them himself. When I pull them from under the faucet, they're clean, the water creating a slight sheen on my skin. I towel them off and leave the bathroom, taking a seat on my bed.

"I am so fucking sorry."

"It's—" More than okay. He held me in my darkest moment, too. Holding him is nothing, but unlike him, I can't make everything okay by just being there. My existence doesn't make anything better. It makes it worse. I am a constant reminder everything was taken from him.

"Not okay. You should slap me." He shakes his head. "Actually, don't, it'll turn me on."

"Stop," I say, placing my hands on the tops of his shoulders. I'm eye-level with his chest, his t-shirt once again unsoiled. Our breaths mix, and for a moment we stand there, inhaling each other's air like its oxygen, all we need. We breathe it in like we don't know what it really is: carbon dioxide, a waste gas, deprived of all we need to survive. Sometimes, I wonder if that's all our relationship is. If we're slowly killing ourselves for wanting it to be more. Metaphorically that is, since Ryne's been dead, but maybe my presence diminishes his final fragile strand of existence. Even so, I can't stop.

What I do next is a compulsion.

Before Ryne can comprehend what I'm doing, I grab fistfuls of his gray t-shirt and yank up until it's bunched around his neck. I run my hands over his lean torso all the way up to his chest where he gouged his heart out. His muscles clench and tighten at the sensation, a ragged breath leaving his body. The skin is smooth and tan, baring not even the slightest scratch. It's like it never happened, but when I peer up beneath my lashes to find his hazel irises swirling with muddy brown and damaged green, I *know* it happened. His pain becomes my own as it pulsates in my own chest like we share a heart. The moment he ripped his heart out, he ripped mine right out with it.

I push up onto the tips of my toes, placing a kiss on his chest right above his heart. "Don't be sorry," I tell him, resting my cheek against his skin. "It's weird coming from you."

Ryne stares over my head, his lower lip wobbling. He clenches his jaw to stop it, but it doesn't stop that one traitorous tear from sliding down his face. "I'd understand if you ran after this," he whispers as he wipes the tear off his cheek. "But I know you won't."

"I'm selfish. I've seen what this investigation has done to you—what being around me does to you, but I can't seem to stop. You should hate me for it."

He shakes his head, swallowing. "We both made this deal to get something we wanted, but then we started wanting other things along the way."

Each other.

As his words hang between us, we're left in silence. This

hasn't been a problem in the past, but after our night at the beach, there's been tension between us and I'm internally cursing myself and thinking of how many therapy sessions I'm going to need for this new category of necrophilia. But I don't just want his body, I want his heart, whole in his chest whether it's beating or not.

I lie down. Ryne lies beside me in the bed, lost in thought.

"What's up?" I ask him, breaking the trance he's in.

"Ever since you made me physical, I've been thinking."

"About?"

He rolls away from me. "I don't know."

"Stop."

"Stop what?"

"Shutting down." I reach out and grab a hold of the edge of his shirt. "Pretending you're not human."

"I'm not."

"You are. Your soul is human. A physical body can't take that away."

"It can," he says roughly. "I'm gone. Who I was died and decayed with my body in some unmarked grave that probably wasn't even a grave but some hole I got shoved into."

He gets to his feet and begins pacing. "Like fuck, Audrey." Pain courses through his features. "I need your light, but I can offer you nothing but darkness."

"I don't need light. Just you."

My words make him recoil, like I've just grabbed the knife sticking out of his chest and twisted it. Like caring for him is the ultimate betrayal.

When he moves, I move with him. Arms reaching toward

him, I barely feel my feet leave the windowsill. Eyes on him, it takes me a moment to comprehend the fall.

"Not this time," I breathe, my body plummeting out the window.

Horror twists his face.

He reaches forward, fitting his body into mine to prepare for a crash. But it never comes. He stops at the last second, his body inches from the grass. His chest moves at a rapid pace, like he's forgotten he's a ghost. He doesn't have to panic or need to breathe, but he still does it, because he was once human and it's all his muscle memory knows.

We're floating in the air, his body a straight plane as he levitates up into the sky, past the window we jumped from until we're floating over the rooftop. Head against his chest, I finally dare to lift my head and meet his astonished face. His eyes are wild, his curls caught in the wind.

"Why did you do that?"

"Because you can't just throw yourself out the window every time you feel something."

He ignores me. "You know I can't die, but you can."

"I can. So what?"

Finally, I'm given clarity, so clear it burns through any doubt fogging my mind. It's like the synapses of my brain have just been reset, information and awareness flooding into every corner of my mind. The world suddenly becomes bright, the sensations strong.

My heart? Ricocheting in my chest.

For the first time in a while, I feel so alive that nothing matters but what I feel for him.

I did it because I knew he'd save me.

I did it because it meant he wouldn't hurt himself.

It's a rush of emotion, a warmth that starts from deep in my heart and flourishes through my chest like a buzz—the best possible one I could find. Nothing the bottles I used to pick up could ever compare to.

Why did I do it? Because Ryne is real. Because what you see is what you get, and Ryne doesn't have it in him to pretend. But most of all, I did it because I've fallen in love with him.

"You know, if it meant you got yours back, I'd trade my life for yours." God knows he enjoyed his more than I ever did mine.

Ryne floats us down slowly, carefully helping me back into the window. I don't let him go. He stumbles forward through the window with me, placing a hand over my beating heart. "I'd die ten times over before I'd let that happen."

I'm pushed back onto the bed, him crawling between my legs. "This is a bad idea," he emphasizes.

"Why?" I ask as his mouth lands on mine.

"Because"—he places a small bite onto the edge of my jaw—"I've fantasized about you so many times, having you might shatter what's left of my soul."

A soft gasp escapes my mouth when his weight settles on me. He lifts himself up and takes in the view of me, my hair spread out around me like a halo and my cheeks flooded with warm blood and this time, it isn't because one of us is covered in it.

That smile. "You're nuts and I'm fucked in the head for thinking I deserve someone so damn gorgeous."

"I'm perfectly sane, if it's any consolation. It doesn't even bother me that you're dead."

His fingers move up my abdomen. "Are you sure I'm a ghost?"

"Yes?"

He glances down at the crotch of his jeans. "Doesn't feel like it."

Before I can say anything, Ryne disappears, materializing by the window.

The good die young and apparently, so did this. We had barely even started.

I push my fallen bra strap up. Ryne tracks the movement, turning around and slamming his head against the wall a single time before facing me, his forehead red from impact.

"Are you okay?"

With eyes squeezed shut in pain, he nods. "Some lines shouldn't be crossed. I can't give you an experience that's real."

I open my mouth and close it, a sigh of frustration exiting my body. He's right and it wouldn't be real for him either, not when every sensation feels like it's happening on the other side of a closed door to him.

"We can do other things," he offers. "Or nothing at all. I'll take you anyway I can have you."

I curl my legs to my chest and pat the spot on the bed beside me. "Lay with me?"

His smile is soft as he presses a kiss to my cheek before lying beside me and murmuring, "Of course, Sweetheart" into my hair.

Life is short and my clock is always ticking, the hour that is my life becoming shorter by the minute. I'm always aware of it, how can I not be? With all these ghosts around me, it's all I think about. There's a constant ticking in my head, but for these past few hours I've spent kissing and laying with Ryne, time is suddenly irrelevant, and the ticking has halted, the hands of the clock stopped.

But time has to start eventually, reality setting in as the hands begin ticking again.

"Ryne . . ." I focus on a strand of hair as I sort my thoughts, my head resting upon the pillow.

"Yes?"

No more kissing. I have to tell him what I saw.

I sit up, my hair falling over my shoulder as I look down on him, his elbow propped on the pillow as he rests his cheek on top of his hand. "There was this girl last night with blood on her hands. I think she killed someone here. Judith saw her too."

Ryne's head snaps up. "What? Do you think she could be the one who . . ." He trails off, grimacing as he remembers his murder.

"I hate to ask, but what do you remember from the night you were killed?"

Ryne inhales a deep breath, his chest rising and sinking as he releases it. "I remember stairs." He wraps his arms around his midsection as he fights back a shiver. He clenches his teeth. "It happened on the stairs."

I lean forward. "Yes, I remember you telling me."

"Until I went with you, I've tried to go down them, but every time I do I get so fucking sick and feel like I'm going to die all over again, so I don't think and jump out the window."

"So you can hurt yourself before anyone else can."

He shrugs. "Who knew being hurt would be the only thing in this spirit world that could make me feel something? Now that I've got you though . . ." he adds, winking in my direction.

I shush him gently. "Don't change the subject. I know this is hard for you but *think*, Casper."

He gives a weak smile at the use of the nickname before a frown takes over, his eyes glazing over as the memory plays out in the cortex of his mind.

"We . . . were sneaking into the lighthouse to have sex."

"Oh. Okay then." I cross my arms.

"Come on, you know I'm no saint. Far from it. But that's why I was there. She said she knew it wasn't bricked in like everyone said it was and that there was a mattress up there and how she always wanted to have sex with a view of the ocean, so I followed her."

My jaw ticks.

"I know," he groans. "Not my best moment, following some girl I just met. But I *didn't* have sex with her," he reminds me when he sees my pouted lips and furrowed eyebrows. "I take pride in not having sex with the girl who killed me. She stabbed me multiple times just so I'd feel the pain. She said something about it. I can't remember what she said, but I remember how the words made me *feel*. Fucking terrified. And you know how she finally decided to finish me off?"

I do know. He doesn't need to tell me.

"She slit my throat." He runs a finger over the scar on his neck. I recall how when I first saw him, I thought he was alive because of it, but he turned out to be as dead as the rest of them, minus the open injuries. He's made up for it though. He's shed more blood than any of them through his own doing.

"So, what if you find the girl?" Ryne asks. "I know how I died, and I still haven't moved on. I've thought about it a lot since you said you'd help me, and I'm not sure if knowing who she was or why she killed me is going to make me move on. I think, just knowing I've got someone out there would be enough. I want the people I love to know I'm dead and that I didn't just disappear off the face of the earth. I want to be . . ."

"Missed."

He looks up at me from beneath his lashes. "I'm selfish for that, aren't I?"

"You're not, Ryne."

"I want you to do something for me." His eyes slice into me.

I don't bother concealing my frown. It can't be anything good.

"You can feel us. I saw you in the graveyard. You were uncomfortable because of the proximity to the bodies, right?"

I think about it. "I can, but it's not as simple as it is to feel your presence. It's something I have to search for if I'm not nearby."

There's never been much reason for me to go looking for a body until now.

"Try then, Melinda. You said you'd find some way to help me figure out why I'm trapped here."

"Fair enough," I trail off, unsure about the whole situation. "Will you be able to handle it if I do?"

"I'll be fine. You?"

I'm not sure, not because it's a body, but because it's Ryne's.

Bones

July 14

The sky is cloudy and the waves slam against the rocks of the cliff like a warning. Ryne and I stand in the middle of the clearing. We're the only two souls in sight. No one lingers on the limestone patio. All the sun basking and picnicking isn't possible today. All shutters are closed, the windows sealed tight in preparation for a storm.

The past few days have been good for him, but I fear finding his body will make him spiral, and this time I don't know if I'll be able to get him back. After all, the past few days have only been good because the ones before them were *bad*.

Ryne and I take advantage of the silence as I try to connect to the land through the other world instead of my own. I scan the property with precision, mentally mapping the trees and the peninsula. Then, once I feel like I have an accurate mental map of the place, I focus on the graveyard, on the anxiety and soul-sucking feeling I nearly succumb to every time I'm in it. The bones are a heavy reminder of the souls they once bared, the density of them like lead in my limbs.

I grab a hold of them within myself, an invisible radar within me rushing from my body before exploring the entire property. Every twig and pile of dirt has a presence of its own. It's so alive I can't help but wonder if there's a soul here too. I overturn rocks, brush, mud, and grass until I find what I'm looking for, the pressure of it building up more and more the closer I get to finding it. My ears pop when I do. It's so intense, I stumble, my head knocking into Ryne's chest as he catches me before I can fall.

I inhale a ragged breath and fall into his embrace, my cheek against the fabric stretched across his chest. "I found something."

"What?"

A grim look pinches my features at this grizzly discovery. "Bones."

Ryne doesn't allow himself optimism—optimism? I want to fall to the ground and laugh at the thought because finding bones *is* something we would be optimists about.

"Graveyard?" Ryne questions, not letting his guard down to prevent the inevitable disappointment if it isn't.

I move my head side to side and lift a shaky finger, pointing straight into the densest and darkest part of the property.

He nods and levitates, his body buzzing with energy. I see it right away: the urge to soar across the land and into the darkness, but he can't. I'm the one who knows where the bones are buried, and since I'm still human, he allows his feet to hit the grass before he shoves his hands into his pockets to restrain them. His legs move slowly, but each step is aggressive and full of power he doesn't know what to do with.

Hoping to take this burden off him, I offer my hand. He gives it a sideways glance before hesitantly wrapping his fingers around mine. I rub his knuckles with my thumb, hoping even though he's a ghost with a muted sense of touch, it can still unravel the uncertainty flourishing in his otherwise empty chest.

A small smile edges up the side of his mouth at the gesture. "I can't tell if you keep forgetting I'm not human or choose to treat me like I am."

"I never forget, Ryne. But whether you're alive or not makes no difference in how I feel about you." I haven't exactly been forthcoming about my feelings for him, but actions reveal all. Actions are the root of who you are. Dad didn't only tell me he loved me, he showed it. Leaving mom after she tried to have me committed showed he didn't believe I was crazy like I convinced myself I was.

He frowns a little. "How do you feel?" He shakes his head at the thought and changes the subject. "I don't know how I'm going to react if I end up in front of my own bones," he admits, twisting his finger in his curls.

"I'd probably go numb," I tell him. "I used to walk by ghosts and pretend I didn't see them. If they were screaming, it was easy to put my headphones in and keep moving. If they were hurting themselves? Simple. Look at anything else, even the tiniest fractures in the sidewalk could hold my attention. How do you think you would react?"

This whole thing is so surreal and while I usually like to deny being fucked in the head, I think we're past that by now.

Ryne and I aren't sane, but we're not crazy either. There's not a word in this world for what we are. We're submerged in a world of ghosts, ghouls, spirits, entities—whatever the hell you want to call the dead whose empty corpses have been buried in the ground.

"Way differently than you. I don't know whether I'd break down on the pile of them or pick them up and throw them at Bryce. Maybe chase Caroline with one of them. She gets on my fucking nerves. She's like the sister I never had." But as he says it, a strange look crosses his face.

"What's wrong?"

"I don't know. I just feel like I said something that's not true. Maybe I did have a sister. Sometimes I can remember, but most of the time I don't. Bryce and Caroline think I'm a middle child because of how I act."

I smile. "You really love them, don't you?"

He snorts. "Sure, and Judith is my mom. We're a happy family." He gives me an incredulous look. "Not everything is so simple, Audrey."

I shove a hanging branch out of the way. "Why call me by my real name now? You never did before."

"I thought if I never called you by your name, I wouldn't think of it, but it's in my head regardless."

Thunder cracks above us, followed by a sheet of rain. He inhales a breath as rain drops cascade down his face. "Caroline and Bryce are like me. They're not real. If it was anyone but you, they could walk right through me and not even feel it, but you? Too real for me. You make me solid. The closest to human I can get. Sometimes I can't even walk with you without thinking I'm just a boy and you're just a girl, and we could be something more, but with me that's not possible.

Audrey, there's no forever with me, and I don't pretend there is."

"That's your problem, Ryne."

"Which one?" He laughs. "I got a lot of them."

"You think I'm more human than I am. Don't forget—I'm a part-timer in your world."

He kicks at a rock. "Meaning?"

"Some girls' criteria don't involve forever. Sometimes we just want something that makes us feel alive even though we know it won't last."

"Stop with the feelings. You're making me soft. Besides," he says almost bitterly, "Wouldn't want another phantom heartbeat."

Ah. Bryce must have explained it to him.

When the thunder cracks again, I mistake it for the sound of my heart. I cried the entire night when I remembered his heart, small and cold in his big hands, a reddish shade of purple. I'm about to mention it, pull back the muscles encasing my own heart so I can bare it to him, tell him how that night nearly killed me.

But then my blood runs cold, like my own bone marrow can sense we're in the presence of another's.

I stop in my tracks. In front of me, the grass is grown over, but the ground is uneven.

"Ryne," I breathe, grasping his arm. "It's shallow."

He looks back to me, eyes simmering with a fear I've never seen before. Swallowing, he crouches and places his hands on top of the dirt. "This is going to be messy. Last chance to turn away, Melinda."

Melinda, not Audrey.

Instead of answering, I refuse to avert my gaze.

Ryne begins. With the unrivaled strength of a spiritual entity, he digs, pulling up roots without breaking a sweat. Mud cakes his hands as he digs, fingers and palms in the earth, tearing it up. The rain causes the mud to splash until it speckles his face, his shirt, his jeans. Abruptly, he stops. The edge of a human radius juts from the ground. His hands become gentle. He carefully wipes mud off the white bone. I try to get a better look from over his shoulder, but before I can, he stands up and paces past me.

"It's not me."

"What?"

"It's. Not. Me," he repeats, his voice taking on an edge as he stomps back over to the grave. "Look at me. I'm huge. Those little ass bones don't belong to me." He kicks the bone hard enough to dislodge it and send it flying into a bush.

"That's . . ." I trail off in disbelief. "All I can feel."

Ryne growls. "Your ability must not be working."

I step back, astounded. "Ryne, that's all there is here. If there was anything else, I'd feel it."

"No," he groans, materializing right in my face, causing me to take a step back, my foot sliding in the mud. "It's not working. I'm bound here, so obviously my body is buried here. There is no other way." He points a finger toward the direction of the clearing, his eyes never wavering from mine. "I wouldn't be stuck wandering around that hotel otherwise."

At that moment my phone rings, the sound cutting through the rain. I pull it out of the back pocket of my soaked through jeans. I answer and press the phone against my ear. "We'll keep trying," I tell Ryne, turning away from him once someone's static voice comes through. "Hello?"

"Hi, is this Audrey Woudstra?"

"Yes."

"Great. I'm calling about that old Mamiya camera's pictures you wanted developed. I'm sorry it took me so long to get back to you. I've been pretty swamped with work."

"Yeah, no worries." I take in our muddy shoes. "We have too."

Has three weeks really gone by that fast?

"Relieved to hear it! Your prints are ready for pickup whenever you're available."

My heart picks up. What was Grandpa taking pictures of before he died?

"So that's it?" Ryne's voice breaks, his brows creased, and mouth turned downward as if he's about to throw a fit.

I rush forward and push myself onto the tips of my toes to wrap my arms around his neck, my finger combing through his soaked hair. "No, it's not."

His arms close around me. "Promise?"

"Always."

Ryne and I stand on the edge of the property. I watch as he attempts to step off the gravel road, but some invisible barrier stops him. He clenches his jaw, his fist balling up at his side before he releases the tension, stretching his fingers before lifting them to my face.

"Hurry back," he demands, his lips capturing my own in a searing kiss. It's like he's taking over every nerve of my being, a possession I succumb to without hesitation.

"Oh yeah," Caleb says from the driver's seat as he waits for me to climb in the car. "This shit definitely just got weird." He slouches in his seat and places a pair of black rimmed sunglasses over his eyes. "Her mouth was moving and everything." He says it more to himself than to us. "God, it's weird when I can't see him."

Ryne glares in Caleb's direction.

"Sweetheart, let him know next time I rip my head off, it's landing in his lap." Winking, he gives me a last wicked smile before one more quick kiss.

I lean my forehead against his and smile. "I'll do better than that."

I inhale dramatically, my hands covering my mouth as I look at Caleb.

"What?" he demands, sitting up.

"Ryne's head! It's in your lap!"

Caleb looks down into his empty lap and screams bloody murder.

"That's my girl." Ryne grins.

I make my way over to the car as Ryne spirits away.

"Get. It. Off."

I pretend to swat the non-existent head out of his lap.

He scowls as he puts the car into drive.

After we pick up the pictures, Caleb and I head back home. The envelope lays in my lap, perfectly sealed.

"This whole thing is crazy." Caleb sits back. "I can't believe you found that camera and saw Grandpa die. What . . . what was it like seeing him in—not person—but spirit?"

"He looked a lot like Dad," I say, my waterline filling.

Caleb sniffs. "Shit, I miss him. And Aunt Rachel."

"I do too."

"You going to open it?"

"Later."

"With Ryne, then?"

I pin him with an annoyed look.

"You know, I've been thinking."

"About what?"

"I don't know. Just doesn't feel right keeping it from Quinn."

"Well, you need to," I tell him as I climb out of the car. "Caleb, she's not going to believe you." She'll think he's as crazy as I am, and it'll make perfect sense to her when she assumes it runs in the family.

"I know you don't like her, and you have every right not to, but Audrey, she's my girlfriend. We've been together for nearly four years, and it wasn't always this way—the constant arguing—she used to be my best friend. She's going to believe me. How else do you think we've gotten to this point?"

I shrug, the topic of relationships bringing conflicting feelings to the surface. Caleb always talks like a relationship is on some level I can't comprehend. Maybe it's not. I've never been in one, and I can't let myself consider one with Ryne. His "my girl" is the closest thing we'll ever get to a label, but it doesn't mean what I feel isn't real. What I feel is the realest thing about me.

"Four years," I mumble, wondering what four years with Ryne would be like.

I wonder and I dread at the same time. Ryne and I will never have four years and if we do, it wouldn't be real. It would be an illusion, because neither of us deserves to be trapped in Windhaven forever. We can't grow like that, not in a way that matters.

"Yes, and see how strong we're still going?"

But they're not.

And it's even more reason why all we have is now, and since all we have is now, maybe it's time I'm honest with my words. We don't need a label, but I need to put a word on love, let him know it's there and solely his to keep whether he's in this world with me or not.

Bones Flying Like Frisbees

July 15

Ryne's knuckles are white, the skin across them stretched so taut that the veins in his hands and arms stand out. Usually, I'd seize this opportunity to greedily take in the contours of his shoulders to the hard line of his jaw and pretty face, but right now, he's menacing.

I want to convey my feelings to Ryne, let him know what he means to me, but the side of my body next to Ryne is frozen, like ice poking through skin, cutting me until I bleed. I fight back a shiver and clench my jaw to prevent my teeth from chattering.

In this moment, it couldn't be more obvious that my Ryne isn't human, but I'm not compelled to run. Instead, I stay and breathe in the dark atmosphere rolling off him in waves. The molecules in the air bend to his command and emit an overwhelming aura broad enough to darken even my most wretched heart.

Leaving today was obviously a bad idea. I left Ryne in a

fragile state and there's no telling what he did to himself while I was gone.

"Are you going to open it?" he asks, tapping a finger against the crisp envelope of photos.

"I can do it later." I set the envelope down on the sleek wood of the dresser. "Let's go back to the grave. I want you to be certain the bones aren't yours."

Ryne shakes his head and kisses me on the mouth. The motion sends a wave of ice down my throat. "No, check the envelope. I've been wanting to see the pictures since we found the camera."

Yet he almost threw it off the cliff and into the ocean. I still don't understand why he tried to do that. Was he honestly that bitter I hadn't found more on him? Ryne is a lot of things, but I've never once thought of him as vengeful.

I shake my head, but Ryne's fingers grip my jaw and tilt my head down to where the photos are hidden behind the folded paper.

"Are you okay?" I whisper.

A wry grin. "Not at all," he admits. "But you make everything a little better."

My heart cracks in my chest, the pieces rivaling shards of glass.

With shaky fingers, I pick up the envelope and break the seal. It contains a thin stack of Polaroids. I gasp when the first picture is of Grandpa and a woman who isn't Granna. There's a sunspot on her face, but the smile isn't Granna's. It's something so familiar that I know I've seen it before. I move the first photo and place it in the back of the stack. The next photo is of the same woman. This time, Grandpa purposely took a photo from the mouth down, the woman leaning back into a pair of fresh purple sheets, her body adorned in a nightgown that dips to reveal her cleavage.

"Whoa." Ryne says. "So, we know he had sex just right before he died. Maybe she killed him. I know I wouldn't mind you shoving a knife in my chest if you fucked me while you did it."

"Hold off on the death by sex fantasies, will you?"

He gives a noncommittal shrug. "I'll try." He floats in the air, crossing his legs and sitting in concentration. He blows out a breath a couple seconds in. "I can't do it. Now I'm picturing you in that same night gown on top of me with a knife in your hand."

I roll my eyes.

I almost don't want to look through the rest, but I do. They're mostly of the same woman. One is of Grandpa's hand on her bare leg and the next is of her face down tangled in sheets, blankets and nothing else. The same old blankets on the musty old mattress in the lighthouse.

Grandpa was having an affair.

Bitterness wells up in me at the thought of Granna being cheated on. Suddenly I feel better about never knowing this man and not having any type of feelings for him.

"Do you think she knows?" Ryne questions.

"I doubt it. You don't remember happy memories and uplift someone who's done you wrong." I groan and touch my throbbing temple. "I keep thinking we've found something, but it always ends up being a dead end or leaving me with more questions."

The shadows stand out from beneath his glassy eyes. "Women kill too, Sweetheart. Don't count that one out yet."

I lay my head on the desk.

Ryne takes the first picture from me and holds it up to peer closer. I watch as his eyes widen a fraction, but one blink and suddenly his face has fallen back to a passive mask. His Adam's apple bobs as he swallows.

"What is it?" I ask, resting my arm on the back of the desk chair.

Ryne tosses the photo onto the desk. "Nothing," he says carefully, walking towards the window. "Come on. Let's fuck around and dig up some bodies."

"Okay." I send Caleb a quick text to let him know what I'm doing.

In a hurry, Ryne jumps out the window. I run to the edge. "I told you to stop doing that—" The words catch in my throat when I see him, hands in his pocket as he floats down. His head swivels up as he gently lands into the grass. "Come on."

My face relaxes. "Give me a minute." I turn on my heel to sprint toward the door when Ryne flies up to the window and picks me up, throwing me over his shoulder. "Ryne," I squeal as his hand grips the back of my thighs. "Someone's going to see."

"I'll fly a little higher so you're harder to spot," he promises before surging into the sky. I grip onto his back, having no choice but to look directly at the ground, which by now is hundreds of feet away.

When we find the half-dug grave of bones, Ryne has reverted into his dark state. Upon further examination, it's confirmed the bones aren't his.

"Are you sure?"

"Audrey, do I look five-six? Hell no. I'm five-eleven. You know that." He kicks at the pile of bones, sending one flying.

The bone surges back toward him, so hard it cracks him in the skull and sends him to the ground. A burst of energy sucker punches me in the gut, throwing me to the ground next to him. When I glance at him, he lifts a hand up to his head, wiping the blood from the gash in surprise.

"What the hell are you doing?" Judith demands, dark energy crackling in the air around her. The shadows of the branches and leaves cast darkness onto her face. Dark stringy hair flies around her head, and she looms above us.

"We found a grave," Ryne says, squinting his eyes as blood drips into them.

"I know. It's mine."

"How did you know?" Ryne demands.

"I'm ancient. I could sense you were near. How dare you defile my grave!"

I use the edge of Ryne's shirt to prod at the wound. "We're sorry, Judith. We didn't realize it was yours!" I curse when more blood exits Ryne's flesh wound. A faraway look sets into his features, the one that tells me he's teleported back to *that* night. The one that killed him. His irises move frantically as if it's happening in front of him.

"Hey," I say, gripping his face between my hands as his form begins to float. "Ryne!"

His form flickers as he squeezes his eyes shut before lowering to the ground. I watch helplessly as Ryne pulls his legs to his chest and rocks back and forth in my arms. "Is it over?"

"You're safe," I assure him, aside from the obvious part where he's dead. I glare at Judith. "You didn't have to hurt him."

Even though he was sending her bones flying like frisbees.

The energy fizzling around her gets worse. She is livid, and I can't blame her. We messed with her resting spot, and I can only imagine what sensation went through her body when we dug up her bones. It must have been a painful, disorienting experience, but it doesn't excuse hurting Ryne.

And now I've got something new for my ghost archives, something I didn't know was possible for ghosts to do. I apologize again, but fury contorts Judith into something unrecognizable. Her eyes burn a glaring red.

"Audrey!"

At the sound of Quinn's voice, Judith snaps out her trance and goes back to normal, the darkness around her receding. As Quinn approaches with Caleb on her heels, Judith growls and spirits away.

"What the hell is going on here?" Quinn demands. "Caleb over here is going on about the fact you can see ghosts."

"Quinn, I'm not lying. Tell her, Audrey!"

"Ryne?" She throws her head back to the sky and laughs. "You're literally such a fucking liar!" Turning to me, she sneers. "Who is Ryne, Audrey? Is he real? Or is he just another one of your hallucinations because you belong in a fucking looney bin!" She takes in the trees with distaste. "And why are you out here, you freak?"

I flinch, my insides clamming up as a familiar clawing takes hold in my chest. She sounds just like my mother. And like I did when my mother accused me of being crazy, I want to deny it. I open my mouth, but I'm cut off as Caleb steps in front of me.

"What the fuck is wrong with you?" Caleb explodes in her direction.

Quinn stumbles back at the volume of his voice, loud, cracked and *broken*. The panic surging in his chest causing his diaphragm to spasm rivals my own and since I can never find comfort when I'm like that, I don't know how to give it to him. I have never seen him in this state or heard him scream at her.

"You're so fucking mean!" he cries out, his body trembling in a mixture of anger and pain. "You hurt me already! Is that not enough? You're hurting my fucking family now too?"

"Caleb," Quinn trails off, frozen in place as Caleb collapses to his knees, tears streaming down his face as all of the emotion he's been suppressing drains out of him.

Quinn tries to reach out for him, but he yanks away as if her touch disgusts him. "We're done," he whispers, the words so quiet Quinn has to crouch to hear him.

"What?"

"I said," Caleb says, his head hanging low, "We're done."

She laughs nervously and stands. "Let's talk about this. You've been a little stressed out, but you know you don't mean it."

Caleb finally raises his head, his blue eyes clearer than I've ever seen them. "No. This time I mean it. We're done, Quinn."

I remove pressure as the wound on Ryne's head gradually heals. He hisses but doesn't tear his eyes off the scene unfolding in front him.

Quinn starts off by cursing Caleb out, then uses any kind of means to degrade him. He simply stares at her and takes it, not because he's weak, but because he's finally seeing the truth: the person who claims to love him treats him like garbage. He takes it in, absorbing every word into his mind, and uses it to build a layer of defense against her, one that'll keep him from ever going back to her again.

When she's done, she must realize the weight her words carry, because she begins apologizing, but it's too late.

Caleb peers at me as if he's been slapped across the face.

My face pinches into a sympathetic frown.

Son of a ghoul, I warned him. He didn't listen and this rotting corpse of a relationship is his to bury.

When Quinn comes to the realization that she can no longer influence him, she plants both hands on his chest before shoving him backward. It catches him so off guard that he topples over, grunting as he lands on his butt. He stays there as Quinn marches away, not bothering to apologize or look back at him.

"Be right back," Ryne says.

"Where are you going?" I demand, wiping the rest of the blood off his face with the edge of his shirt.

His eyes flash in mischief, the burden he bore no longer ramming into the front of his mind and tucked away in a corner for another day. "I'm gonna do what ghosts are supposed to do—haunt. Besides, I promised to send her running. How's that for some romance?"

"Ryne," I sigh. Convenient. Something interfered with his situation, so he's going to use Caleb's to his advantage and forget about it. Classic ghost boy move.

Ryne disappears with a blur. A second later, Quinn screams.

I rush over to Caleb and put my hands under his armpits to lift him, but he doesn't budge.

"Are you okay?"

He says nothing and after a moment, I stop struggling to help, realizing he doesn't want my help. He stands on his own. "No. I'm not okay. I just lost my girlfriend."

"She wasn't meant to be your girlfriend."

Caleb clenches his jaw, fists shaking. "How the hell can you tell me that? Four years, Audrey, and you don't know shit about it."

"I really don't," I admit. "But if that's how she acts in front of people, I can only imagine what goes on behind closed doors."

He shakes his head as if he can't believe what I'm saying.

"Look, if Dad were here, he'd tell you being with Quinn is blocking your blessings. You went to church together. You know he'd be right."

Caleb glances out toward the edge of the cliff. "But he's not here."

"No, but I am." For once, I'm not fading into the background. I'm no longer trapped within the walls of whatever room I enter. I want to be seen. I *will* be heard. "And I'll tell you that being with Quinn is sucking the life out of you."

The words don't taste like my own. They're hopeful, with a hint of honesty and bravery I never imagined myself capable of.

Caleb must not resonate with what I said. Instead of acknowledging me, he makes his way up the rickety stairs and slams the door behind him. Despite the cold shoulder, I stay on his tracks. I'm just about to step onto the first step of the staircase when a hand lands on my arm.

A warm substance coats my skin. I pull out of the grasp, noticing part of my arm is now covered in blood.

The girl from the bonfire stands before me, hands still dripping in crimson blood so thick, it slowly coats the linoleum floors in a puddle. I'm plagued with images of my father in his own pile of blood, the sunrise casting a bloody glow and mimicking him in the sky.

"I need to talk to you about something, but you're going to think I'm insane."

I cut to the chase. "You killed someone, didn't you?"

Her eyes blur with tears. "How did you know?" She wipes her wet cheeks, the blood mixing with her salty sadness.

Bryce appears beside me and takes her in from head to toe. "Jesus."

My face twists into a grimace. "That'll make you lose your breakfast."

He covers his mouth as his throat fills with water.

"Who are you talking to?" the girl asks.

"Ghosts," I say.

Her eyes widen.

I snort, despite the world practically burning around me and falling apart at my feet. "Don't look so scared. You're the one who killed someone."

This Isn't The Fucking Conjuring

July 15

"So, do you want to do this here or somewhere more . . . private?"

If we're going off experience, I'd much rather do stuff like this in seclusion, preferably in a place that scares normal people. The woods provide cover. It's rare that anyone casually strolls up and wonders what I'm doing and why I'm talking to myself. In her case, this is much more than a passerby thinking she's crazy. Someone might call the cops on her if they hear her talking about murder.

Maybe *I* should be calling the cops right now. I could be in danger, but even that sounds ridiculous. I don't fear humans on the same level I fear ghosts. They can do far worse than some local snooping around Windhaven, so I can't bring myself to be anything more than cautious. I will call the cops if she turns out to be some kind of sociopath, but until then, I think it's safe to say not everything is what it seems.

"Sure. My name is Nikita by the way. You're Audrey, right?"

I nod. "Cliff, woods, or gravel road? You decide. There's not much variety."

No wonder everyone here has gone insane.

"Gravel road," she chooses. "The woods scare me."

"The woods scare you, yet you killed someone," I point out.

The horror marring her face suggests I've said something out of the ordinary and considering how carelessly it came out of my mouth, I bet I did, but unlike it used to, I'm not really bothered by the implication of people thinking I'm crazy anymore.

"Sorry," I amend, my sneaker knocking a rock a couple feet in front of us. "I'm used to being around a very different group of people." Dead ones, in fact.

The girl nods. "It's okay. I'm not used to someone else bringing up my life-altering mistake so casually, let alone knowing."

I meet her eyes. "So, why'd you tell me, then?"

My phone is in my pocket. It would take me no time to dial 9-1-1. She's taking a big risk coming to talk to me and even though she may look harmless enough, with her bucket hat and braids, there's a copious amount of blood on her hands that suggests otherwise.

But I recognize something in her that I've seen in myself —fear that you've really lost your mind and no amount of searching will bring back. I know it too well, from the questions whirling in your head to wondering if every interaction or thought you've had is real.

I wonder how she copes with it, if addiction runs as thick in her veins as it does in mine.

"I heard you mention his name at the bonfire and I heard that Quinn girl tell someone about how you're crazy and see things."

Of course, the bitch did.

"I thought you might have experienced similar things to me. I can't even comprehend what happened to me and I've exhausted all options and you're pretty much the last one even if it's a long shot. Look, before we get into this, I have to ask, what did you mean when you said I was covered in blood?"

I stop, folding my arms across my chest to hide the shiver that dances along my skin. I search for the words, her awaiting, worried face clouding my vision as I try to concentrate.

"I don't really know how to explain it, but when someone dies brutally, the blood remains if they become a ghost. You're covered in it, even if you can't see it."

She rubs at her wrists, nails digging in her flesh as if she's trying to scratch the tainted skin away. Reaching out, I grab her fingers with my own. "Don't, it won't come off that way."

"I killed someone," she suddenly blurts out. It must be the first time she's said it out loud, because the impact of the words has her hunched over and ready to hurl.

She wipes her mouth after emptying her stomach. "We were here at Windhaven. It was the end of our senior year and we threw a party. All night I had been flirting with this guy and purposely catching his eye. I suggested we go upstairs."

Pretty girl with a killer smile.

Ryne's face flashes in mind, so distraught, so full of anguish.

"It was *you*," I spit. "You killed Ryne."

She holds her hands up between us. "Hear me out," she cries through clenched teeth as her eyes fill with tears. Both of ours do. "You said you would."

Anger is a snake uncoiling in my stomach, poised and ready to strike as I stare at her, knowing the blood dripping from her hands came from *his* body. I hold myself back, for no reason other than I need to know what happened. His humanity depends on it.

She wraps her arms around her torso. "From there it was weird. At one point, I passed out and lost control of my body. I was talking and knew what I was saying, but I didn't want to be saying it. Whatever direction I tried to force, my body wouldn't work. It was like I was watching through someone else's eyes." A painful swallow.

Possession. It has to be. I haven't been possessed myself, but I've watched ghosts cling to my being and absorb energy as I've been weakened by my anxiety, so full possession must require some kind of altered state to take hold. If they were at a party, I bet on my life drugs and alcohol were involved. But alcohol can barely drown out the Traces.

I tap my foot as I think. What about drugs then? The questions stack up in my mind but have nowhere to go. Nikita is still talking.

"I remember sneaking into the kitchen and grabbing a knife." Her breathing speeds up. "I didn't want to be grabbing it. I tried so hard to drop it, but I couldn't. I didn't even feel drunk at that point, and when I met back up with the boy and walked upstairs I just . . ." Her eyes are two waterfalls. "Started stabbing him. I couldn't stop. I screamed, but no sound came out. When it was over and he was dying on the floor, I took the knife and slid it across his throat."

"Ryne," I breathe, the syllable taking all the strength in my body.

"Oh God, I killed him. I skipped town after that. I came back hoping for answers, but I can't bring myself to ask anyone and Google isn't helping with shit. I can't find an obituary or anything."

"Body," I whisper. "What did you do with it?"

"I don't know! When I woke up, I thought it was a dream, but when I saw blood in the corner of my shower, I knew it wasn't. I didn't stick around, Audrey. I just left. How can you explain that?"

I'm at a loss for words.

"Was I possessed? Because I swear to you, that's what happened. The person who killed Ryne wasn't me!"

I weigh the options in my hand. "Were you drinking? On drugs or anything?"

"Everything. I was cross-faded. I don't even remember how I got home. Come on." She grabs me by the shoulders. "You have to know something. If you can't help me, I don't know what I'm going to do."

Before I detach her from me, that familiar spot of warmth rolls across my back. My head pivots to the east where I find Ryne flying over. He drops beside me, not bothering to glance in my direction. I peer between the two of them, not knowing what to do.

"Ryne, this is . . ."

"He's here?" She looks everywhere except where he's

standing and that itself has him clenching his jaw so hard I fear it'll break.

"His . . ." I trail off. "His ghost is."

Finally, Ryne takes in her face and freezes. His entire demeanor takes a drastic shift.

Everything happens so fast. Bryce appears out of nowhere, followed by Caroline. They each grab onto an arm like they did in the lighthouse when Ryne started to panic. He jerks in their grip, fury taking over as his system is put into overdrive.

"Ryne, stop!" Caroline yells, grabbing onto his arm again when he yanks it free. "You can't kill her. She's going to end up trapped with us!"

"That and the fact you shouldn't be killing anyone!" I interject, cupping Ryne's face. "It's okay," I say in a soothing voice. "You're safe."

Ryne growls, drawling his words out in a slow, languid tone. "She killed me."

"She didn't know what she was doing! Ryne, don't murder her. It's not going to miraculously bring you back to life."

Ryne stops struggling and finally snaps his head toward me, his face pinched in betrayal. "You're defending her?"

"Audrey, what's happening?"

I ignore Nikita and keep my gaze latched onto Ryne's. "Not defending her, but I think something is going on, something that's bigger than what we think, and I've got a feeling she's involved. Ryne, I think she was possessed and we're missing something."

Aunt Rachel. Grandpa. The notes. The affair. This girl. We're missing something. All of this? It has to be connected, and I can't let Ryne risk the last strand of his humanity on a vengeance he'll be worse for. It *has* to be connected.

"She killed me."

"Nikita?" I say.

"What?" she asks, looking around for someone who's not visible.

"Run. Don't stop until you're past the property line. Go!"

Ryne thrashes even harder against Bryce and Caroline, the darkness around him intensifying so much that Bryce and Caroline are thrown off as his eyes burn red. He soars through the air in Nikita's direction, throwing a hand forward to catch her. I gasp when he has her by the edge of her shirt and run over.

"Don't do it," I beg, holding onto his arm.

Nikita struggles against the ground where Ryne straddles her, a death grip on the collar of her shirt. She kicks and screams, but his grip on her is unyielding, his eyes stony and cold.

"Stop!" I beg, throwing my arms around his neck from behind. "Don't!"

"Why?" He fists both his hands into the collar of her shirt, stretching the white material of it. He can't kill her with his own hands, but he can use the fabric of her own shirt against her.

"Once you do it, you can't take it back. You're going to have to live with what you did, but I'm telling you, she's innocent."

"Live?" He laughs. "There's no life for me to worry about living. And possession?" He lets out a cruel, grating laugh. "This isn't the fucking *Conjuring*."

"Killing her won't do anything. What would make you any different from her?"

"Nothing, but it'll sure as *hell* make me feel a bit better."

"Please." I touch the side of his face, my fingers urging him to look back at me.

He allows me to turn his head, eyes bloodshot and wild when they meet mine. "Last chance, Melinda. Give me one good reason why I shouldn't."

As he tightens his grip on her shirt, I yell with everything in me.

"Stop!" The word sends a full tremor through my body and my stomach burns. My words cause Ryne to freeze up, his hand not leaving its clenched position.

"Your eyes," he says as if caught in a trance. It's the fountain all over again, Tilly's mother being thrown back so hard the fountain cracked. It's some control I have over him, and I have no idea how I'm doing it.

Ryne's grip loosens, his hand falling to his side as my words unravel him. Nikita wiggles out from under him, sprinting away the moment she scrambles to her feet.

"Last name!" I call out after her in a last-ditch effort. "What was his last name?"

But she's gone.

"You're even more fucked in the head than I thought." He climbs to his feet.

"You stopped." I press my hand to my chest, feeling it rise and fall in relief.

"We both know I didn't stop because you told me to. I stopped because you *made* me." He says it as if there is a difference.

"Ryne—"

"I had one chance! One chance to take back power that was stolen from me along with my life, and you just let it get away. How am I supposed to move on or gain closure? How? You've practically doomed me to an existence here."

"Ryne, I love you. I did that for your own good."

Slowly, his shoulders begin to shake silently. The silent laughing turns into a contagious little chuckle that morphs into full-blown laughter that cripples him and sends his face into the ground. "*You* love *me?*"

"Yes," I whisper, my voice shrinking.

"Yeah, and I tried to kill you so you're obviously fucked in the head. " He brings his hand up to his mouth, caressing his bottom lip with shaky fingers as if he can't believe what just came out of it.

"What?" I blink, stepping closer.

Ryne curls both hands into fists. "Fuck. Fuck. Fuck. Audrey . . ."

He reaches out for me, but I jerk away. "No, what did you say? You tried to kill me?" My voice is so small I wonder if I've said anything at all.

He runs a distraught hand through his hair. "I—It was the day we first met. I put my hand around your throat and squeezed, but when I saw how alive and fragile you were, how easy it would've been, I felt so sick to my stomach, I couldn't go through with it. But that was then. After that, I never considered—never."

"What am I supposed to do with that, Ryne? You just tried to kill Nikita!" I extend my arm into the direction she fled. "I know she killed you, but why me?"

"I didn't know you. Fuck, Audrey I didn't know all this" —he gestures between the two of us—"was going to happen, or I never would've done it. Judith noticed I had taken an interest in you and put the idea in my mind. You could be a ghost along with the rest of us. At the time, I thought having you here with me would be a good way to pass time."

"A toy. You wanted to kill me so you could have a toy."

Ryne's face contorts with pain. He can't even deny it.

I'm hit with the full-fledged truth—Ryne lost his humanity way before we met. They all did. They've been obsessed with me from the start—the idea I could be one of them. They never once considered that I wanted to live, even if it took me a while to see it.

My legs give out from beneath me. Caroline's fascination with me—had it been the result of the ghosts feeding her delusions of me becoming one of them? How could they even know if I'd become a ghost? Who's to say killing me would've kept me here?

A strangled cry leaves my throat. *The camera.*

"Why did you take the camera, Ryne?"

He shakes his head, but I don't need to hear it from his mouth. The answer is something I know so well it's practically ingrained in me. The fact I have no doubt is sickening. Ryne took the camera, because he knew by doing so, I'd never move on. He actively tried to take away the only thing that was keeping me going—the only reason I stayed *alive.*

"Were you just waiting then?" I scream, dragging myself up from the ground. "For me to die?"

"That was not my—"

"I don't want to hear it," I yell, turning on my heel before pivoting around. "That's why I hid the fucking projector from you. Because even then, I knew I couldn't trust you!" Without another word, I run back to the hotel, wind whipping through my hair and across my face. My thoughts are in disarray, and I've left a trail of my broken heart. I keep going until I'm inside the foyer, but even then, I'm fast on my feet, pushing my way through the library to the next door and into the cover of the kitchen. A cabinet of liquor stands tall against the wall. When I throw the door open, I grab a bottle of liquor and twist the cap off, throwing it back like I've done so many times before. The taste of it assaults my tongue, burns my throat, and makes me gag but I still find myself swallowing.

Slamming the bottle down and wiping my mouth with my palm, I sit down and stare off to the side to find Gavin watching me intently, a video camera in his hand. He lowers it and makes a show of him erasing the footage.

I glare at him warily as he takes a seat beside me at the table.

"Tough day?"

I bring both hands to my face.

"I've got something a little stronger in my room. It may not take all the pain away, but it for sure eases it and makes life a little more fun. You look like you need some of that."

I nod wordlessly and follow him to his room.

Devil's Lettuce

July 17

The final nail is in the coffin, and I'm left buried with Ryne kicking dirt over the grave of my heart. The pain is like a spiritual manifestation of its own, shredding me from the inside out. It's so overwhelming I ache and yearn to feel nothing—to tear my own beating heart from my chest and hope the hollowness would deliver me some kind of numbness to the emotions currently flooding it.

When I bring the blunt to my mouth and inhale, a traitorous tear escapes, the others barely held back at my waterline as if part of a poorly planned war. They threaten to break free, capture my cheeks in a salty sadness. I wipe them away before they can. The smoke burns as it infiltrates my lungs, but it leaves my mouth in soft tendrils, so light they remind me of imaginary, white sheet ghosts. Not the ghost that broke my heart.

"Devil's lettuce," Gavin says, causing Lesley to giggle.

"What?" I cover my mouth as I erupt into a coughing fit.

"Weed," he supplies, passing the blunt to Lesley. She takes a drag, her mouth forming an 'o' shape as she blows circles into the stale air of their room. "You know you're talking to the host of the number two ghost documentary on YouTube. Gotta keep it on brand, baby."

The "baby" out of Gavin's mouth doesn't send heat through my body like it does when Ryne says it, even if what I feel for him is mangled by betrayal.

I drop my head against the back of the headboard of one of the twin beds and sigh, bringing my knees to my chest to keep as far away from Gavin as possible. He edges closer on the bed. More than once, he's tried to send Lesley away, but she's either oblivious or not having it because she refuses his every request.

"Are you okay?" Lesley asks. "You said you've never smoked before, right?"

I nod.

"No wonder you're already high."

I am high, aren't I? I laugh at the thought, my head light and airy enough to float up with the ghosts of Windhaven if I want.

Only I don't.

My gut twists at the thought of never having the three of them hanging around my room with me again or Judith no longer looking out for me as if I'm a daughter of her own as she begs me to be careful. Are they all in on the fact Ryne was going to kill me? They must be. There's no such thing as secrets here unless they're to be kept from me.

Why?

I want to scream and tear Windhaven apart piece by piece for being witness to so much of my suffering. I want to extinguish the presence swirling around my skin and getting closer second by second.

Are they coming to kill me? I try to find the fear through the pain, but I can't. Death doesn't scare me more than living with this feeling does. When the blunt is passed back to me, I suck in until my lungs fill, and I nearly choke on it. I inhale until I'm so high the presences slowly fade out. A slight dwindling, and then . . .

Nothing. Everything is muted.

It's like my core, mind, and skin have been doused in cold water and set out to dry until I'm normal. Just to confirm if what I'm assuming is real, I search within, my senses scanning the premises, delving into every crack and crevice of these old walls, but still, I can't find anything. It's as if all the ghosts have vanished and at this moment, after so much agony, I've finally done it. I've found a way to be completely normal and drag my last foot out of the door between worlds.

It's not as gratifying as I always thought it would be.

Gavin takes the last hit of the blunt and stubs it out in a ceramic ashtray, the orange ashes slowing before turning gray. Discarding the remainder, he washes his hands and grabs a couple plastic cups and a bottle of alcohol.

"Are you old enough to drink?" I question, slightly worried the smell of weed will draw attention.

"Oh yeah, no worries. We're twenty-one."

"Oh."

"How about you?"

"Eighteen," I answer, shifting more into the headboard despite there being no more room.

"Oh shit." Gavin pours a cup and hands it to me. "You just graduated then, huh?" He frowns in disdain as his own cup. "Les, can you *please* go down the hall and get some ice. You know I hate my alcohol at room temperature."

She rolls her eyes but hops off the bed and stuffs her feet into her slippers. "Fine." She pads out of the room, slamming the door behind her and trapping me with a guy who named his YouTube show Ghosted.

Once she's gone, Gavin slides off the bed and drops down to his knees. I lean over the edge to find him looking for something stuffed under the bed. "Ah-ha!" Something scrapes across the hardwood floor as he drags it out from hiding. He drops a black boardgame box onto the bed. "Time for some fun." He pulls a thin board out and unfolds it. An array of golden letters in lines of the alphabet stare back at me, an eerie "yes" and "no" at the bottom of the board on opposing sides.

My blood spikes. I drop my untouched cup of alcohol, the cup bouncing a few times before coming to a complete stop.

A spirit board.

"Whoa!" Gavin grabs a towel from the bathroom and throws it onto the floor. He proceeds to mop it up, dragging the towel across the floor with the heel of his foot.

"Why do you have that?" I demand.

While I don't necessarily fear the spirit board, Dad made it clear he didn't want me messing with it.

"We use it when filming Ghosted. It gets the mood going." He sets the board between us. I cross my legs to prevent the edge of my toe from touching it.

"Do you have someone who's passed on?"

I stare blankly into the empty space, imagining Ryne is somewhere in front of me, trying to get my attention, wondering why his hand is going through me when he reaches toward me.

"There's a boy," I say, my unfocused eyes peering forward, hoping Ryne feels as unseen as I've felt blinded this entire time.

I picture his shadowed face but can't decide whether to picture it as hurt as me or something more sinister. I attempt a vicious look in my mind, but God help me, it's no use. All I can conjure is the vulnerability I've come to know, and that wicked smile that's less wicked and more alluring.

Gavin cocks his head. "Like legit dead? Or?"

"No, he's dead dead."

"Were you together?"

"Yes."

"What happened?"

I meet Gavin's eye. "He hurt me."

"Well." Gavin slides beside me. "In that case"—he places his hands onto the wooden magnifying glass—"no point in getting his permission to date you."

I can't even react, I'm too focused on his hands forming a triangular motion as they shift across the board and where I've seen it before. The motions are so clear in my head, but the more I rack my brain for information on where I've seen this, the more obscured the thoughts in my head become. I watch without blinking, until my eyes burn and my vision blurs in a haze of black and gold.

The second the spirit board goes flying into the air, smacking Gavin in the face, I've found my answer.

Gavin screams at the top of his lungs, the sound echoing off the walls and piercing my ears. I'm unfazed as he runs out of the room and into the hall. I don't need to see ghosts or feel their presence to know this paranormal activity is courtesy of Ryne. I can imagine his boisterous laughter in my ears and hear the words he'd be yelling.

But right now, that doesn't matter.

I turn my back, focusing on the plain sand colored wallpaper across the white space above the headboard on Gavin's wall—Aunt Rachel's wall. Her Trace isn't visible to me, but I can feel the drops of her blood splattering onto my face nonetheless as I peer into the exact spot I know she hangs with her lifeless eyes, the rope creaking under her weight.

I silence my thoughts, the open wound her death left still fresh with nothing to stop the bleeding. Swallowing my hurt down, I run out of the room in desperation, not out of fear.

Granna is perched in her normal spot at the front desk when I skid to a halt downstairs. She calls out to me, but I'm on a mission. I throw the door to my room open, retrieving the hidden projector.

I run back into the hall, crossing into the northern east wing of the inn, down the hallway back to Aunt Rachel's room. When I come to a stop, the door is still wide open. There is no sign of Gavin or Lesley. The room is just how I left it, wet towel of soaked up alcohol on the floor, collecting debris and casting a strong, foul smell into the room. The spirit board lays on the floor, facing up, the magnifying glass slid into the corner, the center of it cracked from the impact.

I set the projector down onto the nightstand gently, as if any harder will make the room implode. The outlet sparks as I plug it into the wall, but when I press the power button, it comes on with no problem. I watch as a blank screen projects onto the wall above the headboard of Gavin's twin bed.

I step in front of the projector for a slight second, the

shape of my body cutting through the screen and casting my silhouette across the wall. I bend down into a crouch, taking in the spirit board. That familiar anxiety creeps in, threatening to consume me like it always does. I shove it down as far as I can because the need to find the truth is more motivating. What really happened here? And why does it keep happening? Hesitantly, I reach my hand out, pausing just before my fingers come into contact with it.

My anxiety begins to spiral, the walls around the room creaking at the pressure. I get a grip on my mind, and everything stills. I give myself internal praise.

I'm nowhere as weak as I thought I was.

I set the board down, snapping a picture of it with my phone before connecting to the projector. The moment the board is projected onto the wall, I gasp. I slowly walk to the bed and stand on top of it, my hands forming a triangle as I move my hands over the letters. The floor is ripped from under me as I connect the zig-zag lines Aunt Rachel made across the wall and realize my initial thought is correct.

Aunt Rachel was messing with a spirit board when she died. With the way her hands were moving, something was communicating with her. It wasn't a *living* person leaving notes pretending to be Grandpa, it was a *dead* one. That's why she acted the way she did. She was trying to comprehend something that should've been impossible.

But who?

Ryne. Bryce. Caroline. Judith. The only ghosts on the property.

There's only one thing I can do now—get sober. I'm not going to see Aunt Rachel's Trace otherwise and right now, I'm going about this entire situation blind. Since I can't see the ghosts either, there's no telling if they're all here right now, watching me.

My skin crawls at the thought, my eyes moving up and down the room and furniture in distrust. Judith could be seated in the corner. Caroline could be crisscrossed in the bed beside me with Bryce lurking near the window. Ryne could be right in front of me with that wicked smile slicing across his face. And the most fucked up part?

I can't bring myself to stop loving him.

A pang in my chest.

I fell in love with Ryne, but I loved all of them. They weren't unrooted beings to me—they were as real and as human as me. They were my friends and the first to make me feel alive in a long time.

"Why?" I howl into the empty room. "Why did you all do this to me?"

In a rage, I tear the sheets off the bed where I imagine Caroline sitting. Picking up the magnifying glass off the floor, I chuck it into the wall with all the strength I have left. The magnifying glass glides through the air, colliding with something. Something that's not the wall. My eyes widen as it drops through the air, but then abruptly stops and slowly rises until it's eye level with me.

Then, it soars right into my head. I'm thrown onto the floor by the impact, my vision blurring as something warm drips down the side of my face. Weakly, I bring my hand to my head, wincing at the pain and pulling it back to find my fingers dotted in scarlet blood.

Black spots bloom in my vision before I'm out cold, what's left of my sight fading to thick darkness.

You Don't Look So Good

July 18

When I wake up, my limbs weigh hundreds of pounds and are loaded to the brink with exhaustion. Sitting up is even worse. My entire body is weak and nearly caves in on itself with soul-wrenching coughs.

I wrap my arms around myself and shiver as I climb out of bed, nearly falling when I get tangled in the sheets. Where am I? My head pounds as I fight through the vertigo and peer around to find myself in my room. I trip over my feet as I make way to the full-length mirror in the corner.

My hands cover my face as I find my complexion a sickly pale, the skin beneath my eyes ringed red to match the blood-shot vessels in them, standing out against the blue of my irises. Gauze is taped against my temple, soiled with my blood. I wince as I rip it off, but I need to see the damage. I resemble Caroline a great deal with this gash in the corner of my temple, blood crusted around the wound.

If I'm being real, I look like I died and came back . . . again.

I'm still in the clothes I was wearing when I was hit in the head, but I don't know how I got back into my room.

Stumbling into the hall, I clench my teeth as they fight to chatter. The presence of the ghosts is back and overwhelming, but one feels strange, like it's right on top of me. I glance up, but no one is there. I expand my reach of the presences, digging even deeper into the sensations, but there's nothing around me, and the other three presences are near the edge of Windhaven. I must still be a little high if I'm missing it.

But one thing's certain. I've got to get off this property. The ghosts can't feel me like I feel them, but they still have eyes all over the hotel and know when there's the slightest change in the atmosphere.

I move swiftly until I'm standing in front of Caleb's door and knocking as soft as possible. "Caleb," I hiss. "Open up!"

The ghosts of Windhaven are trying to kill me.

"Go away!" he screams as if warding off some kind of demonic presence.

"Caleb, please!"

I knock again, only to be greeted with silence. When he doesn't answer, I twist the knob to find it locked. Growling, I drop my head into the wooden panes of the door. Just as I'm about to crumble to the floor in defeat, Granna comes down the hall.

"Granna!" I call, rushing only to nearly collapse into her arms.

"Audrey!" She wraps her arms around me and places the back of her hand against my forehead. "You're cold as ice, but you're drenched in sweat. Sweetie, you're sick. You fell yesterday and hit your head on the side of a bed when you were with Mr. and Miss. Petersen."

"I'm fine," I protest, forcing myself out of her arms. "I have to go to town."

"Not like this," she says, authority present in her tone. "You need to rest."

"No," I wheeze, short of breath. "I want to go into town. I want to go to the doctor. Can I take your car?"

"You're in no condition to drive."

"I'll take an Uber."

"Why don't you ask Caleb?"

I shake my head. "He's not in the headspace to listen. Granna, Quinn left."

She dips her head in sadness. "I know." She contemplates my offer for a moment. "I'll take you myself."

"No!" I burst. "You need to manage the hotel."

And I have no plans to go to a doctor.

She bites her lip and thinks a moment longer before reluctantly agreeing. I thank her and give her a hug before rushing back into my room to change into some clean clothes. I schedule an Uber to pick me up ASAP through the app, with priority even though it'll cost me extra. I don't care. I'm out of my depth here and buried in betrayal.

I throw on some clothes haphazardly, nearly face-planting into the floor every time I move too fast or my thoughts resume cinching around my brain until it's about to burst.

I turn at the notification of my driver arriving and sprint out the door and down the stairs, my sneakers squeaking across the linoleum floor as I run forward, pushing the door open and throwing it closed behind me.

A couple hundred yards away, the Uber waits at the entrance of the property.

Gravel cracks beneath my feet as I kick up dirt behind me, my lungs in agony as I fight to retain air in them.

Suddenly, Ryne materializes in front of me, his face marred by urgency and sadness.

"Aud—"

I dodge him, running right past his form. Adrenaline fills my veins as I glance back over my shoulder to find him cutting through the air, arms outstretched and ready to capture me.

I'm close.

So fucking close.

The end of the gravel road marks the end of the property. There's a sleek black car parked on the side of the road as they wait, not noticing that I'm running like my life depends on it.

"Stop!" Ryne screams, his voice full of desperation in a tone I've never heard from him before. His eyes are wild when I find them, like he's terrified.

I have one foot over the property line when his hand latches onto my arm, nearly ripping it from my socket. I scream at the pain, squeezing my eyes shut. Ryne's hold falters, but he refuses to let go. "You can't go!" His fingers dig into my hip bones as he attempts to pull me backwards. "She's got you."

"You tried to kill me," I cry, tears coursing down my face. "You're a traitor. A goddamn liar." I recall him holding me in the bathtub, how he held me together so I wouldn't just completely fall apart. How could that have been fake?

"I never betrayed you, Sweetheart." My feet slide through the dirt as he steadily pulls me back. "I couldn't."

"Then why're you hurting me?"

His fingers are relentless, like metal tightening around my skin. "Because you're going to hurt a lot worse if you leave."

All the pent-up rage and sadness in me finally snaps. I rip my arm from his grip and muster all my strength to shove him backwards as I yell. "Leave me alone!" Power builds in my core, erupting. Ryne flies back across the land. He slams into the dirt and skids to a stop. He groans and lifts himself up, blood blooming through his shirt at the impact of the fall.

I glance down at my shaky ashen hands, barely comprehending what I've just done. With one last shaken look into Ryne's direction, his face begging me to stay, I run the rest of the way to the car, hopping in before slamming the door.

The driver peers at me through the rearview mirror, taking in my sweaty, out-of-breath appearance. "You look like you've just seen a ghost." He chuckles, shifting gears before pulling onto the road.

I gulp in a fresh breath of air and cradle my hurt arm to my chest, my hair everywhere. "I did," I tell him. "Don't you know the local legends? That place is haunted."

He nods, smiling like I've told him a joke. "So I've heard." He squints at the maps on his phone to see the destination I punched in. "To the square."

We've just entered the city when my stomach churns. "Pull over please," I say, nausea washing over me. The driver is quick to oblige, his brakes squeaking and throwing me forward into the seat as he stops on the side of the road. I unbuckle my seatbelt and lean out of the car and begin heaving, tears streaming from my eyes as I choke on my coughs before throwing up some more.

"You okay?" the driver asks, the leather of his seat squealing as he turns in his seat.

Taking a deep breath, I breathe in and out slowly, the air passing through my lips unevenly. I wipe my mouth off with the back of my hand and pause when my hand is streaked with black gunk.

Blood roaring in my ears, I lean over the side of the car and peer into the gutter of the street. The same black gunk on my hand spills down the storm drain. I yelp and back into the car, my hands finding my stomach.

What the hell is wrong with me?

"I'm ready," I tell the driver.

"You sure, kid? You don't look too good."

All the reason for him to hurry. "Yes."

Shrugging, he drives down the street, stopping when we pull in front of the square. I thank him and drag myself out of the car to the purple wagon parked on the side of the street. I say a silent prayer in my head to God to send my father to watch over me. Once my prayer has been sent to the heavens, I turn to peer across the street where I helped the child, Tilly, find her mother.

I pull a crumpled business card out of my pocket and search for the woman who called me a demon. She knows something about me. While she may be wrong about what it is, she sensed something in me, and I need to know if she knows anything about my ability and can help me.

I move over the cobblestone of the street, relief coursing

through me when I spot it. As I approach, she throws open the flap of her tent, this time wearing a bright pink skirt and decorated in emerald green jewelry that dangles wherever she walks. This time, her hair is down, her long braid over her shoulders.

"You," she says, distrust morphing her face. She backs up in caution.

"I need your help," I plead, collapsing onto my knees, doubling over as I come close to passing out again. "I'm not a demon," I swear to her. "Please."

"What is the matter with you?" she demands, prodding me with her sandal.

"I don't know," I admit. "But you were able to sense something in me, so that must mean you know something about what I can do."

The woman keeps her guard up but steps aside, motioning for me to step into her wagon. I drop my head in relief and climb to my feet, wobbling as I climb in. The wagon is full of trinkets and potion-like bottles and herbs. Most of all, there are crystals everywhere in different colors, shapes, and sizes.

"What is all this?" I ask.

"I tell people they're for protection, but they can't protect someone like me." She takes a seat across from me but keeps a noticeable distance. "So." She narrows her eyes. "Why are you here?

Sitting up straight, I meet her gaze head on. "I see ghosts. I can touch them, and I can even feel their presence and tell you where they are."

She lifts her chin. "Prove it."

"How?"

"The only way you know."

The fountain flashes in my mind, I turn in the direction where it stands, the running water sounding in my ear even from afar. "There was a Shut-Eye in that fountain."

"Which is?"

"A sleeping presence. One that has been around so long, they sleep within objects until they're awakened again. She had a daughter left to wander around by herself, so I woke her. They're both gone now. I don't know where and I know I sound crazy—"

"Tilly," the woman breathes.

I blink. "Tilly," I agree. "How did—"

"I died and came back, much like you did, I take it? I didn't realize there were more people like me."

I nod. "I drowned when I was little."

Her face turns grim. "I was nearly killed by a man when I was young."

Sadness trickles down my heart. "I'm so sorry."

She waves me off.

"There are these ghosts. They're after me, and they're trying to kill me."

"Leave the land," she says as if it's that simple. "They're bound to the land they died on."

"My family is there."

"Ah, that makes matters more complicated."

"What can I do?"

"You can control your ability. Proximity to the ghosts makes you as strong as them. It's hard and I struggle too, but if you really delve into yourself, you can do it. This may not be helpful, but it's all I have."

"What is my power?" All this time I've thought all I had

were senses. Did coming back to Windhaven and interacting with ghosts awaken something I've always had within me?

"Control. You can feel them, so why not bend their energy to your will? As for your illness, I don't know. I'd have to look over you longer if I was going to be able to determine—"

The familiar nausea manifests within my stomach. Bending forward, I heave once again, emptying the contents of my stomach onto her colorful carpet.

The woman screeches when she sees the black gunk dribbling out of my mouth and grabs a bushel of some kind of sage. With a quick swipe of a match from a pack within the pocket of her dress, she lights it on fire.

She waves it my way, the intense swirling around my head filling my lungs with a thick rancid smoke. I throw my hands in front of my face, convinced for a moment she's going to throw it at me.

When there is no impact, I lower my hands to find her whispering some kind of prayer. She pins me with a wild stare, her eyes widening with each word. My core shakes as a sensation burns through it. My stomach jumps as if there are butterflies within it, swarming and hitting the edge of the cage that is my body. With every fiber of my being, I hunch over, my limbs contorting and twisting in pain as I retch up everything within me. It hurts. It burns and I feel like my insides are coming out along with the black gunk that leaves my body. In a small mirror, I see it dripping from the edge of my bottom lip, staining my teeth and tongue black.

A guttural scream rips from my body from the pain.

Then it completely stops. Whatever illness was taking hold of me leaves my body as I regain my strength and my senses, which I didn't realize were dulled until now, refreshed and restored. When I peer across to the woman, her mouth is wide open as she stares at something above my head.

Shaking, I follow her gaze, slowly turning my body.

Judith floats above me, pulling what's left of her form out of my body. She meets my eyes, her face morphing into a sinister stare before she growls, her eyes glowing red as she shakes the earth beneath me.

With one last nasty glance in my direction, she's caught in the wind, dissipating into tendrils of a breeze as she's whisked back to Windhaven where she will be left alone with everyone I love.

To Have And To Bury

July 18

There's a negative energy buzzing in the air at Windhaven and the sky is infused with ugly, darkening clouds. At the edge of the road, I'm caught wondering how I missed it this entire time.

Judith is a Bygone.

The salt in my wound rubs raw from the betrayal. She possessed me. The sickness should've been my first clue. It was the first sign my body had begun rotting from within, because there's no room for untethered souls in the bodies of the living. It's what Ryne was trying to warn me about earlier when I left, but I couldn't even wait a moment to hear him out.

Not when he at one point had the intent to kill me.

As I run up the gravel road, there's static in the air. It rings in my ears, threatens to burst my eardrums. I push it down as best as I can and run into the front doors of the hotel, leaving them banging in the wind behind me. I'm up the stairs in no time, side stepping a couple of guests and nearly slipping on the polished wood. I bang on Caleb's door, begging for him to open it, but there's nothing, not even a call to go away.

Fear creeping into my chest, I latch my shaky finger onto the golden knob of the door. It rattles from my nerves, twisting and creaking as it slowly edges open. The room is empty, but everything is out of place. The sheets lay in a tangled heap on the floor and there's a broken lamp on the floor surrounded by a pile of glass. The window is pried open, fresh blood on the chipped paint of the windowsill. I run over to the window, glass crunching under my shoes as I lean over the edge to find more blood and torn up clumps of grass and dirt like he was dragged kicking and screaming.

My gaze follows the path of struggle into the direction of the graveyard and that's when I spot the ever-growing pile of dirt as Caroline digs a grave. Judith stands there and watches Caleb lying face-down on the ground beside her feet. Sensing my stare, her head twists around on her shoulder, her body not moving. A mixture of fear and anger pulses through me when a smile slashes across her face.

She's going to bury him alive.

I'm outside the hotel in an instant, running because Caleb's life depends on it. I go through the gate, my usual anxiety swallowed by fear for Caleb. Spirits threaten to rise at my command, but I stomp it down and force them to stay in their graves where they belong.

I sprint over, avoiding giant clumps of mud. "Let him go."

Her nasty smile widens, stretching across her face in an unnatural way that rivals the Joker. This close, I can see her bloodshot eyes. The red veins contrasting against the blue of her irises sends a shiver down my spine.

"Oh dear, I can't do that."

"Why're you doing this? Caroline! Stop!"

She pauses her digging, dirt smeared on her face mingling with her head wound. She smiles like she's happy to see me. "It's okay, Audrey," she promises. "We'll be together forever this way. All of us. Judith promised me."

"What about Caleb?" I scream at her.

She blinks once. "He's your cousin," she says as if it should be obvious. "I know you're close to him. That's why I'm doing this, so he can be with us too."

"Caroline," I trail off, finally seeing how truly manipulated she's been. Is this why Ryne took the camera? Did Judith make him believe it was for the best?

"I don't want to die. Caleb doesn't either. Judith is manipulating you." She's been manipulating us all. She was the one who put the bottle in my hand when I was at my lowest and I didn't even think to question it.

Caroline pauses mid-dig to process my words, a frown tugging her face.

"Nobody wants to die! I didn't want to die," Judith hisses. "But your Grandpa decided it was my time. It's only right I put an end to yours."

A speck of warmth sends a shock through my system as Ryne emerges from the woods, flying across the land in a blur towards Judith. With a quick laugh, she grabs him out of the air by the throat.

"Touch her and die," he growls a second before he's slammed into the ground beside Caleb. There's a sickening crack at impact, his back snapping as it bends at an unnatural angle. He coughs, spitting up blood. His eyes are wild as they find me, blood dripping down his chin as he yells, "Run!"

"You shouldn't," Judith warns, kicking at Ryne's crumpled form. He inhales a pained breath, clawing at his throat as he chokes on his own blood. "Don't you want to know why I killed your Aunt Rachel?"

"What?" But it's not my voice that says this, it's belongs to Bryce, who stands behind me, eyes wide in confusion until they land on Ryne. Bryce screams at the sight, but it's lost in a gurgle as water fills his throat. Caroline mimics him, dropping the shovel and covering her face with dirty hands at the sight of their friend, broken and bloody, suffering from a death that would have killed him ten times over by now. But can't.

He's already dead, and there's no sweet oblivion waiting for him.

"Yes, it was me. I'm surprised none of you figured it out. I'd even convinced Ryne to kill Audrey, but the little freak succumbed to his humanity and instead contracted feelings. But the possibility never went through any of your tiny minds. Honestly, you'd think becoming a ghost makes you an imbecile."

"Then you killed Grandpa too, didn't you?" I demand. "You're the woman in those photos he was having an affair with."

There's a revolting satisfaction in her face to this being known. "I am. I was always at Windhaven. We were together for years, and he always talked of how trapped he felt with Margaret and how much he wanted her dead, but when I tried to do exactly what he wanted, he—"

"Killed you," I fill in. "That's why your body was buried in the woods. You tried to kill Granna, and he stopped you."

Grandpa cursed our family. He was a murderer.

"Poison," she smiles. "He caught me just as I was pouring it into her tea. Then, he strangled me." Anger bleeds into her features as she inhales through her nose, the motion bringing attention to the veins in her bruised swollen neck. "And tossed my body into that shallow hole in the woods."

"Why Aunt Rachel?"

Judith tsks.

Caleb stirs, moaning and cradling his head.

"Bryce! Caroline! Take Ryne away," Judith commands. "Restrain him. I don't want to have to deal with him once he's healed."

They hesitate, their feet rooted in place.

Judith sneers, raising her hands, palms outstretched as if they're deadly weapons. "Must I remind you of what I can do?"

How many people did she kill with those hands?

The two grab Ryne, their hands careful as they lift him into their arms. He struggles in their grip despite his injuries, calling my name as they fly away.

"The biggest mistake?" She kicks Caleb over, pushing his body into the hole.

"Caleb!" I scream, falling onto my knees, reaching outstretched hands toward where he lays in the shallow grave.

"Showing emotion. Bryce's weakness? Caroline. He loves her like a sister. Caroline's? The promise of us all being together forever. It's easy to manipulate someone when you pretend you're giving them everything they want. And

Ryne's?" She cackles as if it's comical, her eyes snapping to mine. "You."

My heart squeezes.

"He was easily coerced at first. You're a pretty little thing." Bitterness fills her voice. "You get that from Margaret. Ryne loved the thought of having you trapped here with us. I think he would've gone through with it quickly. But you ruined it all when you revealed you could see us. That's where his morality got in the way. He got to know you instead. You became too real." She starts piling dirt into the hole.

I try to reach for Caleb, but Judith lifts a hand, a wave of her power sending me onto my back.

"Caleb is mine now. To have and to bury."

Pain erupts in my body as I attempt to peel myself from the ground.

"I'm still waiting," Judith sings.

"For what?" I ground out, the wound on my head throbbing.

"The right question. You're asking the wrong ones. It's why *you*. I wanted to watch Margaret suffer after everything she put me through. When your grandfather died, she was miserable, everything was so perfect. But when you came along, all that sadness went away. That is why I wanted to kill you, but I couldn't. I'd never been able to harm a physical being after your grandpa and even managing to land that fatal blow on him was accidental. But one day you were playing by the water. You looked so happy it made me angry, so I pushed you down thinking it would have no effect, but to my surprise, I could feel you. So, I held you under, loving the pure anguish on Margaret's face when she came out and realized you were dead . . . until you weren't."

I sit up, cradling the arm I landed on. "I survived. It made you mad."

More than that. It gave her a taste for revenge and murder.

It's like a cold bucket of water over my head. I didn't just drown that day. Judith killed me. It was before my ability, before I died. I wouldn't have had any idea.

Judith stops throwing dirt down and turns to me. "There was a careful balance I had to keep. Rachel's death was messy and that kept Margaret away for years."

I recall the years Granna stayed away from Windhaven until her wounds healed enough to function.

"So, I made sure for the next two deaths, they were enough to keep her from leaving, but enough to keep her shaken and blaming herself. It all worked out perfectly. It was all about timing. Bryce and Caroline made it too easy. He was already standing too close to the cliff and Caroline had been drinking with her friends. All it took was a little shove."

They have no idea. Bryce and Caroline think their deaths were accidental. She's got her claws wedged so deep into them, there's no telling if they would ever believe it.

"Ryne wasn't a planned one, but thanks to him, I learned how to enter bodies. That girl was so strung out on drugs, so vacant in the head that it made space for me to enter. You being knocked out cold after smoking helped as well. Imagine my surprise when I couldn't possess you as an alcoholic."

Nikita. She possessed Nikita. It's why she offered to go up into the lighthouse with Ryne and knew it wasn't bricked in, because she'd gone there with Grandpa when they were alive.

"Why Ryne?"

Judith begins packing the wet dirt down and I'm left to watch in horror as she shovels the last bit into Caleb's face, his screams muffled by the dirt.

"No!" I run forward, knocking her to the side.

I plow my hands into the mud, throwing handfuls behind me until my nails are caked and bleeding.

I'm suddenly punched in the stomach, a hand wrapping firmly around my throat as I'm lifted into the air.

"Why Ryne? He reminded me too much of your Grandpa! That careless saunter. That cocky attitude. Men like that should *suffer*."

Judith takes over my vision, the woods behind us passing by in a blur. My back slams into the water of the pond. Water fills my mouth and burns my nose as I try to cry for help, but when I open my eyes, Judith's still above me, her form visible in the murky green water as her hands squeeze my throat.

I thrash until she's forced to let go.

I kick to the surface, trying to inhale air, but Judith pulls me back under, forcing me to the mossy floor of the pond. She pins my arms to the ground. I inhale water, my lungs spasming as they beg for the release of pressure. I thrash and kick only to remain captured, my head growing light.

"You should've stayed dead the first time." Judith's voice cuts through the water, sounding further and further away as my head swims.

I remember meeting up with everyone in the woods and how I scared Caroline. What had I been thinking, being fearless of these ghosts?

You're not the only one who can haunt.

Ida's words at the market surface in my mind.

Control.

Suddenly it's like I've been living my life half-asleep. Is that what she meant?

Summoning the power within, I hone in on the presence of the ghosts, feeling for them: Judith right in front of me and Bryce, Ryne, and Caroline somewhere in the woods.

I open my eyes and pin Judith with a glare, concentrating all my energy into her. Something within overflows as the water around me glows, my vision burning white.

Let. Me. Go.

Gaining control, I force us to the surface, wrapping my hands around Judith's wrist as I take control of her power and force us through the air. I remember the feeling of flying with Ryne and focus on that, saying a silent prayer to God to give me the same strength he gave my dad for years.

When we break the surface, I concentrate all the energy and send her flying back with a shove to her chest.

At that moment, Ryne, fully healed, breaks free and soars to me, acting as a shield when Judith attacks. She crashes into him, sending them both through the trees. They crack under the pressure, a line of them falling as they go straight through the thick trunks.

"I'm sorry," Bryce says as he and Caroline circle me with their hands out, ready to grab me. "I swear I didn't know she killed your grandpa and Rachel. I don't want to do this, but she'll hurt Caroline."

"Yeah," Caroline says in a small voice. "She's stronger. Just give her what she wants. It won't be so bad. We can be together."

Catching my breath, I shake my head. "No, she's not. If you two try as hard as you can, there's no way she can hurt you again. Look for it within yourselves, it's there."

"Again?" Bryce asks.

"She killed you both and made it look like an accident."

Their faces shift. Anger. Denial. Realization. Acceptance.

Bryce shakes his head, water flying everywhere. "I—I always had a feeling I wasn't being careless that day."

Bryce and Caroline meet each other's eyes before mine.

I raise an eyebrow in question. "Are you with me?"

They both nod as we turn toward where Judith is on top of Ryne just in time to see her shove her hand through his chest.

He growls at the pain, rolling onto his side before letting out a harrowing scream.

"Your death was by far my favorite," she says, twisting her hand. "I saw the moment in your eyes where you wanted me to kill you just so it could be done with. Possessing that stupid girl was exhilarating."

The two beside me gasp, tears coursing down Caroline's face.

"Why?" Ryne wheezes, each breath a wet rattle in his lungs that causes more blood to spew from his lips, and dribble down his chin.

Judith pulls her hand out and examines the blood on her hand. "I hate men like you. You think you can get away with anything because you have good looks and a nice smile."

She's a complete psychopath.

"Admit it," Ryne hisses. "You loved the idea of holding off on Audrey's death so you could manipulate her to turn her against her Granna. It's why you simply didn't kill Audrey yourself every chance you had. You're just a miserable bitch."

"You little—"

Before Judith can say anything else, I hold out my hands and concentrate all the power toward her.

"I need your help," I tell Bryce and Caroline as a ball of energy forms between my hands, the leaves and wind shifting around me.

Each of them places a hand on my shoulder, their power flowing into me as I aim it for Judith.

"Your eyes are glowing," Caroline whispers.

I've been capable of this power the entire time.

I release everything pent up in me. It tunnels through the air, hitting her. It pins her to the ground, leaving her helpless and fearful just as she has done to all of us—the ones she's killed.

Then, she's gone.

Behind me, Caroline and Bryce drop to the ground. The edges of their ghostly forms lose their sharpness, flickering in and out at the loss of spiritual energy.

"Audrey? Where did she go?"

I shake my head. "I . . . I can't feel her anymore."

"She moved on?" Bryce asks.

"How did you do that?"

I peer up into the sky. "It wasn't me."

"Caleb," Ryne groans, sitting up with his hand covering the wound in his chest.

Panic sets in as I sprint back to the graveyard and drop onto my knees. Before I know it, all three of the ghosts are besides me, scooping away the mud. I cry in relief when I uncover Caleb's face, stopping cold in my tracks when his chest isn't rising or falling.

I begin CPR, opening his mouth to clear his airway of gunk before continuing.

"Fuck!" Ryne curses, slamming his fist into the ground.

"This is all our fault!" Caroline cries. "We let Judith control us."

"Shh, I'm not giving up."

I give Caleb a few more chest compressions and blow into his mouth once more. I pause, hope draining from my body until his own quakes, spasming once more before he rolls over and spits out mud, coughing.

I laugh in delight and launch myself at him, wrapping my arms around him. Weakly, he places a hand onto my back. The three ghosts fall into the embrace as well. Caleb eyes them warily. "Who are they?" he asks, voice scratchy.

I pull back to understand what he's talking about, but the only ones here are us and the ghosts.

"That's Bryce and Caroline," I tell him, pointing between the two. "And this is Ryne."

Caleb backs away like he doesn't understand. "How?"

It dawns on me.

"You must've died," I tell him, panicking.

He drops his head back onto the dirt. "Well, I'm here now. Shit, my back hurts. Who the fuck threw me in that hole?"

"We need to get you to the hospital."

"Actually, screw the hole. Who the fuck dragged me out the window?" he demands.

"I'll explain everything later. I promise. For now, do you want me to call Quinn?" Broken up or not, she's his comfort.

He scowls. "Please don't. I've got enough to unlearn."

"Well," Caroline says, crossing her arms. "I think you should know I never liked her. I definitely did not want her to die and get stuck with us."

Everyone laughs, causing Caroline to smile.

"Actually"—Caleb turns his head away bashfully—"Could you give Hadley a call for me?"

I smile, releasing a breath of relief. "Okay. You got it."

Ryne scoots beside me, the hole in his chest still blooming with blood. "Sweetheart." He collapses into my arms. "Thank God you're okay."

I wrap my arms around him and press his cheek into my chest, my own against the top of his head.

Angels

July 19

Judith moved on, but after what she did to us, I'm not convinced she went anywhere good. She tortured my family for years and killed us off one-by-one to satisfy a vengeance against my Granna for not being chosen over her. She suffered for years because of Judith, in some sick game she didn't know she was a part of. Caleb and I agree we're going to protect her from suffering even more after everything she's been put through.

We make up a story, one that involves Caleb slipping and falling into a muddy creek and accidentally inhaling a mouthful of water. The washed-up debris from the storm accounts for the dirt in his lungs and we keep the fact he died a secret.

"Pack a bag, Sweetie. We're going to stay at the hospital until they release Caleb."

I nod, giving Granna a hug before turning to my half-packed bag. I'm interrupted by the sun rising over the water, shining beams of light so bright, I lift my hand to cover my eyes.

Some people in our life do nothing but wreak havoc while others, like Dad, leave a mark of gold encrusted in our hearts forever.

Bag forgotten, I pad over to the window. I lean forward, my elbows resting on the edge of the window. "What do you see when you look into the sky?"

"Blood," Ryne says as the sunrise burns red. He slouches against the side, one knee up, the other hanging out of the window. But this time, I know he's not going to jump.

"Look closer," I tell him, finger poised as if I'm using it to paint the sky. "See how the yellow burns into the clouds and the red fades to pink? They look a lot like cotton candy skies."

But he's not watching the clouds, he's watching me like the light I give off is brighter. "I love you."

My smile turns shy as I process his words. "I love you too."

"I thought if I denied it, it would reduce the guilt I had about lying to you. I thought accepting the fact we can't stay here together forever would make it hurt less." He places a hand over his heart. "It's not beating, but it fucking hurts as if it is. I think that's why I'm trapped here," he admits. "I'm scared of things hurting me, so I hurt myself so they can't. I could've moved on a year ago, but I was too scared to go into the light. I left it sitting there long enough that it eventually went away."

"That's very insightful, Ghosty. Got anything else?"

I peer over at him.

He shakes his head. "Just selfish words. I want you to stay here forever with me, but you can't. You need to live your life while you have it. Go to college and spend your days out in the city instead of holed up here with me."

My smile falls, tears forming on the edge of my eyes. "I want to be selfish and keep you with me too, but this is no existence for you."

"Maybe not," he agrees. "But you've been the best part of it, even when compared to the life I'd lived. You are the best of everything."

"You've made me the most alive I've been in years," I tell him.

"Guys!" Caroline calls, coming through the walls with Bryce on her trail. "There's a light out on the edge of the cliff. I think we're going to heaven!"

"Or hell," Ryne adds sardonically, true to his nature.

Caroline purses her lips. "Speak for yourself. I don't know about you, but I asked God for forgiveness. I repented!"

"For stealing makeup from the guests, I hope."

"Yes!"

Ryne lifts his chin to Bryce. "What about you?"

He scratches the back of his head, leaning over to heave a mouthful of water.

Caroline steps away in disgust, clasping her hands and looking up to the ceiling. "God, you're going to have to forgive me for my thoughts just now as well, because that shit was disgusting!"

Bryce isn't paying attention and is instead caught in a trance, his gaze locked on the cliff. "We're being called," he says. "It's time to go. Don't you hear it?"

Caroline nods. "I do."

I glance over to where Bryce points to find nothing but the sunrise. "I can't see anything." For once, I'm blind to this.

"It's not your time," Bryce says gently. "Ryne, do you see it? It's a golden glow."

He nods. "I see something, but it's not as bright as what you're saying. Looks more fluorescent."

Bryce shrugs. "Might look different to each of us."

If Caroline can confirm it, she doesn't and instead flies out the window, landing gracefully onto the ground before making her way to it. Bryce follows her, but Ryne stays rooted in his spot.

"You should go," I tell him, my lips wobbling as I smile, the tears building up behind my eyes and threatening to overflow into a puddle of sadness.

He offers me his hand, a silent plea to be with him until the last second. I oblige and place mine in his. For the first time, it's not cold to the touch and instead full of warmth, as if the sun itself has washed over his skin and warmed it.

At the rumble of an engine, I grab my bag off the bed before returning to Ryne's side. "Walk down the stairs with me?"

For a moment, I think he's going to say no and fly out the window. After what happened to him, it's a big thing to ask, but I can't bear the thought of leaving him for a second, of him flying me out the window and that being it.

He nods.

Hand in hand, we walk down the stairs, and I watch in awe as Ryne doesn't give the memories power to hurt him.

"How do you feel?" I ask as he takes each step with precision, the same precision he had when he looked me over the first day I came to Windhaven.

"Like I hold the power. This place can no longer hurt me."

We enter the foyer and push open the double doors, the fresh air flooding our senses and tickling our skin. We walk through the plush summer grass, the sunlight blinding our faces. When we reach the end of the peninsula where Caroline and Bryce wait, I step forward, hugging each of them tight.

"Thanks for everything," Bryce says, soaking my tank top with his soggy clothes and dripping wet hair. "Not just saving us, but for treating us like family."

"Thank you for watching over Ryne for so long."

"You bet." He gives me one last smile.

Caroline clamps onto me. "Thank you. You're the best friend I never got to have. Thank you for giving it to me even after death."

"You've got a special place in my heart," I promise her.

"Also, sorry for trying to kill you, that wasn't cool. It was selfish to want to keep you stuck here with us."

"Very," I agree, laughing lightly. "But I forgive you."

Finally, I come face-to-face with Ryne. His hazel eyes lock onto my own, his beautiful face pulled down in sadness.

"There's nothing I'll ever regret more than having the intention to kill you that day," he confesses. "I just—I liked you so much. I was obsessed with you the second you walked onto the property in the most fucked, up unhealthy way imaginable, so much that I wanted you here with me, but I still couldn't do it."

"Why?"

"I had to see how you were. I wanted to know your heart and soul the same way mine was before I died, untainted. Then, I couldn't imagine condemning you here and risk changing anything about you. You were perfect the way you were. It's sickening, but it's how I thought."

"But you didn't kill me. Your humanity won."

"It almost didn't. But then everything changed when I got to know you. The darkness you tried to hide and the light you claimed wasn't there drew me in. I felt seen for the first time in my life and I felt like I understood you and that you challenged me in ways I never thought of and made me want things I couldn't let myself hope for. I fell in love, and you gave me more life than any I'd been given."

Fingers digging into my hip bones, he pulls me forward into a mind-numbing kiss, his soft lips pressing into mine, calling forth the life within both of us, tangling our souls in invisible thread and binding us together. When he pulls back, he gives me one last hug before revealing his pretty white teeth in a smile. "Fuck me, I am so in love with you."

"I'm in love with you."

"Audrey!" Granna calls from the car. "Time to go!"

I motion to her to wait a moment longer and turn back to Ryne.

He lets go of me and walks backward towards an invisible light. "I'll see you soon enough, Sweetheart. Live your life while you got it. You're gonna blossom just right."

I nod. "My dad will meet you at the gate," I promise him. "You can wait for me together."

"Watch out, Sweetheart. You've got a couple of angels coming your way." He halts mid-step, turning back to me, the most beautiful smile lighting up his face. "Angels," he tests the word, letting it roll over his tongue once more. "It feels so strange to call myself that instead of a ghost."

He steps forward, his ghostly form disappearing from

sight as he's lost in the light of the sunrise. With that, he's gone.

"Granna, I'm fine," Caleb groans from the hospital bed, ripping an IV out of his arm only to get scolded in Spanish by the nurse in charge of him. "Sorry. You can put it back in." She huffs and places the IV back into his arm and glances up to scowl at his mischievous smile.

Granna sighs. "You, young man, are trying to kill me."

Caleb and I snort, knowing who *really* was trying to kill her.

But Granna will never know because Judith doesn't deserve to be spoken into existence. I figure someday we'll tell her about Aunt Rachel, but until then, I need to gather enough evidence from over the years to present a case to her, something she'll believe. Hopefully, it'll be enough to settle the unease that's been shredding her soul. This time, it's not an erratic urge. I don't need to thrust myself into it to keep going anymore.

Now, I can do that on my own.

Caleb glances over to me. "What about you, cuz? You alright?"

"Fine," I say, grabbing his hand. "Now that I'm not suffering from the near heart attack you gave me."

"I meant to say if you were fine leaving Casper back at the hotel."

I wait for Granna to leave the room before answering.

"He . . . they moved on."

"What?"

I nod.

"Are you okay?"

"I'm sad," I admit. I'll probably cry for days and always feel like there's a missing piece of my heart until I see him waiting with Dad at those gates for me.

"I'm sorry, Audrey."

"It's okay," I assure him. "I'll learn to be alright. Besides, I'm happy to finally know what happened to Aunt Rachel."

Caleb twitches and glances over his shoulder. There's no one behind him, but the presence is near us. He's been bothered since we got here and this new world is something he has to get used to, but unlike me, he won't be alone. I'll teach him everything I know and in turn, I don't have to be lonely in it. Who knows, maybe he'll tune into some things more than I will.

Before Caleb can answer, his nurse comes back into the room. "Visiting hours are over," she says gently. "You can come back tomorrow."

I give Caleb a quick kiss on the head and bid him goodnight before turning on my heel. Just before I can take a step, Caleb latches onto my wrist. "Careful," he warns. "Don't step on the green tile over there."

I follow his line of sight to the green tile near a visitor's chair. "Why?"

He furrows his brow. "You don't see how it stands out compared to the others?"

"What do you mean?" I check him over for head injuries.

He scoffs, shaking his head as he smiles. "I'm not crazy"

It's that sentence that makes me realize he's seeing something I'm not. I move back to his side, angling my body to his same position. "What do you see?"

He sits back and blows out a breath. "I'm not sure. It just looks different. You know how we'd watch Scooby Doo as kids? And we always knew what walls were trap doors because they stood out from the backdrop? It's like that."

Could what Caleb sees possibly relate to Shut-Eyes and awakening them?

"We'll figure out what it means together," I promise. "I'll avoid it for now. Goodnight, Caleb. Love you."

"Love you too."

I close his door behind me, going into the hall to take a seat on a lone bench. The hallway's dark, and while I can feel the ghosts here, they're not as strong and lack that spot of warmth I'm desperate to cling to—Ryne's.

The weight I've been carrying on my shoulders finally crashes into me.

All there is numbness, and I'm left alone in the dark to finally cry. My tears overflow, dripping down my cheeks onto my legs as I let out my sorrows, words miraculously forming on my tongue as I begin to pray. It took a while, but I found my faith.

For the rest of night, my heart refuses to ease up on the aching as another sliver of it is gone. And while my heart is no longer whole, there is comfort in feeling sane. For the first time, my mind isn't in pieces.

Epilogue

July 20

"Audrey Woudstra?"

I startle awake, dragging air into my lungs as I awake from a sweet dream into a living nightmare—a world Ryne no longer exists in. No longer in body or soul. The air around me doesn't contain its usual chill, but instead a sweltering heat my body struggles to withstand. To compensate, it kicks into overdrive, drenching my body in sweat to cool me down. My core temperature has risen since Ryne, Bryce, and Caroline moved on.

I glance around in surprise when I realize I've been asleep on the hospital bench. The morning light streams into my face from Caleb's hospital room. The hallway is quiet and lacks the paranormal activity that once occupied Windhaven. The stillness should soothe me. The absence of ghosts used to feel safe, but after meeting Ryne their presence felt like home. Now I'm left to wander empty halls as they once did and ponder where to go from here.

I rub my eyes and squint. "Linda Harper?"

"Hi," she greets, folding me into a hug. "I heard you were here. I'm sorry about your cousin, but relieved to hear he's okay."

"Thank you. How is your grandson?"

Her body trembles in excitement, her hands flailing as she relays the news. "He's woken up! It's a miracle! Would you like to accompany me to see him? I need to go downstairs to get some food, but I hate to leave him alone after all this time he's been in a coma. Do you mind?"

"I do not." Being alone after having not been for so long terrifies me.

Placing a hand on mine, she walks me down the hall of the hospital. The smell of sanitization burns my nose, but overall being here isn't the house of horrors I always thought it would be, and I'm actually content with going to see her grandson.

"The past few months were worrisome. We weren't sure if he was going to make it because his heart rate kept elevating at random times throughout the days. At first, we feared he was going into cardiac arrest, but the doctors did more tests and even a brain scan. Do you know what they found?"

I shake my head.

"Oxytocin. During those heart spikes, his brain was releasing oxytocin. My boy was feeling love while he dreamed."

He was experiencing love?

We stop in front of the room with the last name Harper on it and walk in. The sun is so bright I have to shield my eyes as the orange rays beam into my face. I peer past the harsh light, gasping as the world under me implodes as if it's been dragged from under my feet and flipped upside down. I take in the sight in front me.

A boy in a hospital gown sits on the windowsill, looking out into the view of the bustling city and the sunrise behind it.

"Linda," I whisper. "How long was your grandson in a coma?"

"An entire year."

I've spent the year as a ghost.

"What's his name?"

He turns toward me and my heart plummets.

"This is my grandson, Ryne Harper."

I cover my mouth with my hands as the pink and yellow hues shine behind him, washing him with so much light before fading as the sun takes its rightful place in the sky.

"Ryne, this is Audrey Woudstra, Margaret's granddaughter. You two get to know each other. I'll be back soon." She shoots me an encouraging smile before leaving the room.

The boy in front of me isn't as tan as the one I remember due to being under the fluorescent lighting for so long. His muscles lack the same density from being trapped in a coma, but his eyes are hazel, with the most flourishing shades of forest green I've ever seen. His hair is a deep brown, curly, and he still has that wicked smile playing on the edge of his lips that causes my heart to go off rhythm and my chest to soar.

He's still my Ryne.

But will he remember me?

I hesitate, scared of how he will react. Will he be the golden boy he was before he was attacked, or will he be the one I've come to love after being caught between worlds and developing a dark humor and a taste for pain?

"Hi," I say.

Ryne Harper looks over at me, taking me in from head to toe and back up again slower, steadier. "Hey, Sweetheart."

And that's how I know I've still got him, and my prayers were answered after all.

I run over to him and throw my arms around his neck and when we kiss, the heat radiates from his lips to mine for the first time and the chest under my palm has a throbbing strong pulse that picks up the longer I touch him.

"How do you feel?"

He covers my hand over his heart, his eyes sliding shut as he listens closer to his heartbeat. "Alive. Happy. Scared. Horny. Things I've felt before." He opens those shining eyes. "But what I'm feeling now? I've known I loved you for a while, but it's like my body is struggling to comprehend just how much when it's such a normal thing to my mind. I really, *really* love you, Audrey."

"I love you."

He laughs as his heart thumps even harder against my palm. I grin at him. Ryne sobers up after a moment, turning his head into a beam of sunlight, worrying at his bottom lip as he shakes his head. "My family won't recognize me. I'm not even sure *I'll* recognize who I am anymore."

"I will."

His hand slides up the slope of my jaw, his thumb caressing my cheek. "That so?" he questions, eyes dropping to my mouth, the worry gone and replaced by something more carnal.

"Ryne Harper, I'd know your heart and soul from anywhere."

THE END

Acknowledgments

Some dreams feel so distant that when they're finally achieved, it becomes evident some aspects were never considered—my acknowledgements are one of those aspects. I was so caught up in my dream of becoming an author, putting my all into the writing, editing, and the querying process, that I never fully stopped to think of the pure joy and peace I'd garner from writing something as simple as my acknowledgments.

Right now, I am experiencing all that and more. Thank you, God.

To my wonderful team at Lake Country Press: thank you. Brittany Weisrock, you are the heart of LCP and I am so blessed to have you on my side. I appreciate everything you've done for me, and the love you have for my book. Tara Sexton, thank you for pulling me from the trenches (it was rough in there). I was so happy when Brittany told me you gave THATH rave reviews before she finished it. Your kind words stay with me even now.

Yasmine Garay, you called it. You told me this was going to be my debut. You were so certain about it, even when I had doubts, you made me believe it. Thank you for the late night THATH brain rotting sessions, listening to me lose my mind over plot revelations, and for staying up with me at this very moment at 12:15 A.M (1:15 A.M for you) just to be there for me as I close out this story. You're my best friend. Your support and belief in me are such precious gifts that I cherish.

Thank you to my parents, you've both always encouraged my writing and always told me how proud you each are. Growing up, that went a long way. It goes even further now. I love you both.

Thank you to all my friends in the writing community. Your support means everything.

My dear readers, you reading my book IS my dream and now it has come true. I'm eternally grateful.

Thank you from the bottom of my heart!

True Sloan grew up in a suburb of Dallas, Texas where she discovered her love of reading and writing at a young age. She attended the University of North Texas where she obtained her Bachelors in English with a concentration in Creative Writing as well as a Minor in Technical Communication.

   X

www.ingramcontent.com/pod-product-compliance
Lightning Source LLC
Chambersburg PA
CBHW050012120726
47903CB00006B/1736